The Fugitive of Gezi Park

Deniz Goran

ORTAC PRESS

First published in Great Britain in 2023 by Ortac Press

ISBN: 978-1-8383887-4-4

A CIP record for this book is available from the British Library

Cover design by Jamie Keenan

Set in Scala Pro by Tetragon, London
Printed and bound by CPI Group (UK)

ortacpress.com

The
Fugitive
of Gezi
Park

DENIZ GORAN'S first novel *The Turkish Diplomat's Daughter* became a bestseller when it was published in Turkey in 2007. The novel was also published in the UK, Italy, Germany, Greece and Taiwan. Deniz Goran is the pseudonym of Selin Tamtekin, a Turkish-British novelist and art writer based in London. *The Fugitive of Gezi Park* is her second novel.

Dedicated to the Gezi prisoners and in memory of those who lost their lives during the protests.

———

Also, in memory of Onur Yaser Can.

Öyle bir yerin düşünü gördüm ki: İnsanlar, sabah uyan-
dıklarında hâlâ hayatta olduklarını fark edip, günaydın
demeden önce birbirlerini öpüyorlardı

I dreamt of just such a place: Where people, as they woke
up in the morning aware of still being alive, were kissing
each other before saying good morning

KÜÇÜK İSKENDER

QUINN

'CAN YOU TELL US a bit about the *Dragonfly*?'

'Sure. It's a piece Donald Taffy did in 1991 as a part of his *Fly on the Wall* series. It was exhibited that very same year at his very first show at MoMA. It's such an iconic object. What I love about Donald is his undeniable attention to detail. He's such a reckless perfectionist.'

'How did he make it? I mean, does he cast them or what?' As these words spilled from the old man's lips he extended his right arm, which, for a moment, seemed to freeze in mid-air, an inch away from the creature's transparent, leafy wings. His eyes had caught the sign just in time. PLEASE DO NOT TOUCH.

'Each fly was handmade at his studio by an army of draughtsmen. Did you watch the documentary about it? I highly recommend it. I can lend it to you if you like. Though I don't think I have a copy here with me... I'm sure you can still get hold of one on Amazon. He had a handful of people working on a single fly for months. They're all made from a combination of Plexiglass, vinyl and rubber.'

'It's breathtaking,' the woman remarked, as her fingers wandered around the diamond-encrusted pendant hanging on her creased neck.

'I personally find the *Dragonfly* and the *Mosquito* to be the finest in the whole series,' added Quinn, placing his hand self-assuredly on his chest.

'What is the inspiration, the thought process behind the work, do you know?' the man enquired. He was tall and slender, and generally fit-looking for someone of his age.

'Well, the title of the series really says it all. Throughout his career, voyeurism has been a subject Donald keeps going back to. But what makes his *Fly on the Wall* series so powerful is that there is a possible double reading here. Is it the fly or is it the viewer who's been made to play the role of the voyeur, if you get my drift?'

Pausing to underline the inarguable brilliance of what he had just said, he adopted a solemn look.

'I bought this piece back from a client of mine several years ago. At the time he was going through a terrible divorce,' he explained in a compassionate tone.

'Each artwork has its own story,' remarked the woman.

'It's an exceptional piece that belongs in a museum,' Quinn responded.

The woman blushed with excitement. She brought her body closer to her husband's, discreetly took hold of his hand and squeezed it. Looking composed, he asked for the price. Quinn dropped his head like a shy teenager and gave them a timid smile, as if he was somehow obliged to hold back that specific information. After a few awkward seconds the man released his hand from his wife's grip and repeated his question, this time more firmly.

'*So* – how much is it?'

After taking a deep breath, Quinn explained – with apparent sincerity – as he arched his eyebrows, 'I love exhibiting this work. But, as it's such a rare piece, I'm not entirely sure I want to sell it. I have a feeling that if I do, I might end up regretting it one day – if you see what I mean.'

'Is that so?' replied the man after giving it some thought.

Quinn's face became expressionless and remained that way as their eyes met again.

'Well, in that case,' the man said hesitantly, pausing briefly as he glanced over to his wife, 'Do you happen to have anything similar?'

'From the same series?'

The man nodded, quickly regretting his question for being a bit simple.

'Oh, I'm afraid not,' Quinn replied.

'We have been meaning to get in touch with your gallery for some time now. We always assumed we would one day get to add a Donald Taffy to our collection,' the woman interrupted earnestly. 'And we have been offered many second-rate works.'

'Indeed we have,' the man emphasised, staring at his own feet.

'Donald's an exceptionally prolific artist,' Quinn said. Then, lowering his voice, he added, 'but I'm afraid I have to admit that not all his work is in the same league as this.'

'We're not very keen on his more recent works, nor on the very experimental stuff he did in the late seventies.'

'Not that we don't get it,' the woman intervened.

'Oh, trust me, we get it,' the man added reassuringly.

'It wouldn't really fit in with the rest of the collection, which aims to comprise momentous works by leading contemporary

3

American artists,' explained the woman. Small and delicate next to her husband, she made up for her size with her lively spirit. 'Like Jeff Koons' *Balloon Dog* and a spectacular plate painting by Julian Schnabel.'

'A light installation by Joseph Kosuth that covers an entire wall. One from Baldessari, you know, with the dots. A self-portrait by Chuck Close.'

'How fantastic.'

'Not that we're bragging,' said the man before flashing a brazen smile.

'No, of course, I understand,' Quinn said choosing to overlook the intended humour.

'No, we would never do something like that,' said the woman, shaking her head and widening her eyes surrounded with thick, clumpy mascara. Her husband gave her a moment's glance as if having instantly recognised the potential behind her ingenuous disguise.

'You know, more than anything, I love real collectors who collect with true passion and genuinely adore art.'

'We don't ever sell what we buy. We don't even hang them on our walls. We keep them in a separate warehouse we had built inside our ranch. When Lora and I die, the entire collection will be donated and exhibited, alternating throughout the year, in a room at the Whitney Museum—'

'Which will be dedicated to us,' the woman interrupted, finishing his sentence.

The woman's hand slipped back into her husband's rugged hand, blemished by decades of careless exposure to the sun.

'Listen, to be perfectly honest with you, I decided to showcase this work at the Fair on the condition that I would only sell it if the right buyer should come along. You have to understand that I have the best intentions for my artists and consider the long-term effects of each step I take on their behalf.'

'I hear you,' responded the man.

'I know Donald is a big fan of the Whitney. I think he would be over the moon if he knew one of his most influential pieces was going to go into their collection one day.'

'Isn't it the most wonderful place?' said the woman, before adding, 'We also support a teaching programme there for autistic children.'

'*So* – how much is it?' the man asked again.

ADA

I

I WAS CURIOUSLY drawn to the glint in the stranger's narrowed eyes, the faint smirk on his parted lips as he casually materialised by the entrance of the booth, somehow challenging the dry harmony of the well-dressed individuals shifting before me. I monitored his actions with apprehension, supposing he could sense my inquiring gaze – regardless of the distance between us – the way one is sometimes able to notice another's persistent attention from the corner of one's eye. Catching sight of Quinn – who was absorbed in the company of an elderly couple – the stranger's face briefly took on the roguish expression of someone who takes diabolic pleasure in teasing his subjects, before he pressed his lips together, tilted his head to one side and raised his eyebrows as if acknowledging to himself an element of truth. And just when I had convinced myself he was unaware of my presence, tucked away as I was at the far end of the booth behind a wide desk, its reflective surface decorated with small piles of artists' catalogues that smelled seductively of fresh print, and an open laptop before me which I had yet to find a use for, I found his knowing gaze upon me – as if he had, from the very start, been able to read my thoughts.

He began to examine the artworks cropping up in his way, with the kind of solemn attention driven by duty, prompting sparks of tedium – a small yawn, a hasty rub to one eye and a scratch over his light stubble. Like his sleeves artlessly rolled up just below the elbow, his dishevelled hair demonstrating a new take on orderly chaos and the lack of shine in his distinguished footwear gracefully misshapen through wear, it complemented the look of bohemian anarchy he proudly carried off. But I didn't need to study him any longer – his appearance, together with the particular *feeling* he induced in me was already instilled in my mind, like the memory of a poignant, absorbing dream from the previous night. My growing fascination with him – an individual who seemed at least a decade beyond my years, if not more – did not feel unseemly or rushed.

I sensed his presence approaching steadily, an undistinguishable sea creature gliding through shadowy water. Overwhelmed by this, for a few moments – in which the hubbub of the growing crowd was subdued, as if the volume knob of my acoustic nerve had been readjusted – my surroundings became implausible to me: people and artworks, brutally exposed under the severe spotlights, made to view and be viewed inside this temporary cubicle contrived of detachable, collapsible walls. I had become unsettlingly detached from the shared reality which surrounded me. The dense drone – generated by masses of people continuing to fill the Fair through its wide red swinging doors – resumed, as if a door in my mind had been let open, allowing the monotonous sound to enter and encircle me in an invisible surge. Startled by its blunt intensity, I straightened my posture, as if having sensed a stranger's touch on the back of my neck. By this point, having already passed by me, he was just a few feet away, now pausing in front of a pocket-sized oil painting bordered by an ostentatious gilded frame, a still life executed with photographic likeness.

Embarrassed at having encumbered a single glance with far too much meaning, I remained surprisingly calm, lifting my chin high and facing his direction. By now I was certain he was approaching my desk with the intention of enquiring about the small painting he seemed to have taken a particular liking to; he'd spent more time examining it than any of the other works. I began hastily rummaging through the disorderly compartments of my short-term memory, in search of particulars on the painting in question: the identity of its executor, and its price, which was bound to be disproportionate to its diminutive scale. A two-page document containing such information lay in still darkness amongst gallery stationery inside the top drawer of the desk; it had been passed to me at the start of the day, when the Fair had been possessed by a different energy. It had altogether been a different kind of place – occupied solely by gallery staff and technicians rushing about with screwdrivers, tape measures in their hands; abandoned paper cups of cold coffee stood on chairs, desks, and on its wall-to-wall synthetic carpet covered-floors. White foam packing peanuts spilled from opened crates, some of which still held artworks, while some framed works had been stacked against the walls, waiting for their turn to be hung.

With his sturdy fingers, he pushed away strands of light brown hair which had managed to disengage from the rest of the anarchic disarrangement and extend over to his left eye. He looked questioningly at me; teasing, confident, seemingly intent on unearthing something hidden – of triggering something unanticipated yet which I secretly dreaded (such as the wave of blazing heat which urgently rose from my abdominal region). As I sensed perspiration surface at the roots of my hair, his voice caressed my heightened senses with a soft 'Hi'. A salacious grin emerged on the side of his mouth, as if an admission of responsibility for the state he'd already brought me to.

I gave him the kind of evasive glance I had watched doe-eyed screen sirens perform in monochrome. He pointed at me. An empty reflection filled his eyes, as if the thought prompting his gesture had slipped into oblivion before re-emerging through the choppy waters of his consciousness.

'You're new,' he said, studying my face with unhindered fascination, as if he had just caught sight of something profound.

'I'm just here to help out during the Fair.'

'Really? I'm an old friend of Quinn's. May I?' He indicated the two chairs before my desk. The amused sparkle in his eyes mirrored his childish candour. I nodded, so as not to appear overly keen – but I was also too nervous to react in any other way. Sensing the hard edge of my chair touch my shoulder blades, I realised I had tilted myself backwards, a soft smile seeming to independently form on my lips.

'We met when he still had his gallery in New York. It was over a decade ago. I was working as a curator for the Guggenheim at the time.'

He briefly turned around towards Quinn, who was still engaged with the same couple. 'I am the oldest friend he has in London – although, if I had to be honest, most of the time he cannot stand me. I seem to have that effect on many people, actually,' he continued, with an air of smugness.

'Lucian, by the way,' he added, coming forward in his chair and extending his hand, as if he wished to get the short, ceremonial act over with as quickly as possible. He appeared on edge now, restless in his own skin – as if, regardless of his nonchalance, there was an aspect to formal introductions which made him withdraw into himself.

Feeling the lukewarm grip of his hand, I replied, 'Ada.'

'A-da,' he repeated, unnecessarily extending the first syllable as English speakers tend to do with foreign words.

'Ada,' I insisted, with very little hope that it would catch on.

Staring pensively at an undefined spot in the air, he repeated 'Ada,' with more assurance – and this time, with almost perfect pronunciation. 'Where are you from, Ada?'

'Istanbul,' I responded, at that moment able to block from my mind (as if they had never actually occurred) the incidents that had taken place in the days of my very last visit there. Instead a faint, fictional smell of soot emerged inside my nasal passage, as if I had been descending on foot down one of its many narrow streets leading down to the sea, on either side a tight row of apartment buildings with smoking chimneys and fading facades, stray cats, limping dogs and the odd rugged street merchant drifting from unexpected corners. I smelled the stench of the polluted sea, remembering the opaque waters of the sea churning as a tattered ferryboat manoeuvred itself away from a pier; a group of vociferous seagulls circled the pale, grey skies of my mind.

'Really? How utterly fascinating. I've never been. So when

11

would you say is the best time to visit?' he asked, his eyes tracing the features of my face.

I sighed, sensing the kind of overwhelming apprehension I used to experience giving presentations at university. It was a disturbing irony, being asked to provide travel tips to a destination I was circumstantially prohibited from travelling to.

'Spring, I suppose. It gets too hot and humid in the summer. Late spring is the best. May or early June – but even early June could be risky.' I sensed heat emitting from my cheeks, imagined the crimson of my inflamed skin, its faint reflection dancing about in the space between our eyes.

'Do *you* like it there most in the springtime?'

'No, I actually prefer the colder months.'

'Why do you think that is?' he asked, leaning forward in his seat again, with the tactical curiosity of someone who sought to dig deep through unconventional avenues. Just like Marlene – a psychotherapist I had been having regular sessions with for the last two years. All I knew about Marlene was that she was originally from Munich, and was married with two grown-up children – whereas she had by now absorbed and analysed many facets of my life, not to mention the fine details of what I had to endure before I fled Istanbul. She'd made her very best effort to persuade me to make my peace with what had happened and to move on.

A smiling man approached the desk, having broken away from the shifting, growing number of people inside the booth. He startled me with his sudden appearance – it was as if he'd materialised out of nowhere. Until then I'd registered the people around us as motifs in a wallpaper pattern, parts of an enveloping reality I had mentally secluded myself from. And I'd believed Lucian had done so too – as if we'd been inside a neutral zone within a reflectionless, transparent glass case: unaffected by and uninterested in what was going on beyond the limits of each other's corporeal entities.

'Sorry, can you tell me who painted that?' the smiling man hesitantly asked.

I caught a glimpse of Quinn's profile. The sight of the thick brown rims of his glasses stayed with me moments after I had looked away, a memento of the guilt I had begun to harbour towards him – and then towards myself (for allowing myself to be chatted up, even if it was by someone who claimed to be a friend of his). And, as with every poignant emotion generated by a particular situation, however small or ephemeral, this created a mental imprint of its own – *a feeling* left over from a potent, transient moment – ultimately destined to join the numerous other ones I had been hoarding involuntarily over the past twenty-two years. They occasionally re-emerged, like old, intimate friends from a past era, giving me a taste of the various moments of my life. Having never been fully convinced by the idea of an afterlife, I did however acknowledge the circle of life – of how matter did not altogether disappear, only changed from one form, one kind, to another, in the way that the remains of once-living organisms, plants, mammals, reptiles, microorganisms continued to exist in the layers of the earth's soil. It was *this* aspect of human existence which led me to question the destiny of these mental imprints, which one's conscience accumulated over a lifetime. What became of them once one ceased to exist?

Lucian's cynical, enticing aura brought to mind relationships I had briefly formed during my childhood and teenage years – mainly with girls who possessed seductive charisma and a tendency towards degeneracy, a thirst for immoral pleasures. I was too conscientious and sensible to remain under their manipulative spells; much to my disillusion, I recognised in them a lack of mercy for others, and a gluttonous appetite for self-destruction which demanded the participation of anyone in their company. Yet there had undoubtedly been a side to me, which rarely surfaced – a hidden side of me of which I had little understanding – that was intrigued by and secretly drawn to individuals governed by their inner demons.

Before I could open my mouth, he promptly responded to the smiling man's question, seeming to share the same desire for him to vanish and let us carry on as before – and with less of a guilty conscience, I suspected. Unlike me he didn't seem to be accountable to anyone. He didn't come across as someone who was overly bothered by the consequences of his actions – nor, unlike the shifting, unnoticeable faces around us, skimming through the contents of each booth to get to the next, did he seem to be in a desperate hurry to get anywhere.

Upon hearing Lucian's answer the smiling man responded, 'I thought it was him.'

I was somewhat upset he had acted before me; had I been able to respond to that simple query, the feeling of guilt – undulating like a flag of defeat inside my ribcage with every conscious breath I took – might have subsided. From the corner of my eye I saw the man heading towards the painting. I wondered whether, like a method actor who stayed in character long after the scene had come to an end, he was still maintaining that smile of his now that he had his back to us, or whether he had shifted to an altogether different persona, perhaps one others closer to him would associate him more with – before I altogether lost interest, and the moving bodies of individuals shifted into an abstraction of blurred colours and wordless voices. I found myself again drawn to Lucian's pulse-raising presence.

He leaned his back against the leather chair, balancing the weight of his elbows on its thin leather arms. The shared silence between us surprisingly lacked awkwardness, our interaction carrying on inaudibly through questioning glances and some-times suggestive, sometimes restrained smiles. One of these smiles brought a layer of moisture to my eyes.

'Tell me, Ada, why are you here?'

'You tell me first,' I responded, surprising myself.

'Because I'm showing at the Fair. I have a gallery that spe-cialises in modern and contemporary photography in Fitzrovia and once a year I feel obliged to participate in *this* shambles. You should come and visit if he ever lets you off your tight leash. We're past the Siberian border in E20.'

'But, how come you're not—'

'At my own booth? Yes, you're right. I should be there, shouldn't I?' he asked, almost naively, as if he were consulting a close friend. 'But I really don't like doing this,' he continued, cringing, seeming almost eager to confide in me.

Having barely met him, I couldn't tell if he was the type who freely, casually disclosed passing thoughts – or if this was in fact a form of mental release, one which made him feel less of an accomplice and more of a bystander, the way a similar psychology prevailed in citizens who fervently voiced their discontent with the system at every given opportunity while having to comply with its rules. He turned around, scratching the back of his head as if to relieve himself of an unbearable itch, then extended his neck to catch sight of Quinn's small frame through the silhouettes of passers-by. He turned his face back towards me.

'I'm not like him. I've never been motivated by money. He probably regards me as a fucking idiot and he's probably right. I love putting on shows, engaging with artists, being a part of the creative process, however limited my role in it is these days. And I do occasionally enjoy selling to some collectors. It's immensely rewarding to be in dialogue with people who are as passionate about art and photography as I am and to assist them in making the right choices. But otherwise I leave such soul-numbing drudgery to my employees. Unlike him, I don't have a problem with giving people fixed salaries or trusting others.'

'But you don't like it here,' I said, with a curiosity ineffectively restrained by hesitation, anxious his response would trigger the personal doubt I suppressed. From time to time it faintly revealed its unsettling shadow – a ghostly figure in hiding, eyeing me from behind the thick draperies of my subconscious.

'No, not desperately.'

'But why not?'

'Because I can't stand its hypocrisy,' he said forcefully, even as the playful glint in his eyes suggested he was still in pursuit of a different cause.

'Like all forms of grand-scale endeavour that carry a claim to social responsibility, and also aim to benefit the parties involved, it never achieves what it aspires to. Actually, what it does best is allow people like me to bugger off to the Caribbean or the Maldives in the middle of the freezing winter. The art is stripped of its critical function and taken at face value. That's why everything looks so cheap and crap and pretentious.'

'I haven't seen much of it,' I said in a low, diffident tone. Images – recurring moments from the route I had taken while running small errands for Quinn earlier in the day – played themselves in my mind like a slideshow of frozen snapshots: the seemingly intentional disharmony of pine-green tights under brown clothing worn by a girl who stood behind the art books stand, a dazzling red neon light needily spelling out *Love Me*, a photograph capturing distorted streetlights through amplified rain droplets, and the emotionless expression worn by the gallery owner of the adjacent booth who – unlike his assistant – successfully managed to refrain from eye contact on every occasion I had walked past.

'You still haven't told me why you're here, Ada.'

'I thought I did.' Unsure where his question led, I felt slightly ill at ease, irrationally alarmed he might somehow know something about my past, or perhaps about my temporary position at Quinn's stand.

'Why you're *really* here. Perhaps working at the Fair next to this nob is a sort of a stepping stone to the grand plan you have for yourself.' His cynical tone felt like a pinch to a bare arm.

'I don't have a grand plan,' I responded, somewhat defensively. I could not bear the thought of him perceiving me as an overly ambitious person – someone who already had her life planned out before her. Though I did from time to time aspire to be one of those individuals who possessed the indomitable determination I seemed to lack, I also detected a shallowness in their outlook, a lack of interest in life's details, an emotional blindness towards others – an observation that once again proved to me the inadequacy of all humans. 'Actually, I'm still not certain about what I want to do,' I said. Even if a smile had formed around my lips, the burden of my indecision had begun to weigh my spirits down.

'But surely you're here for a purpose?'

The deep mess I had become entangled in the last time I'd been in Istanbul made it nearly impossible for me to have a so-called purpose, or a plan of any sort, even if I ever wished to.

'I recently finished a degree in History of Art and I was thinking, maybe, I could stay in London a while longer and work in a gallery. You know, try it out for a bit,' I said, doubt hanging over my every word, sceptical of my ability to accomplish such an objective. After everything I had been through, I was uncertain if I wished to follow any career path, or if setting up a permanent address in London was what I had to do, when Istanbul rarely left my mind.

He gazed at me, as if attempting to find hidden clues behind the expressions my face flitted through almost independently of me, as if he believed that they could reveal more of the truth than the words coming out of my mouth. Overwhelmed by this intense, undivided attention, I couldn't help but look away – to notice yet again how alien my environment had become, how insignificant the people, the art and ultimately the Fair was to me at that particular moment. Once I had turned back, I realised – having caught a disguised smile, his bottom lip gradually slipping from the grip of his teeth – that my obvious shyness had further aroused his interest in me.

His eyes went to my mouth, and I made an effort to keep my slightly parted lips still, in the process feeling a kind of physical restiveness, one I commonly experienced when posing in front of a camera.

'A friend told me something the other day. He said it doesn't really make a difference what you do in life in order to be successful. You just need to know what you want and work towards it. Which is, of course, the exact opposite route I initially took. But I'm anything but a role model.' He lifted his eyebrows suggestively, obtaining a particular joy from mocking himself – as if his mockery were a form of self-flattery in disguise. I found myself filled with burning curiosity, wishing to be given access to every detail of his unorthodox life, aspiring to his ways, to the person I presumed he was, my mind quickly conjuring up a prevailing mood I imagined best suited his life – regardless of how little I knew of this near-stranger who had just then unexpectedly turned his back on me to gaze towards the entrance of the booth. It was as if he'd felt a hunch that what was going on beyond us had suddenly gained some relevance to him – and at that point the enchanting energy between us seemed to dissolve, leaving in its place a quickly forgotten sense of shared time between two passing strangers.

When he turned back towards me and our eyes met briefly, he seemed impatient, distracted and distant, as if he had already disengaged himself from *us* and had moved on. I involuntarily, slowly dropped my shoulders, little by little shrinking inside my chair as he hurriedly lifted himself off his own, his tall frame straightening towards the lofty ceiling.

'Listen, I need to go. I'll see you later.'

I responded with another small smile and nod, attempting to give the impression I was untroubled by his sudden departure, accepting the ephemeral and inevitable superficiality of such short-lived interactions. But I felt the faint, persistent ache, the echo of that brief moment of cynicism and undermining in his tone earlier. Although I'd caught a moment's flirtatious gleam in his eyes before he walked off – the remnants of a now-abandoned interest in me – I now found myself lost in a haze of loneliness.

I came across myself, partially reflected in the darkened, smeared screen of the laptop. I felt, then, an awkward moment of personal intimacy – as if, bringing my lower arm to my face, I had managed to capture my evasive scent, while sensing the light brushing of minuscule hairs against my lips. It wasn't until someone approached me that my vision wandered away from the indistinguishable figure before me, steering its way around obstacles to find his recognisable silhouette, diminutive next to a grandiosely overweight far-Eastern man with thick dreadlocks. The ends of the man's pistachio-coloured kaftan swept the floors of the corridor as he and Lucian continued to walk away, disappearing behind the booth.

II

As if lifting my head out of water to a previously blurred image now made clear, I studied the slim, middle-aged woman who stood before my desk – the plain gold ring on her long thumb, a cluster of raised, dark moles which appeared like fungus on a tree trunk on the side of her neck, the flared nostrils at the end of her slender nose, and light ashy brown hair that framed her bare face. She had come to make an enquiry about a black and white photograph. The photograph depicted a woman's figure in a moment of melancholic solitude: her lean body visible from the thigh up as she stood to the left of the composition, her back turned, facing the choppy wavelets of the sea, her angular frame disrupting the horizontal duality of the sea against a blank sky. She was dressed in nothing but bikini bottoms, the darkness of the garment appearing like a dimensionless void against the rest of the picture that, when stared at long enough, lured the vision in as if it were a hypnotic black hole.

'Does it come in editions?' the woman asked, in a surly voice carrying a hint of impatience. When her gaze briefly met mine, she seemed too preoccupied to fully notice me.

'No, I think it's a one-off,' I said, my eyes hesitantly searching for Quinn, who I recalled having seen stepping out of the booth alongside a tall blonde woman.

'That's right. She used to only do one-offs.'

'It's my favourite piece here,' I told her.

'Really?' she responded, studying me as if for the first time acknowledging my presence. I nodded, slightly anxiously; I lived with the fear of my inner thoughts being transparent to others and suspected that with my remark – which had prompted me to acknowledge my dislike of the remaining contents of the booth, their insincere, gimmicky entities unable to move me in any way – she was able to read my opinion.

'It's a great shame she died so young. She died of a... what was it again? Was it some incurable illness?'

'She died in a car crash,' I said, trying to imagine the sudden shock of a lethal collision. For a couple of intensified moments, which brought a flush to my cheeks, I considered the unexpected tragedy of an early death, first as a notion, and then of *hers* particularly. As I did so, fragmented images – quintessentially American (as was she) – wandered through my mind. A diner at the corner of a wide, remote boulevard, where her car had skittered sideways. The red leather upholstery of a classic Chevy spattered in blood, its smashed, compressed, once-ample bonnet engulfed in smoke and flames. These fragments were like storyboards for a short film, one that took its visual language from mid-century American urban aesthetics – like the Tarantino and Lynch movies that captivated me in my late adolescence.

'Wait a minute... yes. Well, of course. I remember it now. It happened while she was holidaying on the Amalfi coast. It's all coming back to me,' she said, leaning her index and middle finger against her temple. 'She drove her car off a cliff. Some thought it was suicide.'

'I didn't know that,' I said, astonished and feeling betrayed by my own presumption. This time, the slow-moving image of a pale-yellow convertible plunging off a cliff played itself in the back of my mind, as I struggled with the embarrassment of owning up to my ignorance.

'I studied her at university. In fact, I wrote one of my essays on her,' I explained, as – moved by my re-enactments of her death – the hairs on my arm stood erect.

'In what context?' she asked.

'Actually, it wasn't just about her. It was about contemporary women artists and how some objectify their bodies through art in order to raise questions about female identity and sexual politics.'

'Very interesting', she said, sounding as if she really meant it. 'Does Quinn Sanderson represent her foundation?'

'Yes, I think so.'

'He is a very lucky man.'

'He discovered her.'

Resting her fingers on her chin she turned towards the photograph and then said, 'She made a few photographic series in her lifetime, didn't she? Which series does this one belong to?'

I took the List of Works, a two-paged, stapled document, from the top drawer of the desk, and replied after glancing through the first page, 'Introspection.'

'It's an enigmatic image,' she said, her words sounding distant as she headed towards the photograph. I lifted myself off my chair. Having managed a conversation with a potential buyer for the first time – and with the airy sense of freedom Quinn's absence granted me – I followed her, feeling profoundly buoyant, as if I were barefoot, walking across a shallow pool of lukewarm water.

'I love her installations, too,' she remarked.

'Quinn launched his previous New York gallery with a solo show of hers,' I said, reminding myself of an exhibition shot I had come across inside a textbook – and, more recently, the same image on the gallery's website: the first installation she had created for a gallery space. She'd covered the gallery with objects that uncannily resembled testicles, and had smeared the word *OUCH!* in what looked like blood across the gallery floor.

'She had a very wry sense of humour, but she didn't always use it. Sometimes she preferred to show a more contemplative side,' she said, her eyes hooked on the photograph.

23

I heard a man's exclamations over the cloud of murmurs, somewhere close by – beyond the partition I stood across from – and for a long second I couldn't place the voice's familiarity. When I realised that it was Lucian's, I was uncontrollably aroused by the thought of his physical proximity. As much as I wanted to hear the voice one more time – I wanted to be certain that it was his – I was temporarily deafened by the rising beat of my apprehension.

'How much does a photograph by her fetch these days?'

I could barely make out her words.

Just as the ear-pulsating beat began to slow its rhythm I sensed someone's soundless presence between us, the eerie feeling it generated uncomfortably familiar – as if from a disturbing nightmare I could no longer recall – while the mere thought that it could be Lucian made my heart resume its cage-pounding beat. Yet I still couldn't bring myself to turn my head and look.

'I'm not exactly sure. I would have to...' I mumbled, gazing vacantly at the pieces of stapled, already slightly creased paper I held between my frozen fingers.

'Not in the price range one would expect from an artist of her calibre, you know,' I heard Quinn's upbeat voice respond. Crestfallen, and yet also a little relieved, I sighed.

'She's an artist whose market value hasn't been fully realised – yet. Since her death her prices have been on a steady climb, but they haven't necessarily skyrocketed, if you know what I mean?' he said, boldly staring into the woman's eyes as if to urge her to properly consider his question. 'It's only a matter of time. From an investment point of view, she's definitely one to keep an eye on,' he continued, lowering his voice, as if he chose to share such valuable information only with collectors he'd taken an instant liking to. 'She's already a part of the canon, but I think, with time, people will understand the important role she played – particularly as a female artist, the effect she had on many artists of her generation, and the lasting effect she's bound to have on the next,' he added, maintaining eye contact with us both. This was a taste of the natural gift of persuasion he possessed, the openness he could project, the charm he could easily adopt.

'Thank you, Ada,' he said, slightly bowing his head in my direction, and lightly tapping his fingers on my shoulder. The energising effect of this unusual courtesy began to dwindle as I headed towards my desk, leaving in its place the artful insincerity that had prompted it.

I thought I heard Lucian's voice again. I hesitated, but could not bring myself to turn around, his maddening omnipresence now pressing its dizzying weight against my ribcage. I imagined him lingering above my head, and then a mere step behind me, sensing the extent of each of my consciously acknowledged, restrained footsteps like a savage hound. In the background, I overheard the woman explain to Quinn how she and her partner collected works of women artists. Her words sounded more remote than they actually were, as if her voice was finding its way to me through a cavernous airshaft. And when I once again heard – or *thought* I heard – Lucian's enticing voice shoot up (as if it were a sudden flare, rising above the indistinguishable utterances), I only managed to keep my weakened balance by pressing a hand on the glossy black surface of a pile of artists' catalogues resting on the edge of the desk. Moving away, I noticed the damp imprint I had left on them.

I heard, or thought I heard, his voice a number of times throughout the next few hours, carrying with me the distressing self-doubt that I was picking up another man's voice, someone I had never laid eyes upon, someone whose presence I could never bring myself to lust after as I did his. While I had once felt assured of my ability to separate reality from the fluid imaginings of my mind, these days it was not necessarily the case. I began to suspect that what I heard was, in fact, random, loud remarks made by other men that I had dubbed over with leftover recordings of his voice.

I saw fewer and fewer people passing along the corridor ahead, even fewer inquisitively poking their heads in to see if they had missed, during their frenzied search, an artwork they could aspire to own.

The chatter and bustle progressively de-escalated, and even Quinn began to abandon his mercantile pursuit. He sat quietly before me, hunched over his phone. My gaze frequently caught on the sporadic, nervous quivering of his right foot. I suppressed the many questions popping up inside my head – assuming that if he felt the desire to chat with me he would instigate a conversation, but unable to banish the doubt (for I could not help but always live in doubt) that my impassive stance was giving him the impression that I was lacking in ambition and uninterested in the goings-on of the gallery.

He sighed wearily.

'The collectors' preview is about to end in a few minutes,' he said in a flat voice, with a spiritless mien – like Lucian, but presumably owing to different reasons, appearing as if he had had enough of the Fair. Having for now discarded the charismatic exterior with which he captivated clients, he came across as any other middle-aged person: strained and fed up with life's petty hindrances and the continuous surge of tasks to see through.

He gave me an evasive glance, as if he found my company awkward, then ducked his head and began hastily tapping both thumbs on his battered phone, at once absorbed by the task. It seemed he was writing a long email; or perhaps he was drafting a list of detailed instructions for his employee, the one who had (with the help of an intern) taken sole charge of his Mayfair gallery, while he remained stranded at the Fair next to me.

Glancing up, he appeared stunned to see me, as if I had slipped through a gap in his perception – when all along I had been there, flicking through one of the artists' catalogues with perspiring hands, helplessly alert to the involuntary sounds made by our subtle movements, which seemed amplified by the silence between us. Perhaps a moment's mindfulness prompted him to lift his bent leg and release it, to straighten his posture and catch my averted gaze.

'Your father – has he ever participated in the Istanbul Biennale?' he asked, in a forced, friendly tone.

'No. The Istanbul Biennale showcases mostly very avant-garde types of practice and my father's paintings became too mainstream for it, I suppose,' I responded. The question conjured up the cerebral atmosphere of nearly bare, air-conditioned exhibition spaces – mostly showcasing conceptual art – the bright blue skies outside, late summer's mostly tolerable heat, and the tumultuous, erratic streets with their perplexed notion of urban aesthetics and bad planning. Magnificent structures reflecting the city's layered past were inappropriately juxtaposed

27

with poorly designed modern buildings of clashing architectural styles. In the haphazardly assembled streets, the majority bearing no visible names – nor sufficiently functioning drainage systems, for that matter – one found dangerously narrow, uneven pedestrian sidewalks built with no regard for the very young, the elderly or the disabled: a testament to unattainable ideals and a lack of foresight, to longstanding and thriving corruption.

'There's one the year after next, isn't there? I might actually go. Maybe you can come with me and introduce me to a few good people,' he said. And though I nodded and smiled at him agreeably, I couldn't possibly see how I could fulfil such a request. I continued to question the genuineness of it: whether it was a passing thought which carried no weight, or whether it was an idea he had already properly considered. By now, he could have realised – from the beautifully printed hardback about my father's work I had brought him – my father's revered status and influence as a local artist. He might have made the sound assumption that, as his daughter, I had access to people he would otherwise not get to meet.

'I'd love to check out all the historical sites when I'm out there,' he said, with an apparent sincerity I found unconvincing. Then, perhaps having finally realised I hadn't had a proper rest all day, he added, 'Oh, do you want to have a little break or something?'

I shrugged my shoulders indecisively. I didn't want to appear too keen to leave.

'Maybe you want to eat something or, I don't know, wander around a bit?' And then, all of a sudden: 'Listen, I'm *so* sorry.' He covered his face with one hand, shaking his head. 'I got totally carried away. Jeez, you must be starving. Did you at least manage to have a snack or something?'

Preoccupied with monitoring his territory during the day, he had only at one point glanced in my direction after nodding along to someone else's remarks. At the time, he seemed to have detected the energy bar I had tried to conceal between the metal frame of the glass desk and my lap (while taking discreet bites out of it). Perhaps he had edited out such trivial details and spared his strength for analysing customers' subtle reactions, random remarks and suggestive gestures in order to glean the seriousness of their pursuits, the kind of art that might best appeal to their acquired tastes, and, most importantly, their spending power. Or perhaps he was someone who, when not ruthlessly goaded on by his sharp commercial instincts, lost the drive to make engaging conversation, which prompted him to ask questions he already knew the answers to.

'I had an energy bar,' I said uncomfortably.

He nodded, already aloof again, seemingly waylaid by another thought.

'I guess now that we're on a break, it would be wise for me to have something a little more substantial.' Sensing the strain of our stiff conversation on my vocal cords, I sustained an unnatural, frozen smile I found hard to undo.

He gave me a sideways glance, then took his time carefully aligning the catalogues at the top of the pile that had tilted a different way from the rest. Guilt trickled through me for not having noticed the slight irregularity.

'It *would* be nice to take a look around the Fair, if I could,' I added, more relaxed than before, having now come to the conclusion it was *his* social ineptness that had triggered mine.

I was somewhat amused by the childlike psychology governing our interaction.

'Well then, now is your time,' he said, then paused and pressed his chin against his neck to suppress a belch. 'Why don't you come back in half an hour? No, actually,' he continued, elevating his chin, 'Make that forty minutes. But you mustn't be late,' he added almost immediately, already seeming to fret about his uncalled-for lenience. 'I need to go through some crucial stuff with you before the preview cocktail begins.' He pushed at the bridge of his glasses. His mood seemed indicative of the kind of solemn intensity which made one fail to recognise undercurrents of humour and serendipity in one's life. I glanced over to the entrance of the booth and noticed a couple of people wander by, each with the Fair catalogue tucked under their arm. Their composure briefly lifted me out of Quinn's bleak point of view, which seemed to be engulfed by his doubt about people and their abilities, and by his constant fear of losing control.

'It's going to be swarming with people knocking their drinks around everywhere. People tend to lose their sense of spatial awareness after one glass. They start leaning on the artworks, stacking their empty glasses on pedestals. It's a disgrace. To see how little respect people have for art, for other people's property.'

The belittling tone, the misanthropic glint in his eyes, had managed to undermine his otherwise undisputable complaint. He dropped his shoulders, grabbed his phone and started aggressively tapping on its miniature keypad, as if wishing to divert his attention elsewhere.

'Each year, it's the same shebang,' I heard him mutter bitterly, in a state of listless boredom, without looking up, just before I left his side. It seemed he was talking to himself as much as he was talking to me.

As I dipped in and out of gallery booths, neither following a systematic trail nor absorbing the surrounding art, I was greeted by the mercenary smiles of gallery staff, who were either lolling around in their uncomfortable seats – some half-heartedly chewing flavourless, ready-made meals – or unflaggingly chatting up the odd collector who happened to still be prowling around. Unable to sense the bond I assumed the shared experience of working at the Fair would generate, I felt dazzled by their alien faces and the intrusively bright spotlights, which laid bare an aloof and unflattering reality I already felt detached from: minimalist gestures, ephemeral impressions, blown-up digital imagery, crudely expressed self-confessions, thick impasto slabs of colour, lacquered surfaces, objects on pedestals and neon lights, all of which I processed as part of an overwhelmingly rich, vibrant whole I was mostly reluctant to separate into its component parts.

Throughout, Lucian's condemnation of art fairs accompanied me as a strong, particular feeling I couldn't assign elsewhere. I became haunted by the nervous anticipation of running into him, often startling myself as if I were just about to do so (I never did), skirting the edges of intertwined corridors, unintentionally returning to familiar corners, entering booths I had passed through minutes ago, and deliberately overlooking in-between spaces. I imagined him to be patiently lurking in these partitions, as if he were an apparition inside a dream I wished to desperately escape from – all the while fervently going round in circles in search of its shadow.

Gradually my fixation ran its course, but only after reliving the same climax of lust and jarring angst I imagined my sudden encounter with him would create. For some time afterwards it left me feeling burned out and numb.

III

'Ada!'

My concise name means *island*, and, in Turkish, suggests a romanticised, quasi-melancholic oasis of seclusion.

As she called out for me with relief, suggesting she had been searching for some time, I too was overcome by a profound happiness to at last be reunited with her. For a few moments her arrival halted everything – and it was only the savoury-sour aftertaste still lingering inside my mouth that prompted me to restore the feeble, involuntary perception of myself that had reigned over me all day, shaped by opinions I imagined people I encountered had of me (however skin-deep, or in fact untrue, they may have been), and by the merciless self-scrutiny I subjected myself to. For a brief moment, the unfavourable tang, reinforced by my thirstiness, returned me to the sushi bar at the far end of the Art Fair, and to the strangely liberating, wistful sense of solitude which had invisibly cocooned me away from the refined, poised strangers who had surrounded me. It had granted me a clarity of vision and inner contentment I didn't these days naturally possess: a rare moment of insight – which I now, perhaps with childlike naivety, found comfort in reading as a prelude to Tijen's much-anticipated arrival at the Fair, as if there were a hidden, whimsical logic behind it.

'The minute I arrived I went straight to your stand. I introduced myself to Quinn. He said you were out on a break. I've called you endless times.'

'My phone was on silent.'

She joyfully embraced me. Her strong, loving grip soon became too uncomfortable to physically withstand. As she kissed my cheeks, I sensed the gooey consistency her glistening lips left behind, while the musky floral perfume rising from her skin brought to my mind an idealised essence of the life I had left behind in Istanbul.

'Gosh, look what I've done!' she exclaimed, leaning back to examine my cheeks with an exaggerated, comical expression. Then she stared with genuine affection into my eyes in the intense way she usually did, as if she was trying to intuit whether Quinn had rushed to offer me full-time employment at his gallery after I had worked alongside him for less than a day; a highly unlikely possibility, in my view, but one which had unavoidably dominated our recent phone conversations (along with Turkey's unpredictable, worrisome future).

As she began to rub the smudges off my cheeks with an elder-sister attentiveness, her eyes, faintly enhanced with neutral, shimmery eyeshadow, seemed to contain a taciturn sadness which only revealed itself when she was far more tired than her desperately hectic life (mother to six-year-old twin girls, head of one of Istanbul's most successful contemporary art galleries, sustaining a loveless marriage) permitted her to be.

'That's better,' she said, after a long pause, her unsure expression suggesting otherwise.

I involuntarily touched one of my cheeks and said, 'I was worried about you. I thought you'd get here by noon,' while admitting to myself, with remorse, how throughout the day, in the face of various distractions, the prospect of her arrival had lost its pressing significance.

Rolling her eyes, she let out a terse, humourless giggle and then responded, 'That makes two of us.'

'But what happened?'

'Oh, don't ask,' she responded with a wide, unbothered smile. Her usual initial reluctance to share occasional mishaps – or personal issues she chose to underplay – with those who were closest to her had permitted her to maintain a relatively non-confrontational marriage for the past decade. She and her husband shared the same bed but not the same life.

'How come you're so late?' I rephrased my question. She calmly reached forward to shift a lock of my hair that had been covering nearly half of my face; as she carefully fastened it behind my ear with her elegant fingers (bearing several modernist rings with huge semi-precious stones), I was momentarily taken aback by the unobstructed view that appeared before me: one I had been deliberately depriving myself of, and what little sense this all made.

'Sweetheart, my flight got severely delayed because they couldn't get the TV screens to work. In the end they made us switch planes.' A spark of humour appeared in her eyes.

'Oh, that must've been awful!' I found myself imagining the stifling boredom and frustration, the disquieting unpredictability and purposelessness, of being trapped inside a stationary aircraft.

With a sigh, she said, 'But I'm here now.' Wearing a wide, content smile on her face, resting her hands serenely on her abdomen (above the even, wide pleats of her halfway-buttoned, high-waisted black coat), she eagerly gazed around. Her intellect, grace and magnetic warmth infused her well-proportioned yet unremarkable face with an endearing beauty.

'It's so good to see you. I've missed you so much,' I said, in a well-intended but clearly futile attempt to divert her curiosity from the scarcely populated corridors of the Art Fair. But the heartfelt reality of what I had said nearly brought tears to my eyes.

'Oh, sweetie, I've missed you too,' she responded tenderly, tilting her head; she gave the impression that, like me, she was also reminiscing: remembering our guileless discussions, our idle ponderings in the late afternoons. Every other fortnight or so, still dressed in my school uniform, I used to drop in on her after school, energetically trotting across her vast gallery whilst schlepping a bulging backpack. Exchanging perfunctory greetings with her soft-spoken employees – who continued to work and move about with thoughtful discretion – I would vanish behind the closed doors of her sleek office, situated at the far end of her gallery. For nearly a century prior, it had been a sought-after residential flat, taking up the entire first floor of an arresting Art Nouveau building on the youth-populated İstiklal Avenue; a bystander to the untold chronicles of now-deceased individuals, to uncountable instances of domestic routine, to moments of familial bliss, needless disputes and much avoidable heartache. And all this had left no obvious residue in its airy high-ceilinged rooms.

Now predominantly occupied by art galleries and graphic design studios, the building was a short stroll away from Taksim Square, a site that – since witnessing the violent massacre of 1977's May Day – had achieved an eternal, symbolic resonance with Turkey's perishing left-wing struggle. Countless civil protests fired up by inequality and the injustices common citizens found themselves up against had taken place there.

35

And, quite recently, with the Gezi Park protests – sparked off by disproportionate, severe police brutality – a small, peaceful group protesting the destruction of Gezi Park in the square had prompted a wave of unprecedented demonstrations that lasted for several weeks, and which rapidly spread across the country. They quickly spiralled into a polyphonic, ardent uproar against the ruling establishment's misconduct – its reckless abolition of urban green space for personal profit; its increasing reliance on excessive police force, even during peaceful protests; its systematic efforts to infringe upon the secular order; the growing restrictions upon freedom of expression and the freedom of the press; its haphazard eagerness to plunge the country into a war with neighbouring Syria. Above all, against escalating authoritarianism, conveyed daily through polarising rhetoric.

'I was at your father's studio a couple of days ago. We're planning to have the show in late April.'

'That's wonderful news,' I said, with the dedicated zeal of a proud daughter. All the same, I felt an unforgiving resentment, an aching sadness. I remained silently ashamed by the yearning and envy I couldn't help but harbour – for not being present in his studio at that decisive moment, as I had been on so many occasions in the past.

'It's been definitely worth the five-year wait.'

'I wish I could be there at the opening.'

'I have a strong feeling that you will,' she replied, with a clairvoyant's confidence.

A few seconds of contemplative stillness drifted between us before she added, somewhat cautiously, perhaps concerned that she was intruding, 'They both miss you terribly.'

Reflecting on the text message I had received from them early that morning (*Best of luck on your first day of work! We know you'll do brilliantly! Love, Mum & Dad*) I was filled with their warmth, then by a deep longing for their company.

'I wish they could come over again soon.'

'I'm sure they will.'

Marlene had advised me many times during our sessions that it was within a person's ability to reverse negative feelings once they arose – as if flipping a light switch inside one's awareness – by placing oneself in a positive state of mind. I gazed upwards at a couple of charmless spotlights – repeated fixtures on an expansive, industrial metal grid which hung ungraciously throughout the entire exhibition hall – and sighed deeply, intending to purge the heavy gloom with which I deliberated the uncertainties in my near future. I quickly came to regard my difficulty breathing as a psychosomatic delusion of this mindset, from which, at present, it didn't seem easy to disengage.

'If I somehow find a way to remain here a bit longer,' I managed to say with very little hope, 'my mother said they can come to visit me in February when her university goes on a month's break.'

'What a brilliant plan,' Tijen responded cheerfully, as if urging me to take a more optimistic view. She then pleadingly added, 'Dearest Ada, I'm so sorry I'm unable to stay for even one night to be with you.' She reached over to caress one of my motionless hands, arching her eyebrows and dropping her bottom lip, an infantile expression momentarily passing over her face which, rather than being laughable, appeared sincere, and further highlighted the distinct traits she had passed to her nearly identical daughters. I hadn't seen them in the flesh since the turn of unforeseen events – to this day nightmarishly unfathomable to me – had caused me to flee Istanbul in the summer of 2013. Nevertheless, I had been kept up to date with, and continued to be fascinated by, the degree to which their physical features and behavioural quirks had developed and shifted over a two-year period. Tijen – the devoted mother that she was – continued to share photographs and videos with me regularly.

'No, don't worry. Of course I understand,' I hastily replied, composing a believable façade of confidence. While I was beyond grateful to finally have her next to me, regardless of how transitory our encounter was to be, I couldn't help but feel disenchanted by our friendship, even choosing in this moment to overlook the brief visit she had made to London, two years ago – almost immediately after I had left Istanbul. She had come to be by my side at an exceptionally difficult time when I'd needed her the most, and had given me dedicated support since. It raised the much-evaded yet lingering question: *why*, given this rare opportunity, she hadn't set her gruelling obligations aside once again, when I required her consoling companionship nearly as much?

'Tijen is a very ambitious businesswoman, but she's also a very loyal friend. Otherwise she wouldn't be calling you as frequently as she does. You have to accept people for who they are,' Marlene had pointed out at our last session, in her usual hypnotically calming voice.

Not someone who displayed tactile affection as Tijen did, I nevertheless momentarily caressed one of Tijen's hands to reciprocate her gesture. I felt relieved as I gently pulled away.

'Sweetheart, everything's *so* crazy right now,' she said, rolling her eyes in an exaggerated manner. From time to time, she found it difficult to tolerate the all-consuming intensity of the routine she had set out for herself. It conveniently left her little time for contemplation, particularly in relation to her drained, dead-end marriage – which she no longer saw any point in discussing at great length – and how she was intending to spend the rest of her life with a man who seemed to plan his life around how he could best avoid her.

'I promise that as soon as things quiet down in the next few months, I will make the time to come and see you. I'll stay with you in that bijou flat of yours. Don't worry about me, I'm more than happy to sleep on the sofa.'

'Don't be silly. We can share my bed, like we did before. And this time I can take you to some of my favourite places,' I said eagerly, attempting to recover some positive momentum. Meanwhile, I privately reflected on the sullen, forlorn mood that had clouded her previous visit to London. We had barely left my stifling flat, owing to my mortified, self-blaming state of mind at the time, as well as my distorted sense of reality, governed by repetitive, paranoia-infused thoughts of the highly improbable yet distressing kind.

'And maybe one night you and I can go on the prowl,' she added, winking at me playfully – a selfless plan, all in the name of restoring my interest and faith in men. Her unyielding, difficult-to-justify faithfulness to her husband – notwithstanding her years of perpetual marital discontent – had steadily blunted the confidence she used to project towards men, along with the visceral desire that had once inhabited her.

'I actually miss the days I could leisurely stroll about the streets of a foreign city, walking for hours and even developing blisters on my feet!'

At thirty-two, she was ten years older than me. Her earnest comment had caused me to wonder whether, when I reached her age, I would also be constrained by obligation to the extent that she was – until I realised I had *already* involuntarily placed myself in a position where I had much less freedom than she did.

'Last evening I attended Wagner's *Walküre* at the Royal Opera House in Covent Garden,' I said, apropos of nothing.

'Sweetheart, I'm so envious of you.'

'I bought the cheapest ticket there was – nine pounds, months in advance. The seat was an uncomfortable, creaky wooden bench at the top edge of the amphitheatre. Once I adjusted to being so high up, and accepted the restricted view of the stage, I loved every second of it,' I said, still entranced by the rousing, dark melancholy of Wagner's complex score. I'd managed to sweep aside my initial unease as I sat snugly between two strangers I never got to fully observe. As I listened to the ludic free-jamming of musicians tuning their instruments, the growing clatter of the expectant crowd filled every square foot of the dimly lit venue – limbless, relentlessly swirling creatures. I faced the deep fall descending beneath me, my remarkable proximity to the majestic gilded dome above my head and my bird's-eye view of the curtained stage below: both, from time to time, threatening to draw me into the emptiness. Once the lights had been lowered, and the rising applause indicated the emergence of the conductor – who remained out of my visual range throughout the duration of the performance – I focused on a group of string instruments generating an intensifying quiver, which aroused within me anticipation of the turbulent narrative ahead, and my anxiety faded into the background.

'You'll see. Once they manage to turn the regime into a dictatorship, under the flimsy disguise of a so-called presidency, they will soon put a ban on opera and classical music performances, claiming that such practices are against our cultural heritage and moral values. Who knows? Maybe they will make the same claim one day when they decide to put a padlock on the front door of my gallery.'

'Do you really believe they will go so far?' I asked, still somewhat unsure if I should fully give in to the strengthening consensus. Since the current order in Turkey had first risen to power – a vague event in the background of my childhood when, like most ten-year-olds, my interests lay in friendships, assumed romantic affiliations with distant boys, and Harry Potter – many believed the doomed republic had been on its cautiously and tactically plotted course towards one day becoming a fully fledged Islamic autocracy under the sole jurisdiction of one leader. If this was true, my parents later argued with remorse, it had been a rather difficult thing to determine at the time. They were using a line of genuine but weak defence, just as other likeminded frontline liberals had, for their initial trusting support for the new proprietors of the country, who had rather convincingly sloughed off their stern Islamic nationalist convictions and re-imagined themselves as moderate conservatives. But my parents also regretted their naive optimism, created by their desire to see their country move forward, to catch up to its European counterparts and become a proper democracy: first and foremost by declaring the prevailing constitution obsolete, and by the drafting of a new, relatively progressive constitution – one of the early ambitious undertakings of the freshly appointed administration, never to be achieved. At the time, it had ardently claimed it would honour and grant necessary freedoms to all segments of society: to ensure the Kurdish minority's entitlement to speak and teach in their mother tongue, and to solidify the right to openly practise one's religion, revoking the much-disputed ban on headscarves in the public sector. It seemed an all-embracing, non-interventionist stance on personal liberties, appearing to support the liberal vision that one day soon Turkey was to become a true democracy – provided it could set itself free from the interventions of a self-serving army through clever manoeuvres carried out by the new ruling class – and thus finally gain its acceptance as an exceptional yet vital member of the European Union. A country where atheists, Christians, Jews, Muslims, Alevis, Shias, Armenians, Kurds, ultra-liberals, nihilist bohemians, pragmatic moderates, loyal Kemalists, hardline nationalists and devout Islamists could peacefully exist side by side.

'Oh sweetheart, I no longer know anything. I take things one day at a time. Serkan and I have stopped watching the evening news. There's no point in being reminded on a daily basis that we have absolutely no hope left for the future,' she said, weariness and hostility briefly seizing her face. Upon careful inspection, I saw barely visible lines on either side of her mouth, and under her eyes slight dents which had not been there before.

'I've missed you so much,' I said once again, the same words taking on a broader meaning. I watched her expression lighten and, as I did, I considered the gratification I obtained in being able to identify the different guises her face could adopt, and how I recognised an element of her subtle beauty in every one.

When she spontaneously pulled me towards her and wrapped her arms around me, I sensed her floaty perfume again, now in a warm, concentrated fusion with her bodily scent.

'Istanbul isn't the same without you,' she said softly into my ear, while I hugged her with equal, unrestrained intensity. I could distinguish the density of her bones under her winter attire and her flesh; embracing her with all my strength, I had to hold back the titanic surge of emotion, which felt as if it were trapped at the far end of my soft palate. I could not bring myself to swallow. Its urgency began to dwindle but not entirely disappear – and as we began to gradually, with mutual unspoken accord, loosen our tight grips on one another, Marlene's frequently voiced, comforting statement entered my mind: *there's absolutely nothing wrong with crying*. I suppose it gave legitimacy to the tears gathered at the rims of my eyes, waiting to spill over the moment I blinked.

'Sweet Ada, we all miss you terribly. But it would be mighty selfish for us to want you to come back just for that reason. Istanbul has got a lot worse since you've left. It's lost its grace and dignity. People are so inconsiderate of one another.'

I nodded in silence, swiftly eliminating a few tears just as they began their journey down my hot, dishevelled face, as the combination of loneliness and undignified self-pity that hounded me on some nights fought my fragile temper.

When I looked back at her I was greeted by her concerned stare.

'It's not that I don't value being here,' I said, having reminded myself of the irony of the effort I had made, over three years

43

ago, to convince my protective parents to support me in my move to London to study for a bachelor's degree in History of Art (a choice of subject my father had initially frowned upon). In those days I had an urgent desire for self-sufficiency, and an overpowering want to be exposed to a fundamentally different cultural mindset than the one I had grown up in.

'I don't mind the weather and I have made a few good friends. I appreciate the fact that drivers stop at zebra crossings, policemen don't carry guns, that I hardly ever get verbally or physically harassed by strange men when walking down the street, and that there's a sufficiently functioning underground system.'

'These days we seem to have round-the-clock gridlock,' Tijen said, with an air of habitual discontent. 'If I didn't have a gallery to run, I would refuse to leave my neighbourhood, like your father,' she added with conviction, which – knowing she would never willingly surrender herself to such a restrictive life-style – I found highly amusing. 'I'm happy I've managed to put a smile back on your face. You look so pretty when you smile.'

I did continue to smile, somewhat shyly, aware that the recent flood of emotion (which had left me flushed) was likely to disguise my blush – an inevitable outcome of such a direct compliment, even coming from her.

'Istanbul is my home. Despite all its faults I still miss my country terribly,' I said, as trifling opinions and comparisons were altogether replaced by an ingrained devotion and an una-bated longing for my homeland I could not casually dismiss.

'Of course you do. One should never forget one's roots,' she replied, her dutiful tone reminding me of the framed poster she had of Mustafa Kemal Atatürk. It portrayed him in his senior years: a blond receding hairline, a composed, fatherly posture, and immaculately dressed as always. He sat in a double-breasted summer suit, complemented by a white matching tie and handkerchief, pensively staring ahead – as if into the uncharted future of a country he had founded, against all odds, with unyielding courage, idealistic conviction and fortitude. Virtues that were absent in today's leaders, who mostly exhibited limited abilities, fraudulent intentions and insular worldviews.

The poster, originally a one-off supplement to *Hayat* – once an in-demand weekly, now no longer in print – carried a caption underneath which read, *Our Father, We Follow Your Trail.* It took pride of place across from Tijen's neat desk, right beside the door, as if to constantly remind her of – and to assert to anyone who entered through her office – her unyielding commitment to the legacy Atatürk had left behind. With its poor print quality and bold colours – which over the years had acquired a tint of yellow that added to its retro appeal – it stood out from the rest of the artwork gracing her walls. Among the works was a painting belonging to my father, intricately executed with layers of confluent, abstract signs, painted in strikingly compatible hues. She had acquired it from his previous exhibition; she did this with all her artists, as a part of their agreement with her.

I had got to know *Hayat* through my father, who had inherited several volumes of its leather-bound copies from his long-deceased paternal grandparents – who had been Turkish-stock Balkan migrants, and who had to face displacement, separation and loss. Forced to abandon their possessions, and in their haste to evacuate their homelands during the breakdown of the Empire, most of them had chosen to settle in Istanbul, lured there by its lively splendour and rich prospects. They were the first generation of the newly formed republic – where westernisation, implemented in more cautious measures during the late Ottoman era, was being adopted assertively and in all aspects of life. They conformed to the new social order, to a Muslim society where for the first time religion had been pulled from the public to the private sphere.

Along with well-maintained, chronologically arranged copies of *Hayat*, intermittently covering the late sixties and early seventies, my father had also acquired through a different source a few copies of its American counterpart *Life* – also no longer in print – from roughly the same period. Side by side, one could see how the Turkish equivalent had borrowed its name, and a nearly identical visual format, from its predecessor – with its weekly covers predominantly featuring glamorous, décolleté actresses with beehive coiffures and well-practised smiles.

'Of course, if they hadn't so effectively brought the army to its knees, and infested it with their own people, like they did with the police force and the justice system, things would be very different today,' she said. She had voiced the same opinion to me numerous times; it was as if repeating it as often as she did allowed her to gradually come to terms with an irreversible, agonising state of affairs.

'The previous army would've intervened long ago,' I said, more to please her than anything else. Since Turkey's secularist foundation seemed under substantial threat, and the country had already retreated from democracy, a further coup by the army, however dishonourable, might be seen by some as a less devastating scenario (and stern Kemalists such as Tijen, who valued secularism over democracy, would likely think so). While I could recognise the pragmatic intention in decisively removing power from those who had so brazenly abused it, I (like my parents and their close friends) couldn't ignore the feebleness, the shameful hypocrisy, and the regressive effects of replacing one wrongdoer with another – even as the question of whether secularism and true democracy could ever be fully implemented in Turkey (and if so, if it could last) retained its disconcerting relevance.

Tijen sighed, hopeless. She took a couple of steps back and looked me up and down for the very first time.

'Have you lost a bit of weight?'

My skinny jeans *were* somewhat looser than usual. I shrugged my shoulders at her.

'Sweetheart, I hope you're looking after yourself and eating properly. I know how you can get when you're left to your own devices,' she said.

'I feel as if even if I am acquitted at next month's hearing, and I happen to find a legitimate and effective way to stay and build up my life in London, I will be continuously haunted.'

'Of course you're going to be acquitted. Haunted by what?'

'By the guilt of turning my back on what's happening, of putting myself first.'

'Dearest Ada. You're so young. What I now cherish most about my early twenties is my complete ignorance and self-centeredness back then. I used to think the entire world revolved around me and my issues. You're so very different. I wouldn't want you to waste your youth on something you lack control over. You cannot imagine how quickly the years pile on. It only feels like yesterday I was the same age as you,' she said.

I found her well-intended advice hard to relate to, if not slightly bothersome.

'We need to think of ourselves first, and the well-being of our families. Look at what happened in Ukraine. All those courageous protestors died for no reason. Russia will never allow Ukraine to enter the European Union, in the same way the European Union would never have granted us membership. Even if we sussed out how to catch lightning in a bottle,' Tijen said – and for a moment I sensed my opinions bending towards her levelheaded, compartmentalised vision, before defaulting to my usual frame of thought.

'We sometimes think everything is set in stone when it is, in fact, in a state of constant change. The current political climate in Turkey has become too grotesque to sustain itself. It will inevitably come to a breaking point.'

'Of course it will, but *when*?'

I shrugged my shoulders. I was frustrated that my viewpoint could easily be disputed by a single, rather basic question.

'In the meantime, they are letting more and more Syrians through our border. The Syrians are their latest currency. Before the Syrians it was the Kurds and before the Kurds it was the liberals and of course the *Cemaat*. How on earth they plan to look after all those Syrians, when already such a large fraction of the population – many of whom ironically happen to be their main supporters – live in such disgraceful circumstances, is beyond me. The Syrians are everywhere in Istanbul, begging. I frequently come across small families with forlorn expressions; they're outcasts in a city which has no mercy even for its own. They've escaped war and now they need to escape extreme poverty.'

As Tijen expressed her frustration with an intensity that bordered on the comical, my mind was drawn to the absurdity of all the injustice in the world – fully aware this was by no means a new phenomenon. I considered the subtle tension in the air at the start of the Fair, as VIP collectors competed with each other, discreetly negotiating with dealers in a multitude of languages over ludicrously priced artworks, while across the world queues of people were desperately waiting to be let through at the barren Turkish–Syrian border, guarded by soldiers with expressionless faces.

'They're shrewd tacticians. They can detect a lucrative opportunity in the most destructive of circumstances – they can deliberately create those circumstances in order to win an election. The Syrian migrants, the ignorant, impoverished segment of the population who continue to vote for them, the foolish liberals who once happily sucked up to them, the treacherous *Cemaat* who initially were their greatest ally, and their latest enemy, the Kurds, who they have cornered into a compromised position – for them, they're just chess pieces they can strategically shuffle around to prolong their sovereignty.'

'But how come the entirety of the country isn't outraged by the deaths of civilians in the southeast?'

'On the day the Kurds declared they would stand in the way of the presidency they were rebranded as public enemy number one. Since then the partisan press has gone to great efforts to blur the distinction between Kurdish civilians and Kurdish terrorists. On the whole, people have very little compassion for terrorists,' Tijen responded tactfully, as always careful in my company to show how she was of course fully accepting towards a portion of the Kurdish population (primarily those who had moved to big cities and had managed to assimilate

49

themselves convincingly, to such an extent that any traces of their ethnicity had vanished under an imposing Turkish identity), while playing down her underlying discontent and apprehension, shared by most Turks, towards Kurdish people's demands to be granted some autonomy in the southeastern domain – an area chiefly populated by them for centuries, and neglected by all governments past and present.

'But is it that simple to deceive people?' I asked, and as I did so the implausible narrative of a late sixties Yesilçam movie I had watched one afternoon entered into my thoughts. It was a movie with patchy, dubbed audio and shoddy editing, portraying a heartbroken brunette heroine with clownish glasses who, having been callously abandoned by her wealthy, conceited boyfriend, re-entered his life after some time as his new love interest. As part of her revenge plot, she hid her real identity by dyeing her hair blonde and vamping herself up with excessive makeup and fancy clothes. The crude storyline, astonishingly able to keep one keenly hooked, effectively identified our susceptibility to deception and the cunning ability we possess to deceive others – predispositions that are, to varying degrees, present in every one of us.

'Oh, sweetheart, people only see what they want to see,' she answered in a reluctant tone, her bright eyes projecting the empathetic warmth she nevertheless continued to foster. Her behaviour seemed to indicate that we had to somehow hope for the best, even when most people's perceptions were skewed by prejudices that had been gradually ingrained in us from an early age – like patterns of destructive behaviour picked up during childhood – and which we rarely possessed the strength of will and skills of self-reasoning to abandon. That probably applied to me to some extent, as it did to Tijen, considering her unchallengeable commitment to Kemalism and its defects, and her compliance to an elitist order she would happily want Turkey to return to.

As she tilted her head and frowned pensively, her demeanour once again brought forward the still-vivid memory of her bubbly daughters, and for a moment I imagined myself back in their enchanting room, filled with glitter and shades of lilac, sturdy wooden toys and an abundance of pretty dolls and soft animals. I recalled our games of hide and seek, which they always insisted I play whenever I visited Tijen's flat. All this entered my mind. Their lovable gullibility, which caused me to smile internally as I remembered how, amidst plenty of giggling and ear-piercing screeching, I would find the girls hiding in the same spot they always hid in.

'You know what's really sad? I keep coming across more and more enlightened, beautiful people who are looking at ways to leave. They fear they have no future in a country where their civil liberties are at stake.'

Not wanting her to carry on – concerned it would in no time lead to me and how I intended to stay in London, a subject I had become tired of thinking about (and even more so of discussing with her) – I nodded silently as I reflected on the growing number of young Turkish people I had met lately. Most of them had impressive degrees and solid work experience, and had recently arrived in London, having plucked up the courage to leave behind their families, their friends, their lives. Most of them were just about able to maintain a living in this costly city by cleaning homes, working on building sites and waiting tables in shady restaurants, with the fragile hope that, if they managed to stick around long enough, one day they would be given the opportunity to practise their real occupations and reclaim their quality of living.

'Do Dilara and Ceylan really still remember me? It's totally normal if they don't. And I promise I won't be upset, I'm just curious to know the truth, that's all.'

'Trust me, they do!' she insisted, seeming amused by my eager bid to retain my hazy, fading image inside the fluid minds of two six-year-olds. 'They might not remember you as thoroughly as an adult might. But whenever they see a photo of you on my phone or on my iPad they always say, 'That's Ada!'

Imagining the adorableness of their responses made in precise unison, I smiled, for a moment enjoying the light-hearted optimism this brought – until the question of when, if ever, I would see them again shifted my mood further into the oppressive pit of darkness that, now and again, it kept stumbling back into.

Two men with sharp English accents passed us, creating a current of air I sensed at my fingertips. Tijen paused. Taking her time, she observed the towering sculpture in soft pastel hues showcased by a South Korean gallery, which appeared to mimic the floating tentacles of a sea anemone. It was accompanied by intricately detailed, abstract pencil drawings on large segments of thick paper, each one carefully pinned to the walls of a single panel. Then her gaze continued to an assembly of soft sculptures with interconnecting units spread across the floor of a Peruvian gallery's cubicle. These were enhanced with colourful beads, a peculiarly decorative amalgamation which rather cleverly took its inspiration from a blood pressure monitor, a toilet pump, and the Peruvian weaving tradition.

They were fine examples of artworks present at the Fair which were most unlike any of the local art she regularly came across in Istanbul; her eyes glistened with an exhausted kind of happiness, I suspect, reinforced by the privilege she ascribed to attending the VIP collectors' preview – however short this visit was intended to be. It probably made it worth her while to endure the laborious day's journey from Istanbul to London, and then back to Istanbul, which would have her tiptoeing into her flat in the silence of the early morning while her children and Serkan remained fast asleep in their rooms.

'Dearest Ada, you're so very lucky to be here. If I were in your place, I would do everything in my power to stay.'

Involuntarily, I rolled my eyes at her.

'You're just making it sound easy.'

'We both know it's not impossible for you to stay here. I already told you, I could easily help you. If you're unable to get yourself a job between now and the end of February when your visa runs out, you can apply for a self-employment visa through the Ankara Agreement, which will allow you to set up a limited company in the UK.'

'I don't know, we'll see. I suppose I should,' I mumbled, with little desire to continue the conversation in this vein.

'You told me yourself: there are Turkish lawyers in London who specialise in the Ankara Agreement. Go and speak to one. Do it next week. Do it before it's too late.' We had discussed how seeking asylum in the UK was never an option, unless I absolutely had to – it would prevent me from going back home for five whole years, irrespective of any changes to my situation that might occur during this period.

'But what will I say?'

This was perhaps manipulative of me, but I felt able to say it in front of Tijen, whose understanding disposition made her tolerant of such remarks. Additionally, it seemed to me indicative of my morale, brought low in the last few weeks by my indecision, which intensified as the date of my court hearing drew closer. I was terrified by the verdict I would receive, and felt a profound sadness for the bleak future of my country. Sometimes I saw it as a colossal, sinking liner I was being made to watch from a distant shore.

'You can say you wish to set up an art dealership that specialises in Turkish contemporary art,' she replied, unaffected by my unseemly question.

I hunched my shoulders and nodded, ill at ease for having made her spell out what I already knew. I had discussed this strategy, and a few others, with her multiple times over the phone.

'Do you secretly believe they're going to sentence me to prison?' I asked in a lifeless voice.

I had been charged with assisting a criminal organisation, resisting public officials and assaulting a police officer. I could receive up to thirteen years in prison. Regardless of people's reassurances, I assumed they would find me guilty in the end. If not for all the charges I had been wrongfully accused of, then on the grounds that I had fled the country a day before having to appear in court.

'Sweetheart, of course not! We all know these hearings are just another way for them to intimidate people. In your case, they already know they're at fault. This is just a formality which has been unnecessarily dragging on due to our wretched bureaucracy. The judge has no choice but to decide in your favour.'

'You really think so?' I asked, desperately trying to cling to the very little hope I harboured.

'Yes, with all my heart,' she responded, her eyes charged with empathy. She reached out briefly to caress my chin with her fingers, an act which took me back several years – to a time when the nature of our relationship had been fundamentally different. I had been too young to be her friend, and instead had to observe her with the awe and admiration teenage girls foster towards young women with grown-up lives.

For a moment, her zealous spirit was able to convince me that the court ruling was bound to clear me of the charges. I considered the other Gezi Park protestors who had also been arrested. Like me, their participation in the protest had been met with open-ended offences. After being driven from pillar to post within the dreary Turkish judiciary system, nearly every person was acquitted; a few were given fines.

'Oh Tijen, I cannot begin to imagine that soon my days as a fugitive will be behind me!' I said almost breathlessly, as if I had been walking briskly. I smiled a fragile smile – astonished that a situation I had unwillingly learnt to accept and adapt to in the course of two years could one day become something I would only associate with my past.

'Sweetheart. You never did anything wrong. We were all there, remember?'

I shrugged my shoulders. Then I nodded.

'Remember the many times I dropped in on you, after having to close up the gallery early? It was like having a massive carnival right on the doorstep.'

Her one-sided recollection of what it had been like brought to my mind a panoramic view: at the time it resembled a modern rendition of an epic warzone. I had instinctively followed a few protestors I had not previously met into an unfamiliar building; many considerate residents in the area had left the entrances to their buildings unlocked for us. Up a flight of stairs and into a small, squalid top-floor flat – a charitable old man, overdressed in a saggy knitted cardigan, insisted we take our shoes off before entering his flat. He offered us lukewarm glasses of water and a box of stale, bitter chocolate, which we keenly consumed. We had watched from his little balcony (housing numerous terracotta pots of neglected, dry plants) as events unfolded in Taksim Square. Tight rows of heavily armed men in helmets, with plastic shields, machine guns and batons, were attempting to break up the protest without any prior warning, systematically advancing on unarmed protestors. Smaller units chased and cornered singled-out individuals amidst white smoke from exploding teargas canisters which had been recklessly fired at people. The canisters slowly disintegrated in the air, releasing a toxic amalgam able to inflict temporary blindness, breathing difficulty, chest pain and skin burns. They gave our faces a ghostly, pale complexion that day. Water enhanced with teargas gushed from a fast-moving vehicle, targeting waves of screaming, vulnerable civilians along the way – children and pitiful stray cats and dogs among them.

'One weekend I even showed up with Serkan and the girls. We started off at Beşiktaş and walked pass the stadium, then up Gümüşsuyu into Taksim Square. Remember how on the Asian side my mother came out with my aunt one night around midnight with thousands of others, banging their pots and marching all the way down Bağdat Avenue? Serkan's friend Ümit had passed through the Bosphorus bridge at five o'clock in the morning, just before dawn, with thousands of other protestors. He told me it was the most magical experience.'

'What made it so special was that it all happened so organically. Hierarchy never came into it. Everyone had an equal stake in everything,' I said.

For a moment I was back amongst the multicoloured, igloo-shaped tents, the perennial wisdom of tall, shady trees, the approachable, bright faces of other protestors – some of whom I had established genuine friendships with overnight. Fluttering banners carrying graffiti with earnest, but sometimes humorous anti-government, pro-freedom statements. Suspicious-looking men we assumed were civil policemen hanging about to dully observe our expanding haven of communal solidarity – a constant reminder of the seriousness of our aim, and the severe repercussions it could entail. I recalled the warm, soft summer breeze on my bare limbs occasionally moving the dense curls of my hair as I sat cross-legged on the patchy grass and chatted with friends. We overheard impromptu live musical performances, and fed happily on donations of warm homemade meals. Sometimes I would flick through the yellowed pages of a pocket-sized French existentialist novel I had borrowed from our makeshift library, its provisional shelves cobbled together with breezeblocks and tiles some protestors had borrowed from a nearby construction site. I remembered the peculiar joy of gradually falling asleep inside a flimsy tent with my closest friend Elif and her boyfriend Kaan in the heart of Istanbul – amidst comforting voices, coughs, and laughter, the sound of car engines, horns and police sirens travelling from afar – and waking up surrounded by our safety net of people, who may have believed in incompatible things but found a unity in this mission: conservationists, Islamists, Kemalists, socialists, liberals, football fanatics, gays, trans people, feminists, Kurds, socialites, Alevis. I lacked common ground with most of these people, yet they cordially offered me tea and *simit* every morning before I eagerly got to work with a group of keen volunteers, taking great pride in clearing up any leftover rubbish from the previous day. The rubbish mainly accumulated in front of a string of cafés and sandwich bars by Taksim Square, and at the beginnings of İstiklal Avenue and other adjoining streets. Along the way we would receive warm compliments from local shop owners and residents; they'd often remark that the area, a point of attraction for both tourists and Istanbul's massive youth population, had never been so clean.

'Even your father, who normally shies away from big crowds – even he went there once, didn't he?'

A day after my trial, attended by my lawyer (whom I had only met once), and two days after I had taken an early morning flight from Atatürk Airport, having barely found the strength to wave at my distraught parents as I passed through passport control – they appeared to have aged years in a few days – my father received a visit at home from the state prosecutor, accompanied by two police officers. My mother was away at work. When they had questioned him about my whereabouts he had responded calmly, saying I had done nothing wrong. I'd merely used my constitutional right to freedom of assembly, and I had since left the country to resume my studies in London. As the men walked towards the elevator, he added: 'Gentlemen, by attempting to slaughter the Gezi spirit you're aiding those who wish to abolish the little freedom we have left in this country.'

'Sweetheart, I can guarantee you that in about a month's time there will no longer be any legal impediment to prevent you from returning. Even so, sadly our country is no longer the right place for young bright people like you. If you do manage to stay here, then you'll be able to come and go as you please. And, if you think about it, London is really only a stone's throw away.'

Both Tijen and I knew that even if I were to be acquitted of the ludicrous charges, my documented participation and prosecution during the Gezi Park protest would remain an ineradicable stain on my record. It was likely to continue to creep out of the woodwork of Turkish bureaucracy and threaten to inhibit the unassuming life I wanted to build for myself.

'If you do decide to apply for a self-employment visa through the Ankara Agreement, I can provide you with all the artists – and you can be my right hand in London. Can you imagine how amazing it would be if you were able to create a client base here in London for your father's work?'

Momentarily stirred by Tijen's own excitement, and by the thought of being able to generate substantial foreign interest in my father's works – and the huge boost this would provide to his career – I responded, 'I wish I could be instrumental in something like that.' But I remained doubtful I truly wanted to become an art dealer, and if I could be any good at it, as she was. I felt I lacked commercial instinct and was inept at asserting my claim on things.

'If your business becomes a success – which I am certain it will – perhaps one day it'll give me an incentive to move out here with my family.'

'Would you really ever consider it?' I asked, finding it nearly impossible to imagine Tijen anywhere else apart from Istanbul.

'If the gallery wasn't doing so well right now, and if Serkan were the more adaptable type – and considering where Turkey's heading – yes, I would, actually. More than anything else, I would want to do it for my daughters. But Serkan could never live anywhere else besides Istanbul. His English is pretty appalling, as you know, and he has no interest in improving it. No one would hire him. And besides, I can't picture him being separated from his friends or his favourite football team. You know how he is.'

I kept my thoughts to myself, no longer inclined to confront her about her decision to continue to plan her life around a man who remained emotionally unavailable. Over time, one becomes reluctant to bring up persistent, major defects in the lives of close friends or beloved family members. Such actions, as well-intended as they are, in the long-term bring no constructive results, only resulting in bruising disputes that leave hard feelings.

Yet still I studied her in a vain attempt to once and for all grasp whether hers was an acute fear of being left on her own, or some other entrenched form of insecurity that made it seem viable to continue to devote herself to a loveless marriage, barely held together by a halfhearted friendship. Perhaps it was the force of habit and practicality brought on by many years of a false togetherness. Considering he was also an absent father much of the time, it would be a weak argument to suggest she was letting it carry on for the sake of her children. Unlike many other women, who found themselves helplessly trapped in a similar situation, *she*, one would have thought, had the financial leverage, personal success and the self-sufficiency to walk away.

'The roles between partners are established very early on in a relationship,' I remembered Marlene once saying. 'Of course certain situations, especially having children, can somewhat alter this balance, but only to a certain degree.' I recalled how a childhood girlfriend of Tijen's, whom I had coincidentally met in Tijen's absence at a social gathering, had confided in me about the troubled early days of Tijen and Serkan's union. She reiterated that it was Tijen who had initiated the relationship and had clung onto Serkan. She found a certain irresistible appeal in his aloof manliness, an artistically defiant streak in his non-conformist, utopian views and his egotistical sense of entitlement – even if he was someone who possessed very little interest in art apart from some fondness for mainstream American cinema and, oddly, sappy Turkish pop songs from past decades. He had sustained his reluctance to fully commit to anything; indecision, to this day, was his default mode in the face of the simplest conundrums. It had been the pestering of his ailing mother that had pushed Serkan to propose. An overbearing, stern matriarchal figure, regardless of her initial reservations, over the years she had grown to accept Tijen and appreciate her loyalty. Her longing to become a grandmother, and the conventional life of marriage and children she obstinately envisaged for her only son, blinded her to Serkan's awkwardness in social situations, the difficulty he had relating to other people (unless in the company of his male friends, with whom he shared obsessions for watching football and for sailing). This blindness had led her to push him into a fixed arrangement he lacked the interpersonal skills ever to adapt to.

My mind travelled away from Tijen and Serkan and their complicated relationship to the devastating thought that my break might already be over. My pulse galloped. I pulled out my phone and nervously looked at its illuminated lockscreen.

'You have to go, don't you?'

I nodded reluctantly, wishing I could stay with her instead and stroll from one gallery booth to another together, leisurely observing the art and discussing whatever came to our minds.

'We haven't had a chance to talk about how it's been going with Quinn so far.'

I shrugged my shoulders with little enthusiasm. 'It's going OK, I suppose.'

'I'm sure we'll have plenty of opportunities to discuss it over the phone once I'm back in Istanbul.'

'I'll be working for him for only another three days.'

'This is a great opportunity for you. It's really wonderful your professor recommended *you*, out of all the other graduates in your year. It shows how much promise he sees in you.'

'I guess it will look pretty good on my CV.'

She paused, then tilted her head and gave me a teasing glance that carried a hint of disapproval.

'Sweetheart, please don't stand in the way of your own future by supposing he won't ever consider hiring you just because you haven't got a work permit.'

'I'll try not to,' I said, and smiled earnestly, finding humour in my own pessimism. At that particular moment, the heavy armour of despair I usually felt weighing me down seemed to lift, even though I was certain my experience of working alongside Quinn would not extend beyond the Fair.

'Actually, quite a few Turkish collectors recognised me. They all seemed very eager to chat with me. I think he was quietly impressed and a bit surprised. I was, too.'

Photos obtained in the summer of 2013 from my Instagram account (which I had since deleted) had been cropped, enlarged and appropriated to meet the required standards for front page leaders in Turkish newspapers; they'd also been circulated on news websites, blogs and social networks. I had become the focus of repetitive arguments explored in long articles and television discussion programmes that extended into the middle of the night. Arguments were put forward by individuals who seemed to know my intentions, the elaborate details of my life, the salacious specifics of what I had been subjected to during my arrest and lengthy detention, the outrageousness of my offences, why and how I had fled the country – all better than I could or would wish to remember. I had simultaneously been referred to as a viciously targeted, wrongly accused, courageous martyr; the environmentally aware, virtuous daughter of an artist who was considered a national treasure; a poster girl for the Gezi Park protests; and a good-for-nothing looter, a sly traitor who had cowardly absconded from prosecution in her homeland and had renounced her Turkish citizenship to become British – a radical who had close ties with ultra left-wing extremist groups. Such an image of me, created for public consumption – rashly formed out of assumed facts and absurd lies, fabricated to dampen the fervent Gezi spirit – had become an entity of its own, a version of myself I could not altogether relate to. Without having wished for it, I had acquired the compassion and loathing of people who now had the outline of my face etched into their minds, alongside their presuppositions of me. And yet, unaware of my traits and idiosyncrasies, the habits and passions I harboured, my ingrained values and beliefs, the essentials that made me the person I am, I remained nearly as much a stranger to them as they were to me.

'Really? Who?' Tijen's eyes gleamed. She paused to glance around with sharpened senses, attempting to catch a glimpse of a recognisable face; part of her motive to attend the Fair was to be seen by and to mingle with Turkish collectors.

For her sake I thought hard, but the disconcerting pressure of the limited time I had left dragged their names further into the dim strata of my short-term memory, even while their distinctive faces, with lively, sometimes peculiar expressions, remained at hand.

'I'm so terrible with names. I promise I'll remember and tell you later.'

'Has Quinn figured out anything about you?'

Having by now become fully accustomed to *that look* people generally reserved for someone who had managed to gain nationwide notoriety, I shook my head and responded, 'I guess he hasn't yet felt the need to google me.'

'I'll come and visit you at your booth in a bit.'

'I wish there was a way we could spend more time together before you leave.'

Her eyes bore a look of provisional sadness and guilt as she reached her hand out towards me. We both knew that, once in Quinn's inhibiting company, our interaction was bound to revert to something more restricted and contrived.

I felt the reassuring warmth of her palm press itself against my cheek, a motherly gesture I had witnessed her perform many times in the past – mostly after appeasing one of her disgruntled daughters.

'It's all going to be fine in the end. You'll see. One day, when you look back and reflect on these days, you'll wish you hadn't agonised so much over things.'

In a melancholic mood, I nodded at her encouraging words without properly reflecting on their content – conscious that once I left her side and rushed over to Quinn's stand, the influence of her fleeting presence, imbued with the beautiful, painful memories of Istanbul, of my parents and of my childhood, and the intimate friendships I had left behind, would be replaced by the commanding reality of the Art Fair.

IV

I listened to the harmonic patter of rain, interrupted by what sounded like a build-up of rainwater cascading from the gutters onto the pavement outside. After closely observing the people in front of me, I too struggled clumsily with opening my umbrella as I set foot through the red, bulky doors of the Fair into the daunting rain and cold of a late November night. Once outside, my tired eyes were dazzled by the chiaroscuro surroundings: the rustling shadows of people on the move, their obscuring umbrellas set against enticingly bright signboards; the black tarmac wet and jewel-like; the abundant, drenched leaves of a large oak tree, shiny and metallic under the streetlamp. As cars passed by, I watched raindrops come into prominence under the prying glare of their headlights; a sudden, sharp gust of wind brought the smell of burning tobacco – despite the relentless rain, someone had managed to light up. Trying to avoid plunging into puddles of water that only revealed themselves at the last moment, and as the rain maintained its assertive rhythm on my umbrella, I was lost in thought under the darkened cosiness of its shield, reliving certain moments from the day. The gratifying exhaustion of a long day at work – a phenomenon new to me – made itself evident in my body, while anxieties about my performance at the Fair continued to orbit in the distant background of my consciousness, like floating debris hauled in by a typhoon. All these thoughts were trivial, though, next to my urgent wish to open the front door of my snug little flat, discard my coat and soaking wet umbrella, and prepare myself a warm meal.

Suddenly sensing someone beside me, I turned and saw him walking briskly along. He didn't have an umbrella, nor was he wearing a coat, his only shield against the turbulent rain the lifted collars of his jacket.

'I can give you a lift if you're heading in the direction of Mayfair,' he said, translucent beads of water dripping down his hair and clinging onto the tips of his eyelashes. He took a quick drag from his cigarette; as he dropped his left hand to his side I caught a glimpse of its bright burning end, peeking at me from within his palm. I extended my umbrella out to him, as if to suggest we could share it, but felt instantly intimidated by my boldness – of it being read as anything other than an act of courtesy, which it was, and one I would still have made had it been someone else in his place.

'No, don't worry about it,' he said, grinning as the rain hit his face.

I awkwardly pulled the umbrella back towards myself, my heart jolting against its cage of surrounding flesh. A hot flush began to travel up my neck like a horde of ants crawling up a tree trunk.

'I find it's cleansing for the soul,' he added, taking a quick but earnest drag from his warped cigarette and looking up at the raindrops darting down at him.

I quietly nodded at his comment, then slightly lowered my umbrella.

Accelerating his pace, he asked, 'Coming?' with an impatient, suggestive look in his eyes. I shook my head and smiled, as if to suggest it was ludicrous of him to think I would, and watched him toss away the now soggy, lifeless cigarette, further straightening the raised collars of his jacket – some segments of it more soaked than others by rain that had yet to be absorbed by the bristly woollen fibres. Lifting his shoulders, he buried his hands inside the misshapen pockets of his jacket and then ran in short, nimble steps across the tarmac, disregarding the approaching traffic and forcing it to slow down for him.

I continued to monitor his swift advance until I eventually saw his shrinking figure slip into a side street. Yet, in a fiction, I continued to follow him down a quiet, dead-end street, set against the shadows of old three-storey buildings and the fresh fragrance of wet soil and manure – as if we had been transported from the bustle of the city centre into the contained calmness occasionally found in the rural outskirts of Greater London.

The heavy rain slows to a barely noticeable drizzle. No longer in need of, nor in possession of, an umbrella to hide behind, I soon catch up to his dark, enticing frame. We exchange a few words, charged in tone but not content, until I unexpectedly stop and kiss him.

The repeatedly imagined climax of this lusted-after encounter made me short of breath each time, and caused a moment's internal quiver. I continued to walk ahead on my designated path, somehow managing to avoid collisions with passing traffic, remaining almost completely disconnected from the hectic reality of my surroundings. I yearned for this stranger who had triggered in me something I had shunned. In the past two years I had become convinced that desire was an emotion someone like me could no longer experience.

As I descended the steps at the entrance of the underground station, alongside a rapidly multiplying crowd, I felt a sliver of relief, as if I had saved myself from a minor hazard, or at least an inconvenient situation. My overwhelming attraction towards him was bound to have caused awkwardness – not to mention the extreme anxiety his presence might generate if I'd been trapped in a confined space with him. I contemplated – while nursing an undeniable longing for the situation I had just shied away from – the direction things would have taken had I accepted his offer. At the same time, I was making the rational argument that to do so – Mayfair being in the opposite direction to where I lived – would've meant foolishly prolonging the tedious journey ahead of me.

LUCIAN

I

YOUR BODY JUST doesn't take these reckless beatings any longer. The late nights and the worsening hangovers. You know you can't carry on like this; you're getting too old for this senseless shit. It seems some people never do; it's as if their bodies are geared for excess, have an extraordinary resistance to it. Your good friend Rex, for instance. You recently celebrated his fifty-eighth birthday with some mutual friends and these two birds he'd met on the plane passing through London, as he frequently does – this time on his way to Cannes. The guy still smokes several joints a day, can easily knock down a bottle of vodka and resorts to doing the *occasional* line whenever he needs sobering up. You've been falling off the wagon more often than usual since your divorce. But you cannot deny it – you've always been a sucker for the recreational.

The last time you glanced at your watch it said five in the morning. It was a given – the week of the Fair was going to be yet another test of endurance for your poor, maltreated liver. Not to mention a kamikaze operation on your brain cells. At the start of the evening, you were already considerably boozed up on the cheap, flat champagne they served at the VIP preview cocktail – and that was before you turned up at a dinner at the Coxes', looking dishevelled and reeking of fags, alcohol and damp clothes.

Linda and Howard Cox are collector royalty, and they take it upon themselves to give a massive, catered sit-down dinner for fifty-odd people at their six-storey residence in Mayfair every year, around the time of the Fair. *Shameless fucking self-promoters*, you can't help but think to yourself – even if you've become unfazed by what some rich people get up to in order to publicise their *love and support for the arts*. The Coxes wish to remind people of their vast wealth, the abundance of art-world celebrities they're naturally affiliated with, and the priceless load of rubbish they have hanging on their walls at every opportunity. *Bling Art*, as you like to call it – not that you came up with the definition yourself – is what mostly constitutes their hefty collection, the majority of which lives inside a warehouse in East London, waiting to be upgraded to something more substantial. It's frightful how one's behavioural tendencies and outlook on life can easily be decoded by the type of art one buys and the way one collects.

You've always considered Howard Cox to be a very peculiar and unlikeable person. Guided by his massively inflated ego, he's determined to make his mark in the art world. A few times a year, he curates exhibitions of devastatingly bad works by unknown artists on the ground floor of their soulless house. *Curates* – it's mind-boggling how exceptionally limited a meaning the word has when at the mercy of some visionless twat who hangs a few pieces of artwork with the help of able technicians. Howard's got an awful plaster sculpture on a plinth in the hallway on the first floor of his house, one he apparently made himself. It's just outside the room where he keeps his collection of antique telescopes. He once walked you to this great creation – a nude plaster figure, resembling a bad copy of a Marc Quinn sculpture – and said, somewhat snootily, 'This is a piece I made recently,' as if it was only natural and inevitable that a man of his intellect and calibre should take a stab at becoming an artist. All you could say in return was: 'Really?'

Then he gave you this tedious spiel on the influence of the principles of neuroscience on the making of the sculpture. He lost you half a minute into his explanation. There's no better way to intimidate and silence people than to assert ideas too incomprehensible to be challenged.

The only thing worth mentioning about Linda Cox is the massive brown mole she has on her right cheek, easily the size of a rabbit dropping. You'd expect someone as vain as her would have had it removed. Maybe it's surgically impossible.

You'd called Linda from the Fair yesterday, to ask if you could bring someone to the dinner. Knowing how seriously these women take their seating plans, you're pretty confident your last-minute request had instantly annoyed her, if not encouraged a deep-seated dislike for you. Provided she hadn't developed one already. With such dinners, one could not be naive and assume that one was invited because one was *liked*. It was more to do with how your name either complemented or diversified a given guest list. When you revealed that your plus one was Hiroki Asano her voice softened. She said she would see what she could do, as if it wasn't *you* who was doing

71

her a favour by bringing along someone who, with his recent
big retrospective at the Tate Modern, had reached artworld
stardom.

She was ready to get you out of her hair and hang up but,
you said, there was just one more *little thing*. Since Hiroki was
off to Berlin early next morning, was there any chance he could
be seated next to you at the table? Now you were pushing your
luck. But, as much as you felt professionally obliged to show
your face at such flashy engagements, if you could help it you'd
rather not sit next to a complete bore for two hours. You went
on to explain that you had just run into Hiroki at the Fair. You
exaggerated a little, saying he was an extremely close friend
of yours; you even lied to her, claiming you were working
on a big public project together, funded by the Arts Council,
knowing it was the only viable technique you could use with
such people. She remained silent for a considerable time, then
sighed wearily and said, again, that she would see what she
could do.

At the table, you happened to have an oligarch's leggy blonde
wife seated on your other side. Mesmerised by her beauty, you
ignored Hiroki for the first half an hour. She had flawless white
skin, striking blue eyes that resembled a Siberian husky's, and
the most amazing bone structure. At first, her breathtaking
presence and her short, standoffish responses had given you
a bit of a stiffy under the table – yet, having consumed several
flutes of champagne at the Fair, you were also desperate to take
a leak. All the same you were reluctant to stand up and make
your way to the cloakroom. The long dining room was lit by
large pillar candles rising from the floor, and a seemingly endless array of candles floated in water-filled glass bowls placed

on the table, as if you all were crazed cult members feasting before your annual sacrificial ritual.

To your disappointment, by the time waiters turned up with your starters, you'd figured out that the oligarch's wife's interior wasn't as alluring as her exterior. Having covered the basics, you had nothing left to say to each other. Her blue eyes projected an energy that was cold and dim. If you ever got the chance to shag her, you could easily picture yourself forcing a pillow over her head just to avoid her lifeless gaze.

For the rest of the dinner you listened to Hiroki while he explained, bits of foie gras pâté stuck to the spindly ends of his scruffy goatee, his latest venture: a massive installation project in an empty warehouse outside Tokyo that involved stacking up thousands of out-dated Japanese consumer electronics: computers, stereos, DVD players, mobiles, headphones, television sets – before smashing them into pieces with bulldozers and shaping the piles of waste so they resembled mountains of shiny, volcanic black sand. Apart from its visual splendour, the installation would draw attention to Japan's extravagance, its waste from mass production. You're never too stimulated by art inspired by environmental issues, but you still liked the concept – or perhaps the way it was so passionately and articulately explained by Hiroki despite his broken English. Hiroki is a computer nerd turned artistic genius. You've always been very fond of him – he reminds you of a mad mathematician.

The colossally long dining table was populated by other celebrated artists – some of whom were trying to conceal the deranging effect their unimaginable success had on them with their loud, uninhibited voices, and others who were engaged in a silent discussion only with themselves. Scattered around were socialites dressed in skimpy, weird designer outfits, as if to distract from the inept sentences streaming from their lush, brightly painted mouths. Other than yourself, there were a good number of cocky, opportunistic art dealers looking out for their next prey, and a few distinguished alcoholics – also prized art critics in their own right – who regarded such lavish dinners as perks of their miserably paid jobs.

The table was also adorned by international jet-setters, museum directors, art advisors, world-famous curators – who had all flown from God knows where to dandily mingle together for the remaining days of the Fair at other private events: major exhibitions, plush dinners held in their honour, evening auctions, book launches, specifically organised to coincide with London's busiest art week. You now and again listened in on other people's conversations. One would expect intellectual or provocative discussions to arise occasionally from such a well-selected bunch, but that was hardly the case. You overheard drivel about the rainy forecast, about their full schedules in London and the preview of the Fair. Petty gossip: who they had bumped into, who had turned up with whom, who had the best booth this year – and, most important of all, of course, who had purchased the highest-priced artworks.

After the dinner, you tagged along with Hiroki to a party held at a large residence in Notting Hill. You can't remember how, but there you started talking to this average-looking girl. It turned out she worked for a West End gallery, though its name escapes you right now. By the time you arrived there they had run out of booze, which was for the best; you were still sloshed from the pudding wine they'd served at the end of dinner. Linda Cox had shrieked with unease when, just as you were heading out, you grabbed her by her bony waist and planted a wet kiss on her mole.

Soon you, the girl, and Hiroki decided to go on a little expedition. Sneaking into the kitchen, you discovered a bottle of vodka in the deep end of the freezer. It felt like your little triumph. You drank it straight, from white plastic cups you found in the reception room lying on the table next to all the empty bottles; they'd also run out of juice, Coke, tonic and ice. Hiroki apparently knew the host, who was some forgotten eighties pop-star-turned-collector-turned-conceptual-artist-wannabe, but, oddly, you'd never ran into the guy.

Once your three-way conversation began to ebb, Hiroki whispered in your ear: he had a gram of coke. It felt like the best news you'd heard in a long time. You started making individual trips to the loo, but soon got tired of it: the lack of privacy in a house crowded with strangers, the constant queue in front of the only available bathroom. Even more discouraging was the noticeable drop in hygiene levels with each visit. Hiroki suggested going back to his hotel room. You hadn't looked, but you're guessing it must've been around one in the morning. Getting impatient after several last-minute cancellations by Uber drivers, you all decided to try your luck hailing a black cab.

There were only a few cars passing by on the main road. Restless and bored of waiting, Hiroki got to work. With his fat, stubby fingers he wiped a small section of the roof of a parked M3 with some tissues, tipped out a portion of the coke, and then started dividing the white powder into precise, neat lines. Conveniently, there was no breeze in the cold, damp air. Everything was very still. You and the girl froze and stayed silent, as if to move or speak would be to distract him from the delicacy of his mission. One by one you leaned over the car to sniff two lines each through a silly trimmed straw you'd found inside your jacket pocket, a souvenir of past misconduct.

When you eventually saw the yellow light of a black cab steadily approaching, you all jumped up and down, waving animatedly, your uninhibited voices echoing down the empty road.

The driver lowered his window. He was a balding old guy with sagging olive skin. The bags under his eyes revealed a bit of the red flesh underneath the lid. He looked fed-up as he briefly examined all of you. You couldn't blame him; you were rowdy and reckless and behaving as if you led lives uncluttered by quotidian responsibility, as if you existed in a parallel time to most Londoners, tucked up in their warm beds. Hiroki told him the address, but the driver continued to stare blankly; when you leaned over and repeated the address, he turned away and gave a short nod. He released the central locking system and you all gladly jumped inside.

You were being driven along the Knightsbridge end of Hyde Park. You couldn't see anything beyond the park gates, but you continued to stare, your hand resting on the grab handle so you could prevent yourself from leaning against the girl's small frame whenever the bulky vehicle took corners at speed. You were half-heartedly contemplating if you ought to drop the other two off and head home. You never knew when to leave a good party – or any party, really, regardless whether it was a good one or not. You tended to lose your sense of time, your sense of reason. It was one of the factors that had ultimately put an end to your marriage with Tabitha.

Hiroki and the girl were having a heady discussion about the poetry of Philip Larkin. You remember them referring to Larkin's love of jazz. They were talking about him as if they had both known him intimately, which you found terribly irritating. Your father used to be like that, easily irritated by others' behaviour. You don't know if such things could be hereditary.

You turned around to observe the girl's face in profile. Although they shared no physical resemblance, her youthfulness reminded you of Ada. You had thought about Ada the entire day, like a desperate teenager who rarely managed to get laid. Had she accepted your offer of a lift, you would (much to Linda Cox's disbelief and annoyance) have arrived with your second tag-along on your arm. In the worst-case scenario, she could have stayed for a drink – and besides, even with such highly rated dinners, there were always a few last-minute drop-outs. And people tended not to mind squeezing in an extra chair for a pretty young thing who would have most of the table drooling over her. These days, chasing after twenty-somethings had become a *thing* for you, even though it couldn't altogether eliminate the torment of the recent dissolution of your marriage. It seemed easier to impress younger women with your charm and eccentricity. The older ones saw right through you.

The girl in the cab wore a near-black maroon lipstick which had lost its creamy consistency a while back, though her lips were still covered with a thin layer of the cosmetic paint. The severe colour didn't suit her; it emphasised how slight her lips were in relation to her wide, angled face. For a moment, without listening to what she was saying, you watched her mouth move and noticed that a denser layer of the colour remained inside the creases of her lips. You felt remarkably aroused by this. You imagined Ada's succulent lips in place of hers, and then acknowledged the girl's lips again, as you pictured yourself leaning over and snogging her. She didn't look a day over twenty-five. Philip Larkin had probably kicked the bucket before she was conceived. You let them carry on talking; your mouth had gone dry. Besides, you couldn't stand poetry – it bored the shit out of you. Clenching your teeth, you watched as the cab passed near-empty side roads. You used to frequent these streets when you were an art student at the RCA. In those days you had big dreams for yourself. Big dreams brought to their knees by self-doubt and anguish.

You have a long day ahead of you at the Fair tomorrow, you remember thinking – yet you couldn't bring yourself to make the sensible choice. Instead, you told yourself you'd be letting Hiroki down if you back-pedalled at the very last minute. The girl could easily change her mind and say she wished to call it a night, too. She did seem rather keen to tag along, but you could never tell with women. So far, you weren't sure of her motives and couldn't suss out why she had chosen to be sandwiched between two older men in the back of a cab, making her way to a hotel room in the middle of the night. It could well be that she was after the charlie. Some women would do just about anything to score for free, or to get shitfaced with anyone. Or maybe she wished to brag the next day at work about how she had partied with the great Hiroki Asano.

But, if you had to be honest with yourself, it wasn't solely Hiroki's welfare you were thinking of. You suddenly convinced yourself that you'd started fancying the girl – when, in hindsight, she was a mere substitute, channelling the desire stirred up inside you earlier that day. Moments before you'd left the party, you were already becoming fixated on her. She had a certain way about her: a sweet, childlike temperament. The wicked sense of humour she exhibited as the night progressed drew you in further. You recall her teasing Hiroki about his hair, saying that he could easily smuggle explosives through Customs by hiding them in his big dreadlocks. You had found this very funny then, more than you do now.

Initially, you had failed to notice the compact little figure she possessed – her perky round arse in that tight, short skirt. Once it grabbed your attention it was all you could think of. An image of her naked arse swam around your intoxicated mind, a tempting oasis you wished to reach by the end of the evening. Earlier, while waiting for a cab to show up, she'd been shivering and complaining about the cold. She was wearing a shaggy faux-fur coat that only reached her waist. You had put your arm around her, giving her an affectionate rub on the shoulders before your hand proceeded downwards, wrapping itself discreetly around one of her butt cheeks. You were hoping that she was sufficiently coked up, that her body had become too numb to notice your subtle grip, or her mind too narcotised to be bothered by it. Sadly, you were wrong. Flashing you a warning look, she'd pushed your hand away.

You wished you could remember her name. Not now, but then – it annoyingly kept slipping from your mind, despite you having heard Hiroki say it numerous times. You eventually ended up at his hotel room, had a few more lines, and drank whatever you could get your hands on. You offered him a twenty-pound note for the miniature bottles of hard liquor you were consuming, so you wouldn't feel bad about going up to the minibar and helping yourself to another bottle every so often, but he wouldn't take it. He rested one hand on your shoulder and said you needn't stress about it: his gallery would pay for all the expenses. You told him he should be glad *you* weren't representing him. He laughed, then went off to find his portable speaker.

Soon the gradually intensifying gloomy chords of Górecki's third symphony could be heard beneath your heated yammering. Such music was totally unsuited for the occasion. You suspect that Hiroki was trying to come off as a deep and tormented soul to impress the girl. The coke suddenly stimulated your bowels into movement.

When you returned from the loo, after what seemed like a good hour, you found the girl sitting on his lap. It looked as if they had just been kissing, or were about to. You doubted he could score as easily if he hadn't been a celebrity artist, looking the way he did. At first, you were appalled and insulted that the tasteless bird had gone for him instead of you. But you managed to hold back your frustration and head out without creating a scene. After all, you didn't even recall her name. You can't seem to remember if you said goodbye; if you hadn't, you doubt that it mattered to anyone.

By the time you'd walked to your flat in Fitzrovia, you had calmed down somewhat. Yet it still took you quite a while to fall asleep. You tossed and turned in your bed, worrying whether you were going to get any sleep at all, and how you were meant to cope at the Fair.

In bed, you carried on thinking about *the girl*. You re-imagined her as an irresistible hybrid of herself and Ada, reliving the moments before you left Hiroki's plush hotel room.

It was rather annoying – and ironic, you supposed – that you couldn't remember whether what had prompted you to walk out had actually happened. You couldn't remember if you had in fact seen Hiroki and the girl kissing. You felt as if they had been, or that they were just about to, but you weren't entirely sure. She had definitely changed positions, having moved off the sofa. That was the only thing you were a hundred per cent certain of. You were no longer sure how accurately you had interpreted their body language, or if you remembered clearly what they had been up to when you walked back in. Had her arms been around his neck, or had she been holding something in her hands and examining it – an artist's catalogue or a book cover? The more you thought about it, the more you realised you weren't sure whether there had been anything sexual going on between them at all.

You got up from bed to pee at least half a dozen times, as your body tried to flush the poisons out of your system. Eventually you resorted to half a Xanax; you must've dozed off shortly after that.

11

When you wake up and lift your unbearably heavy head, it feels as if it has been wedged inside a metal bucket that is being kicked around by a couple of playground bullies. The combination of uppers and downers was bound to give you the most excruciatingly unmanageable hangover the next morning. For a long time, you stand still under the showerhead as rivulets of water stream down your naked body. You get dressed and force yourself out the front door of your flat.

The subdued light reflecting across the overcast sky is enough to sting your hyper-sensitive eyes. Then you notice that your hair is still soaking wet; you'd forgotten to dry it. The cold gives you a false sense of revitalisation now and again, distracting you from the chemicals seeping through your pores.

You see a tall blonde girl standing by the large set of windows. She smiles at you before waving. You give her a flirty smile and wave back. It takes you a few seconds to register that she is one of your new interns, looking out from the front window of your gallery. Imogen's parents are wealthy collectors; at one of your recent post-opening dinners, her father walked up to you and spoke at length about her passion for art and her desire to get herself a career in the art world. He had the vilest breath. You felt obliged to offer her an unpaid internship at your gallery.

You drag your feet and go into the little café on the corner of your street. Pawel, the Polish manager, is behind the counter as usual – his back to the door, cooking on a steaming griddle. He turns around; his eyes shoot you a glance from above his fleshy cheeks. He nods at you with a discreet smile – as if by now he can tell from your appearance exactly what kind of a morning this is for you. Since your separation, his tiny café has become an extension of your flat – it's where you have your breakfast every weekday.

'Can I please have a fresh orange juice? A large one?' you blurt out. You are thirsty as hell.

He signals to Magda, behind the register. She's been working at Pawel's café for a couple of months now – the daughter of a family friend from the small town in Poland they are all from.

After turning over the fat sausages sizzling on the griddle, Pawel rubs the side of his plump nose and then asks you with a sombre expression if you wish to have *the usual*.

'No, give me an English breakfast. Eggs, sunny side up. White toasted bread. I want bacon, sausage, baked beans, the whole business. Followed by a double espresso – *please*.'

The café is relatively empty apart from two builder types seated by the counter. It feels as if lightning is flashing inside your dehydrated skull as you walk away, picking up a bunch of newspapers you have no intention of reading, and sit at one of the tables.

Some mornings, when you're feeling less delicate, you perch by the counter and chat with Pawel if he isn't too busy serving other customers. You mostly talk about current affairs. Recently, a topic of discussion was the referendum scheduled for next year. Pawel hinted at his unease about the prospect of getting kicked out with his family if the UK ever decided to leave the EU. You told him to relax and said it was sheer madness to even contemplate that this country's citizens would vote for such nonsense. If only politicians spent taxpayers' money on more worthwhile causes.

Pawel drives up all the way from East Croydon at six in the morning to get to Fitzrovia five days a week, but he's never moaned about it – or about anything else, for that matter. On the contrary, he seems to be rather pleased that he got his life in London sorted out relatively quickly. He arrived in this country speaking only broken English, with a seamstress wife, two toddlers to feed, and not much else. Under the same circumstances, you probably wouldn't have achieved what he has so far. If it wasn't for your inheritance, you probably wouldn't have a penny to your name – or a business, for that matter. Next to a self-made man like Pawel, you feel pretty fucking useless.

When you arrive at the Fair, you're feeling worse for wear. The double shot of bitter espresso is threatening to flip over the contents of your stomach; you're struggling to shake off an uncanny detachment from your dead-beat body. Passing through the crowded, brightly lit corridors, you stop to say a brief hello to people who look frightfully familiar, though you're unsure who the hell they are and how well you really know them, if at all.

As you walk into your gallery's booth, you're met by the suspicious, questioning gaze of Eloise. Eloise manages the gallery, delegates all the work amongst the staff, and does most of the sales. You don't know where you would be without her.

Already over two hours late, you stagger towards Eloise like an ailing octogenarian and immediately confess to her that you had an exceptionally awful night. With a look of genuine concern, she rubs your upper arm; she can be very affectionate, in a sisterly way, but she can equally be bossy with you if necessary. You need such a figure in your work life to sort you out: to pamper you with compliments and encourage you when you lack confidence, and to whip you back into shape whenever you lose focus.

'What happened?' she asks, still looking concerned until she's distracted by an art critic who is passing by. Eloise eagerly calls out the woman's name. The woman sends both of you kisses in the air. Eloise instantly returns the affected gesture. When you first hired her, she was just another provincial girl trying her luck in London – these days she's on first-name terms with some of the most revered people in the art industry.

'I spent the entire night holding the toilet seat and throwing up,' you explain in an exhausted voice.

'Oh no!'

Food poisoning is your favourite alibi. You nod, slightly guilty; you hate having to lie like this – it's silly and requires way too much effort. Touching your sweaty forehead with your shaking fingers, you add, in a lifeless voice, 'I didn't get to sleep till about five a.m.'

It is the only ounce of truth to fall from your lips. You sincerely doubt that she fully believes your story – it really doesn't matter, as long as she plays along with it. After all, you're her lousy boss and she's your employee; she's occasionally obliged to turn a blind eye to your lies and screwups. Though there have been many instances when it feels like you've switched roles – that she is the gallery owner and you some useless help turning up late again – and this is no exception.

Unsure how you're going to make it to the end of the day, you falter towards the corridor. You watch streams of people pass by. The first day the Fair opens to the general public is tremendously busy, as expected. On your way in, you came across the long tail of sad sods who hadn't been sensible enough to purchase their tickets online, queueing outside in the miserable cold and rain. You wonder what people will leave with once they've been subjected to what's inside; any artwork that is remotely interesting and worth one's attention is easily lost inside the vast homogenous commercial banality of the venue. There are about a hundred and seventy galleries exhibiting this year, so it's unlikely anyone will have the perseverance to see the entire Fair in one day, or the desire to cough up another thirty-five pounds for a second ticket. You know it's all a bit of nonsense, clever marketing more than anything else.

Then your tired vision catches sight of Ada approaching – she stands out like a goddess, otherworldly amongst the bland crowd. Almost instantly, she notices you too and smiles back. Cutting through several people's paths, you walk up to her and take hold of her hands – she's been holding them close to her chest, guarded.

'I was waiting here for you the entire afternoon yesterday,' you tell her. She pulls her hands away gently, while her smile becomes less containable and her cheeks catch colour.

'Come with me,' you say, and she happily follows you. Then she stops at the entrance of your booth, as if she's just remembered something very urgent.

'I really can't go in – I have to go!'

'But why? Let me at least give you a short tour of my humble abode,' you insist, amused by her erratic behaviour.

'I *can't*. I *have* to go to the cafeteria. There is a cafeteria at the far end, isn't there?' she asks, pointing ahead. 'I hope I wasn't going in the wrong direction.'

Her panic-stricken stare brings you close to laughing your head off. 'Let me think,' you say, rubbing your chin. 'Yeah, I think there's a cafeteria next to the French bistro if you follow this corridor to the very end.'

'Quinn is with an important client. He asked me to get them some coffee. I can't be late.'

You notice the crumpled banknote poking out of her fist. It's rather sweet that she is taking it so seriously – terribly foolish, but sweet.

Yesterday afternoon, when you returned to Quinn's booth to find that Ada had gone off for a break, he pulled you to one side and demanded you stay away from her – at least until the Fair was over.

'Some of us are trying to make a living here, buddy, and my gallery stand is not a pickup joint,' Quinn complained, wired and sweaty as usual.

Quinn was always under severe levels of stress. He often appeared on the brink of a breaking point, like a lava-spitting volcano that continually came close to erupting but rarely ever did. He suffered from high blood pressure and diabetes, but often forgot to eat anything, and drank endless amounts of coffee, as if to keep the tension rolling. His entire life revolved around his gallery, the cold, beastly English wife he deserted New York for, and their three feral boys who lacked the capacity to greet anyone verbally. All this was part of the constant misery he faced, which he seemed to wholly embrace.

You introduce Eloise to Ada as the *Boss of Everything*, explain the situation to her, and ask her whether she can fetch those lousy coffees in Ada's place. Eloise, competent and assured, responds, 'Sure, no problem at all,' and heads out to the cafeteria.

After you walk Ada around your small booth, talking to her about the artists and giving her some backstory concerning the photographs, you ask her, 'So, how's the miserable bastard been treating you today?'

If she hasn't already, she's bound to find out how utterly impossible Quinn can be. He represents some of the most successful contemporary artists, selling their works to the highest-brow clients: the richest of the rich, art foundations, banks, museums. His massive, high-ceilinged Mayfair gallery is every Art History graduate's dream destination – yet no employee lasts. It's the constant paranoia, the unrealistic expectations, when he's just too repressed to openly tell people what he demands of them. They eventually run off to somewhere more tolerable, more zen – or he fires them out of the blue just because he's having a bad day. Whenever you pay him a visit, you always come across new faces. You hardly ever get to leave his office without hearing him moan about the incompetence of his newer employees. He can be a piece of work, though very occasionally you've seen him get emotional when someone suddenly decides to leave. He's an oddball.

'He's been all right,' Ada answers back tactfully.

'How are the sales?' you ask, just to observe her reaction.

She looks away timidly and replies, 'I don't know. Quinn's dealing with that side of things.'

'I bet they've been selling like hot cakes.'

She shrugs. 'I don't know. I suppose so.'

Quinn is an impressively secretive and cunning operator. To exercise power over his employees, his rivals, and people he does deals with, he keeps them in the dark, manipulating the truth to his advantage.

When Eloise returns, and Ada is ready to set off with her newly acquired coffee and some loose coins, you ask her if she's up to anything immediately after the Fair. Considering the terrible shape you're in, you'd be out of your fucking wits to ask her out tonight – but, in matters of the heart and groin, you believe it's essential to strike while the iron is hot.

III

Around five in the afternoon, you hear Eloise say, 'Lucian, I think you should head home.'

She has been giving you the cold shoulder ever since you made her fetch those coffees for Ada. She didn't make a fuss about it, but you can tell from her unusual silence that your selfish request has made her feel undervalued and overlooked. The only drawback to working alongside women is they take everything very personally.

As you bring your head forward, you feel a sharp pain in the back of your neck – and what's more, the inside of your mouth has completely dried up. You realise that you must've briefly dozed off like a bum. You see Eloise standing before you; she doesn't look happy.

'I beg your pardon. Was I sleeping?' you have the audacity to ask, while straightening up in the chair.

'There was a group of people, they all heard you snore. Didn't you hear their giggles?' she asks. Tetchy.

'I never snore,' you point out, pretending you're baffled by the accusation. Tabitha once claimed, donning a pair of noise-cancelling headphones before bed, that the best part of being married to you was that you never snored.

Initially, humour was one of the things that kept you together. You once made her laugh so hard she wet herself in the dairy aisle. When you left the supermarket, you could still see a damp patch on her trousers. But sarcasm eventually replaced humour, and in an unravelling relationship nothing backfires more easily than a sarcastic remark. Nowadays texting has become the main mode of communication between you; you very seldom speak to her over the phone. When you do, you sometimes get carried away, briefly forget about the unmendable rift between you, and say something funny – a comment you instinctively know will have her in fits. Yet she carries on with the same indifference, as if you haven't said anything remotely funny.

You yawn as wide as your jaw allows, rub your face, and begin massaging the back of your stiff neck.

'Lucian, I really think you ought to go home and get some rest. You don't look well,' Eloise says, this time with concern.

When you walk out of the Fair, the sky has turned a murky brown that is strangely atmospheric – it has just started to rain heavily. You lift the collars of your jacket and walk against the raindrops. You have never owned an umbrella in your entire life; the hassle of carrying one around has always outweighed the inconvenience of occasionally getting soaked.

You need to recharge your batteries prior to meeting Ada – but you can't remember where you parked the bloody car in the morning.

Then you decide it would be absolute madness to drive yourself back home. By the time you find the car, drive through hopeless traffic – bound to get worse by the minute – you will barely have time for a nap before you have to drive all the way back to pick Ada up. You cross the road, pass between two sets of vehicles at a standstill. You remember noticing a small hotel on the same road last night.

To your surprise, a few yards down the road, you recognise the metallic finish of your car and realise you had parked it on the same street this morning, out of habit. Your father left you the Mercedes 500SL in his will. It is the same model

Princess Diana had been killed in; he bought it several years after her death from a secondhand car dealer, as a tribute to her. He had a huge crush on Lady Di, and used to say she had the best pair of legs to ever strut up the steps of Buckingham Palace. He was a peculiar fellow, your father: cold and very opinionated, with the sort of old-fashioned sexist ideas only considered acceptable amongst public-school types with strong right-wing sentiments and a fondness for hanging out in stuffy gentlemen's clubs. You had never shown an interest in the car. While he was alive, you drove an old red Mini. Like you, he was quite tall and well-built compared to the average Englishman, and on the rare occasions you gave him a lift, he complained there was not enough leg room. Your guess is he left you the Mercedes 500SL to solve that problem.

You turn into the small hotel's oppressively stagnant reception and check into a double room. The male receptionist who assists you is painstakingly polite and courteous.

'This way, sir. After you, sir. To your left, sir. If you will follow me, sir.'

You have a problem with people calling you *sir* – deep down, you assume they're taking the mickey. And they probably are. For one thing, you lack the composure and gravitas to be addressed that way. Despite your age, you feel at best like an adolescent who still has some way to go before maturing into a proper adult.

You both walk down a dispiritingly windowless corridor on the fourth floor. You pass by an abandoned wooden tray on the floor holding a plate with a half-eaten club sandwich and a few dried-up potato chips. There is also a tiny white vase, with the pathetic, fallen head of a red carnation poking out of it. The whole composition has an unsettling undertone.

'Here we are, sir,' he declares, unnecessarily cheery. He inserts the plastic key and begins to fiddle with the handle of the door. For some reason, it isn't opening. The thought of having to wait for him while he rushes downstairs to get another is too much for you. Nibbling bits of skin off your thumb, you watch him re-insert the key into the slot a couple of times.

'Do you have many guests at this time of year?' you ask, partly to dilute your shared, growing frustration, and also since you feel a hint of guilt for being put off by his insistence on addressing you as *sir*, when he probably hasn't much choice in the matter. Dressed as he is in an austere tie and pristine white shirt, it must feel belittling and unnatural to have to be so courteous around a man like you. Your clothes are damp, your shirt rumpled, and your jacket has long lost its shape and dignity. They have the pungency peculiar to clothes drenched in the rain. And you haven't even bothered to shave the last three mornings. These days you can't be arsed. Shaving your face every other morning, cutting your nails and toenails once in a while – the thought of repeating these tasks causes your spirit to plummet.

You had mentioned this to Rex halfway through your lunch at St. John in Smithfield, when he was back in London to meet with a British director for a project he was trying to get off the ground – an epic movie on the Arab Spring. Both of you were in the habit of occasionally sharing personal matters. Like your discussions about art, cinema, literature and world politics, it gave your relationship – otherwise driven by your shared fervencies for booze and narcotics, and more recently for philandering – the profundity and integrity it urgently needed. Savouring a juicy piece of bone marrow held between his greasy fingers, he replied, 'You must be a little depressed because of your divorce.'

'It hasn't exactly been easy.'

He nodded back in silence.

'At least I wasn't made to pay a fortune in child support.'

Yours was one of the most straightforward divorces in Great Britain; through a lawyer, you proposed a relatively modest amount (considering what some women could claim these days), just enough to cover the children's ludicrously expensive private school tuition. She accepted it through her lawyer the very next day. It helped that she has a huge following at home and abroad, and makes a reasonable living as a successful novelist (twice shortlisted for the Booker prize). Also, she is the only child of an affluent family. What you reckon is it was her way of telling you to fuck off.

After scooping out and eating more of the marrow, Rex wiped his fingers on the napkin, leaned back, and cavalierly poked his little finger between his teeth. Then he said, 'She's a nice girl, much nicer than most of them.'

Over the years you were with Tabitha, whenever she came up he would use those exact words; he would say he thought she was *a nice girl* – and you could tell he was sincere. Rex was a sharp old fox: he carried enough impurity and vice in his system to swiftly pick up on someone else's. Yet not once had he made an effort to engage with her.

'You probably got too comfortable with the routine of marriage. Even an incorrigible outlaw like you can fall into that trap. Anyone can – anyone except me,' he boasted, wearing a self-righteous grin, before picking up another piece of greasy bone marrow.

You could say Rex has unresolved issues with women. He will resort to sly attacks on those who happen to possess the lethal combination of youth and good looks. He will do his utmost best, employing poorly disguised insults and misogynistic remarks, to bring them to breaking point. Once, he caused a girl with gnawed fingernails to burst into tears.

There have been a few who have rightly told him to go and fuck himself. One leggy bird had poured a full glass of red wine over his shiny bald head before dashing out of a restaurant. But most choose to remain in his company. They tuck into meticulously prepared dishes and quaff the fine wine and overpriced cocktails placed in front of them; they happily snort his high-end charlie, pop his pills and smoke his fat spliffs. People from the movie industry seem to have special powers over others. For most of these girls, Rex's blunt rudeness, sagging body parts and expensive dentures are just about tolerable for one evening. Then there are always a rare few who continue to accept his swanky invitations. Those with no pride, who have dubious ambitions of their own. Thick-skinned types with expressionless faces, able to react to his malicious humiliations with a shrug of the shoulder. The odd one becomes a girlfriend, but so far no relationship has lasted longer than a year.

The hotel receptionist turns around with a complacent smile on his face. 'We've been pretty busy, sir. There's a massive contemporary art fair going on right now, very close to us...'

'Oh, is that so,' you say, and leave it at that. Frankly you can't be bothered to start up a conversation about your gallery and your participation at the Fair. If you do, he will probably feel obliged to ask you all sorts of questions. If you can help it, you avoid engaging in forced dialogue with strangers. Continuing to smile, he nods, and then turns around and inserts the card in the slot again. This time, when he presses the brass handle of the door it opens effortlessly.

'Well, that is just very strange, but here we go, sir,' he says pensively, trying to maintain a cheerful appearance.

'Thank God for that,' you mutter, deeply relieved. You enter and he follows you. It's a pretentious old room with shoddy brown furniture. He asks whether you would like to be shown how things function. You tell him you can probably figure them out yourself and hand him a two-pound coin.

Right after he leaves, you draw the bulky curtains together. You strip naked, dumping your stale clothes in the corner, then climb into bed without attempting to remove the bedcover; it weighs about half a ton, made from the same nauseatingly pat-terned fabric as the curtains. You briefly pick up on the distant echo of screaming sirens; you would think London was on the brink of major catastrophe.

You check the time on your phone, switch it to silent mode and then throw it further across the bed to prevent yourself from obsessively monitoring the hour. For a few seconds you stare into the dimensionless void, the alienation of trying to sleep in a foreign space creeping up on you. Then you notice the TV remote lying by the bedside table. You half-reluctantly pick it up and turn the TV on.

Immediately, the room is lit up by a massive screen fixed to the wall. You absolutely cannot stand it when they do that: attach a commonplace TV screen onto a wall as if it were high art. Right beneath the TV is a wooden cabinet with a large bottle of Evian and a basket full of crisps, chocolate bars and what have you, for all the lazy gits who are willing to pay three times the price for a given snack rather than nip down to the nearest off-licence.

With murky floral carpet clashing with the curtains and the duvet, and a badly executed portrait of some tosser who probably never existed hanging on one of the walls, they haven't exactly been able to pull off the classic English look. What's more, on the bedside table is a printed list indicating the rates for prepay blockbuster movies and porn channels. Frankly, hotel rooms have always depressed you terribly. You should never have come here unless you were actually contemplating suicide. You should just have driven home. Especially when you're paying two hundred and ten pounds for this misery.

You turn up the volume on the TV and start uninterestedly flicking through the channels. By the time you reach the sixty-fourth channel, an insurmountable exhaustion washes over you. You can barely keep your eyelids open. You give Mary Berry the middle finger just as she's giving advice about lemon drizzle cake and switch off the TV.

When you open your eyes again, you find yourself lying flat on a pillow, your arms spread apart like a cruising eagle. You look around you: the TV screen on the wall gives you the first clue to where you are. One by one, the oppressive silhouettes of the furnishings surrounding you and the stiflingly heavy bedcover compressing your burning nakedness brings you back to the room you are compelled to camp in. As if you've just half-heartedly bonked a bird whom you are dying to flee, you lean across, snatch up your phone, and leap out of bed.

I V

You pull up outside the Fair. There are still some people – mostly exhibitors, by now – coming out of the venue, hurriedly attending to their lousy umbrellas and rushing in the direction of the Tube station. You spot her by the edge of the pavement; she's standing upright, her long legs clasped primly together, holding a stern black umbrella over her head as if she's beside someone's open grave, watching the casket being lowered at her feet. You flash the car lights to grab her attention. According to the dashboard clock, you're running twenty-one minutes late; idiotically you forgot to set the alarm on your phone before passing out on the hotel bed. Aware it was only going to make you even later, you jumped into the shower and washed yourself frantically, as if trying to rid yourself of a flea infestation – like the one you had many years ago as a kid, after smuggling a box of stray kittens into the house behind your mother's back. In the hotel shower, you smothered yourself with what you could squeeze from the miniature shampoo bottles. You couldn't allow yourself to pick her up smelling like a filthy dog.

She lifts her umbrella a bit higher and stares at the car, but you doubt she can see inside; it's dark and raining intensely. Behind you stretches a long line of impatient drivers, so you lean across the passenger seat, open the door, and shout for her to jump in.

She awkwardly positions her legs – clad in a pair of slim-cut jeans – inside the spacious passenger footwell. She clumsily struggles to close her soaking wet umbrella. Once she has managed that, she lets it drip over her coat before dropping it alongside her boots. One of the cars behind you sounds its horn, and a few others quickly join in.

'What a bunch of wankers!' you angrily mutter to yourself, not intending to speak the words aloud in her company, then set the car in motion a fraction of a second before she's able to close the passenger door fully. You don't feel like your usual self; your head feels heavy, subtle waves of pain now and again manifest themselves. Your mind is blurry and filled with unfinished sentences, partial thoughts. Late afternoon naps almost always make you feel this way. It is as if neither your mind nor your body can adjust to being awake again.

'Sorry I'm late. I had to meet an important client back at the gallery. The traffic on the way back was insane,' you lie, your eyes set on the moving traffic in front of you.

'It's OK.'

She must be pretty pissed off being kept waiting that long in the rain, but she's obviously trying to be polite about it. She seems like someone who's been brought up to have good manners.

'I didn't have your number. Otherwise I would've called,' you add, thinking how foolish it was of you not to have asked for it.

Things could happen, you know, you internally mutter to yourself, exaggeratedly mimicking Tabitha's manner of speech. When you've lived long enough with someone, you start repeating their words as a reflex. Tabitha frequently imagined the worst possible scenarios. She worried a fire might break out in your home while you were all fast asleep, and had made you buy a tall stepladder so you could escape to the roof in case the floors beneath you were in flames.

'It's OK,' Ada repeats, sounding as if she would rather you stop making excuses for yourself. The air inside the car is clammy and charged with tension. For a passing moment, stopped at a red light, you imagine slipping your hand between her legs. The thought of it gives you a light erection.

The demister doesn't seem to be doing its job properly. When you stop at the next set of lights, you lean over on your squeaky leather seat and messily wipe away most of the condensation covering the windscreen. Your limbs feel awkward, unwieldy. Now that you have contemplated the idea, you're afraid of accidentally touching her – though, given the amount of space between you, it's unlikely. You glance at her; the dampness in the air has fluffed out her dense curls. Her head is turned away from you.

'Is there a particular place you'd like to go?' you ask, just to appear courteous. You don't have anything particularly interesting to say to her at this moment. She shrugs, then briefly turns towards you and smiles. She looks quite tense, as if she would rather be somewhere else, and for an extended period you drive in silence. Sometimes the acknowledgement of her presence feels all too arousing, and sometimes you're drawn so far inside a cloudy haze of nothingness you actually forget she's there right beside you.

'Are you hungry?' you ask, approaching an amber traffic light. Your right foot automatically presses on the accelerator.

She is wiping the steam off the window beside her with the back of her hand. She shakes her head and says, 'I'm fine, actually. I had some food around six. I'm not hungry yet.'

'Really? I did the same.'

You had emerged from the bathroom with a stiff towel wrapped around your waist. Famished, you had gone straight for the basket of snacks. To your great satisfaction (and slight reservation) you devoured a packet of Walkers salt and vinegar crisps, followed by a Mars bar. Their combined residues are still lodged in your back teeth.

'Tell you what. I have a photography collection of mine hanging in a friend's basement on Cheyne Walk. I'd really like for you to see it. My friend won't be there, but he has live-in staff who can serve us some drinks and nibbles, and I can walk you around my collection.'

'What kind of a collection?' she asks, glancing in your direction. Then she looks away again. You can't tell if she is watching the changing scenery or avoiding eye contact. You are driving down Park Lane, towards Hyde Park Corner, where you were loitering like a useless fuck less than twenty-four hours ago. You remember how, after you had passed Green Park, you had sidled alongside the iron railings of a shopping arcade to release a warm stream of urine. It had splattered generously, releasing a cloud of vapour on its way down. If she knew the state you had been in, she probably wouldn't be too impressed.

'It's a photography collection with a few other bits and pieces. Mostly late nineteenth century.'

She tilts her head in your direction again. You catch her enigmatic gaze as you're turning the sturdy wheel of the car clockwise at the big roundabout, scarcely managing to signal before the appropriate exit. Driving the car, you often find yourself picturing your father behind the wheel.

'What kind of photographs?'

'I won't say. But they're unlike anything you've seen so far.'

Tabitha had prohibited you from hanging any of the photographs from the collection in the three-bedroom house she now shares with your two kids and the diabetic Bengal cat who is starting to go blind in one eye. They are definitely not everyone's bag.

'Are they portraits?' Ada asks after a long silence.

'They can be regarded as portraiture, I suppose. Well, as much as any photograph of a human being can be regarded as one, but they weren't executed with that purpose in mind.'

She silently nods. You're not going to give her any clues.

There's this fuzzy video footage from your childhood. It must've been taken when you were about three or so. Your parents were still together, pursuing their ill-fated marriage filled with raw sparks of discontent and fury. Your father had once remarked at a dinner party that the only time he and your mother properly enjoyed each other's company was in the process of making you. At this point he was married to his third wife and she was also present at the table. You suppose it was intended as a tasteless joke and a compliment to you – that, or a tribute to his insatiable sex drive, which had left behind half a dozen offspring he seemed not to have wanted, and a whole series of lethally dysfunctional relationships. Your father – an arrogant minor toff – had been inflicted with severe intimacy issues, you suspect, when aged seven he had been shipped off to boarding school. And your dear mother was a fun-loving hippy-eccentric with an overly soppy disposition. Their absurdly incompatible union was never going to last.

Anyway, that fuzzy video footage was filmed in your backyard on a snowy winter's day. You're not sure what the occasion was; it might just have been the snow. There's plenty of *you*, dressed up in a baby-blue down coat that resembles an airbag, running and rolling around the place as if you've been topped up with steroids. Close-ups of your face sporadically appear. Your eyelids flicker to keep flecks of snow from getting into your eyes. There's also a bit of your father, posing unashamedly for the camera. You hear your mother energetically saying, 'Isn't it a glorious day?' while she shakes the handheld camera. Your father half-nods to her and then starts readjusting his hair unconcernedly, as if standing in front of a mirror admiring himself. Your father used to love staring at his own reflection. Whether you were having one of your usual disagreements, or he was giving you a lecture about how to get on in life the way he had so successfully done, if there happened to be a mirror close by, he would sneak glimpses at himself.

Your mother: 'Why don't we make a snowman? Surely there is enough snow here to make a snowman?' She never lost her positive attitude, even when she was dying from an ugly, malicious tumour that had branched inside her colon. She died just before you graduated from the RCA. Tabitha frequently thought about the possible death of *her* loved ones; such pessimistic deliberations would somehow lead her to the possibility of your unfaithfulness. She said it made her feel more prepared. Imagining the worst probably gave her the illusion she had some control over her life. She also superstitiously believed that to think about your worst fears meant there was less chance of them actually taking place.

The flecks of snow dropping from the sky multiply. Your father smiles flirtatiously at the camera, then attempts to casually slide his hands into the pockets of his winter jacket – which seems to be brand new, or at least worn for the first time, because he cannot get his hands through the stitched-up pockets. He loses his cool and stares helplessly at the camera; he knows he appears an utter fool. It cracks you up every time you watch it; it's hilarious and yet somehow quite touching.

When you park the car, astonishingly finding a spot right in front of the house, you're still feeling heavy-headed and not altogether yourself. Still, your situation will soon be resolved by a couple of strong snifters. Ada tilts her long legs sideways as you reach into the glove compartment to grab your leather gloves. They were a purchase from Barneys last year, when you were in New York for the Armory Show. It's a miracle you haven't yet lost them. You always lose things: keys, phones, scarves, lighters. You even lost your boxer shorts one evening. You had them on upon leaving your house, and by the time you got back in the morning they were gone – such a mystery. They could be hanging inside a gilded frame in some mad bird's boudoir, for all you know.

You push your fingers forcefully inside a glove. There's no urgent need for you to wear them – yet you do anyway, sensing her curious, timid eyes upon you. It makes you think of your father in that video.

ADA

I

'ART WAS THE ONLY thing I was ever properly good at,' he said.

Swinging the antique-style, oxidised lighter he had borrowed, he repositioned himself and leaned backwards, the undulating spirals of smoke from his newly lit cigarette rushing to fill the space. The smoke quickly accumulated under the faint light of the lamp towering between us. Its base had been crafted to resemble the monstrous claws of some fictive predator that could only come from the imaginings of the fruitful human mind. The lamp's gracefully aged velvet shade reminded me of old interiors I imagined once existed, where it had been – and still continued to be – a silent, inanimate witness.

Our eyes briefly met. I shook my head at him softly, as if to say *I understand what you mean* – I believed I could. Though I had spent most of the afternoon at the Fair anticipating how our shared evening was going to proceed, and despite being momentarily mesmerised by the openness with which he spoke about himself – an innately un-English quality – my thoughts wandered off, trying to predict what kind of an aftertaste our current moment would leave me with.

I brought my attention to the cushions of the low-set sofa I was sinking into, the cold touch of the cocktail glass against my fingertips, the strong vodka martini mix I wasn't sure I was fully enjoying, the subtle floral scent I picked up on, and a teasing warmth from the electric blue flames moving dispassionately inside a gas fire. I shifted my attention to the majestic interior, desperately trying to suspend myself from the here and now while still focusing on its trimmings.

Meanwhile, flashes of pulse-raising erotic acts between us that I had obsessively conjured up that afternoon were resurfacing in my mind with incisive potency.

'Then why didn't you—'

'Become an artist?' he said, staring intently back at me, as if intending to ask the very same question.

Running his fingers up and down his thigh, he left soft, barely visible trails on his trousers – reminiscent of tyre tracks on a snowed-in road – while the distant echo of quickening footsteps from the opposite end of the house reminded me that we were, after all, not alone.

'You know,' he began with a smirk on his lips, which in time dissolved, 'I could give you a tiresome, self-pitying explanation. My mother's unjust suffering, followed by her traumatic death after my graduation. My father's lack of belief in me as an artist – mind you, he was dismissive of anything creative – and his nagging insistence that I should work alongside him at his lucrative property business. I rejected him time and again, and he never seemed to quite grasp exactly why – or ever acknowledge what a total disaster it would've been for everyone had

I accepted. And, of course, despite my efforts, being unable to find a decent gallery to represent my work. I can list all these elements in my life as reasons. But, truth be told,' he said, leisurely stirring the liquid around a sunken green olive with his index finger, 'Somewhere along the line I lost focus.'

As he sucked the dewiness from his finger and took an unrestrained swig from the wide-mouthed glass, I glimpsed the deepening lines under his curious, impish eyes. I wondered how old he was. In my first year in London, I had briefly developed a particular interest for older men with youthful spirits, who lived precariously and in the moment. After deliberating on this I caught up hastily with the present, anxious and relieved – as if I'd just managed to climb onto the back end of a departing double-decker bus – and reflected on how tired he seemed, as if the hours in a day were insufficient to fulfil his objectives and desires. As if he'd had to exchange his sleep, and his health, for extra time.

His weary gaze seemed to be projected inwards, perhaps absorbed by a passing emotion, as he popped the olive into his mouth and started chewing – until a sudden crack startled us both.

'Blimey,' he said, removing the egg-shaped stone from between his lips and disposing of it inside a small ashtray the surface of which was covered with a rocky landscape of grey ash. It reminded me of a black-and-white close-up of a planet – an image I had possibly come across inside a textbook in high school.

'Why do you think you lost your focus?' I asked warily, concerned that the eagerness in my tone signalled my unruly fascination with him. I was confident he wouldn't be offended by the intrusion, though, and he might find comfort, as some people did, cross-examining key decisions they had made in the past to make sense of their lives. Yet, in the farthest corner of my mind, nascent fears concerning Lucian moved about; dark, nomadic sharks in the silent depths of the sea.

Stretching out his arm and taking a final drag, he glanced at his fingers and watched the burning end of the cigarette between them. Turning towards me, the tip of his tongue briefly tracing his upper lip, he said, 'I suppose I got distracted. I somehow lost faith in what I was trying to achieve.'

We stared into each other's eyes intently, knowingly, before I spoke.

'The very same thing happened to me, I think.'

'Really?' he asked. His own lips slightly ajar, he followed the shape of my mouth with his eyes, as if to suggest our parallel experiences should inevitably reshape themselves into a more carnal form.

'Not exactly the same thing, but it was similar, I suppose,' I said. I smiled apprehensively, resisting the urge to look away. I wished I had a less transparent demeanour, as rapid pulses of my heart heralded an impending influx of warm blood to my cheeks.

'I thought I would follow in my father's footsteps and become an artist, a painter. For a very long time, until I was about seventeen, all I wanted to do was paint. I spent my evenings, my weekends, my summer holidays painting at my father's studio.'

The heavy tang of paint fumes; paintbrushes springing out of murky water-filled glass jars; paint-smeared tea cloths; tubes of acrylics and oils, their printed labels nearly illegible. Past exhibition posters, torn around the edges, that covered most of the wall space overlooking my father's wide-angled desk, where he executed preliminary drawings for his large canvases. Volumes on Anatolian and Mesopotamian history and anthropology, exhibition catalogues, artists' monographs, *Hayat* and *Life* magazines, CDs, LPs methodically stacked onto the shelves of an imposing walnut bookshelf inherited from my paternal grandparents. Apart from one or two works in progress, the rest of the paintings were safely stored inside a colossal unit of metallic sliding racks, away from light and prying eyes. A jazz quintet's record would be humming from a turntable; artist friends turning up unannounced, infatuated with certain current motifs, passing ideas and lingering fears, only an old, wrinkly foulard wrapped around their unshaven necks to shield them against the damp chill of Istanbul's winter outside. Two well-fed stray cats, regulars of the studio, would be stretched out leisurely like vainglorious concubines beside flaming-hot radiators, shaking their plush tails and narrowing their eyes condescendingly at self-indulgent utterances about art theory, meticulously chewing away the residue of dirt from their sickle-like claws. At the anxiety and gloom being expressed over Turkey's near future they might apathetically lick their paws – confident that a radical change in the country's regime, if it ever happened, would hardly have a direct impact on them.

'Did you paint side by side?' he asked, the mischievous spark of sexual pursuit briefly absent from his eyes. I wondered whether, like me, he was able to form through someone else's description a picture in his mind of people and places that gradually strengthened with each explanation, until they became entities that had very little in common with their counterparts in reality.

'We used to paint at separate ends of a very spacious, L-shaped room. The studio is on the ground floor of an apartment building—'

'Do your parents live there?'

'No, they live on the sixth floor of a separate building, but it's on the same street as the studio.' In my mind I steadily followed the bendy, narrow road uphill – imagining it on an early summer's evening, when the sun had barely set. I was accompanied by the smell of the sea I had recently left behind, and the warm, sour stench of rotting garbage from bulky aluminium bins, a stench that clashed with the aroma of smoked aubergines, of homemade yogurt whipped with crushed garlic and of slices of still-warm bread, freshly baked in the local bakery's stone oven. All these sensations found their way to me, together with voices and laughter from open windows and family verandas. I longingly recalled the freshly watered grass I often enjoyed the scent of while treading up the long, narrow path. I remembered, too, the sweet incense of peach roses, and the pepperish bouquet of vermillion geraniums, peeking through masses of concrete. Without intending to, I imagined a boy I would encounter, standing idly next to the local grocery store, wearing the burgundy and blue striped T-shirt of his favourite football team, bouncing a ball beside plump watermelons and honeydews beleaguered by a few insistent house flies. I remembered, too – with a fondness one sometimes reserves for near-strangers – the grocery store owner. A self-contained, austere man who sometimes would not reciprocate a salutation, so preoccupied was he with solving newspaper puzzles between taking payments, indifferently bagging each item. His inert detachment was occasionally interrupted by a shy, vague smile; the lines on his greasy skin and the look of discontent in his eyes seemed to suggest turbulent internal arguments that never reached a conclusion, as if he just about managed to tolerate life's burdens, while continuing to thoroughly examine them under a giant magnifying glass.

Moving further along the ascending road, its bends resembling a snake dangling from a branch, I was only able to recall random minor details of some of the mismatched apartment buildings, most of them erected at some point in the previous century, when the secularist doctrines of Mustafa Kemal Atatürk still resonated in the minds of most Turks. I then found myself standing at the edge of our balcony, my fingertips resting on the railing, sensing the soft southwesterly breeze bring a salty tang as I gazed intently at the lively sea traffic. Glistening yachts; small, timber fishing boats; packed ferryboats moving swiftly, leaving their white, frothy trails behind, while in the middle of the enclosed sea some foreigners mistook for a river a couple of mammoth transport vessels appeared stationary, as if they were stranded whales misled and straying too close to shore. Further ahead, minarets resembling colossal spears penetrated the murky layer of pollution, unable to ever reach the pristine blue sky they aimed for. They stood among arbitrarily, imprudently built throngs of apartment blocks, the great majority of which – lacking the physical resilience required in a critical earthquake zone – were cramped together ungraciously, even foully, carpeting the hilly landscape of the metropolis as a concrete form of vegetation that, from a distance, resembled a chaotic assemblage of old harlequin matchboxes, like the ones my mother kept in a ceramic bowl. (The bowl itself was placed in a cupboard which was hardly ever opened; leftovers from a cavalier phase in her life, cherished souvenirs from when she still used to casually smoke.)

Licking his bottom lip attentively, Lucian commented, 'Your dear father and I are much alike' – as if to hint that, by a remarkable twist of fate, he had actually met him.

'How so?' I asked, naively contemplating the probability of the encounter, nonetheless unconvinced by the comparison, despite knowing Lucian for slightly longer than a day, and not yet having seen a painting of his. Besides their commitment to art, the two men exemplified conflicting guises the artist might embody. On the one hand: a scholarly thinker, an unwavering individual driven by the challenges of the medium, possessed by an obsessive nature, preoccupied with adapting new techniques of painting, which predominantly relied on foresight and restraint, to an abstract language of his own creation intertwined with arcane symbols borrowed from ancient Anatolian and Mesopotamian civilisations. On the other: the erratic, dreamy, and eternally impulsive *visceral artist*. The kind of artist I imagined Lucian to have been – who, like a child, had lost himself in paint's viscous tactility, discovering temporary pockets of escape from the mundanity of living. His raw sensitivity and acute observation would have captured many fine peculiarities overlooked by others – I imagined him to have surrendered without hesitation to his subconscious, and to the artistically riveting places one arrives at through encounters with chance and error.

'I live above the gallery,' he said. The bitterness in his voice, the temporary lack of animation in his eyes, suggested that the convenience in his living arrangements was actually a cause of distress for him.

'My father hardly leaves our street,' I told him. 'A few times a year he visits the gallery which represents his work, and sometimes there's some social event he cannot bring himself to say no to, like a relative's wedding or a close friend's exhibition preview.' I lowered my voice at the end of my sentence, suddenly worried that it carried no obvious interest for him. I sensed, inside the secluded corridors of my psyche, the particular mood I reserved for the art scene in Istanbul. It instantly embraced me with its potent familiarity, its sentimental resonance, and took me on a brief journey through my childhood and early adolescence, when I would pay spontaneous visits to galleries and artists' studios alongside my father – who, as a younger man, a less acclaimed painter, relished exposing himself to other artistic influences and to the general bedlam of the city.

'Why do you think your dear father's such a recluse?' he asked, sunk comfortably in his green armchair, his legs spread out. He periodically pressed his knees together with playful nonchalance. The unassuming shimmer of the damask arm-chair now and again caught my attention.

Reflecting on his question, I imagined stark, high-ceilinged spaces, inside historic, grandiose apartment buildings with marble staircases and tiny, coffin-like elevators, their ornate façades reflecting the undeniable dominance of European aesthetics in late Ottoman-era architecture. Most of these art galleries had prospered in the last decade or so, when Turkish contemporary art had woken up from its deep slumber, rapidly attempting to catch up with internationally recognised avant-garde art practices – and questioning its own relevance and future, resurrected under a government which possessed little genuine appreciation for artistic expression.

'He says unnecessarily over-exposing himself to foreign influences might affect the concentration and discipline required for artistic productivity. In some ways, my father lives the life of a monk. His art is his meditation, his studio is his temple. On a normal day he goes there at eight in the morning to self-reflect, study and ultimately *produce*. He finds the word *create* too presumptuous, at odds with what he does. He considers himself more of an artisan than an artist. His success has never fazed him. Instead it has made him withdraw. Simplicity governs his life. He has a very restricted diet. He only eats fish, fruit, vegetables, wholegrain bread, pasta and rice, and bulgur wheat. He cannot drink alcohol, tea or coffee. He says his system has become too sensitive to process such strong ingredients.'

'Our frame of mind has a much stronger effect on our actions and inclinations – even the way our bodies process other substances – than we're led to believe,' he said, reaching for his empty cocktail glass. He glanced into the space behind my left shoulder, his wandering eyes travelling through the open door and through an oak-panelled passage – on to a vestibule where a cumbrous chandelier had been hung. The chandelier resembled a tall wedding cake flipped upside down – rows of suspended, delicately arranged crystal droplets, reminding me of jewellery handed down to my mother by my late maternal grandmother. She had been a quick-witted, compassionate, fiery old woman, in the final years of her life, haunted by the apprehension she felt for the future of her country. She had once explained to me how, a couple of decades before I was born, during the Cold War, the overblown threat of Bolshevism had prompted the uniformed defenders of the secular regime to torture and slaughter left-wing youth, Turkey's future intelligentsia, and consciously encourage the expansion of religious fundamentalism. My grandmother thereby showed me how longstanding governing powers could create a route to their demise, by unintentionally conjuring their own enemies.

Lucian's attention seemed to have drifted off. Perhaps he was curious about the whereabouts of the elderly man who had let us into the house. He had assisted me in removing my coat, restrained and attentive, before leading us inside to the double reception room with an authority he seemed entitled to while the owner of the house was absent. The collars of his shirt swam around his gaunt neck, worn at the folds from recurrent wash and wear. Along the way, he responded to Lucian's questions with short, conclusive answers.

The old man had returned once, his footsteps hardly noticeable in the background. His ghostly reappearances barely had an effect on the flow of our conversation. He grasped a circular tray with his ancient fingers, a few of them crooked and swollen at the joints. Blue veins branched out on the backs of his hands like tinted, jagged maps. He'd brought us a couple of freshly prepared vodka martinis, and a bowl of Japanese crackers which so far neither of us had taken a liking to.

A few minutes after my most recent mouthful, gentle surges of lukewarm brilliance began to travel inside my bloodstream, their anaesthetising and invigorating influence rapidly taking effect. My sentiments, like the way I perceived my surroundings, sharpened then softened.

Lucian retrieved the lighter, then released himself back into his armchair while exhaling smoke from his lungs with a deep sigh, as if the action had enabled him to exorcise frustrations clogging up his psyche, like clearing a clump of hair from a bath plug.

'What did you paint?' he asked.

His probing side-glance generated a moment's shockwave. Inhaling sharply, I moved backward in my sunken seat, as if I'd stumbled upon an invisible electric barrier.

'You can have what's left of mine, if you like,' I said, referring to my glass. It was as if I had allowed myself to loosen the taut buckles of a corset; intoxication had allowed my boundaries to become elastic, my immediate thoughts less probing and urgent. Yet I still didn't want to entirely lose my composure.

'He should be back any moment. He's probably delayed due to some bodily necessity which requires *immediate* attention,' Lucian said, arousing in me a juvenile laughter I was unprepared for. He returned to carefully moulding the tip of his cigarette on the ridge of the ashtray. Almost immediately he looked up again and directed his amused, intrigued attention to my lingering giggles. They felt unrelenting and redemptive at once, before dying out along with the hilarity of what he had said.

'I used to paint objects that didn't actually exist. They only sometimes had a slight, uncanny resemblance to real objects. I called them fictitious still lives. I worked with both acrylics and oils. And very occasionally with oil pastels. The scale of my paintings was usually pretty small,' I explained, without feeling the uneasiness and inevitable frustration I felt attempting to describe the contents of my paintings to someone new.

I watched him press his thumb over the soggy, yellowed end of his filter, seeming preoccupied with what I had just said. Then he lifted his head towards the ceiling, took a hurried drag, and repeated with a smile, his eyes glimmering, 'Fictitious still lives.' He laughed. 'I fucking love the sound of it!'

I smiled back at him, dropped my gaze, and began to carefully observe the geometric pattern repeating itself on the vast carpet beneath our feet, noticing its resemblance to the sun symbol of the Hittites (the ancient Anatolian civilisation my father had done extensive research on). I felt my smiling lips ache as I tried to suppress my gnawing shyness, bubbling up alongside the joy his reaction had created in me.

'What objects did they resemble?'

I shrugged my shoulders.

'Not anything in particular. I suppose like small, abstract sculptures on a pedestal – but their lines, their detailing, sometimes suggested a vague resemblance to something else. Most of the time I didn't notice these resemblances until some-one pointed them out to me, or until I could distance myself from the painting for a while. I never consciously planned my paintings, or thought deeply about what they were meant to resemble, to represent, the way my father does.'

'Frankly, I find works that come out of such forced endeav-ours insincere, lacking creative fervour.'

'What about you?' I asked.

I picked up on the old man's cautious, nearly silent steps but did not turn around to acknowledge his arrival, to respect the scant level of interaction he wished to have with us, for the sake of our privacy and possibly his own peace of mind.

Spreading his arms animatedly, Lucian replied, 'I painted huge abstract canvases,' demonstrating the peculiar gratification men derived associating themselves with large-scale objects. 'In oils, acrylics and spray paint. Pretty often I incorporated graffiti, cartoons and digital printing. I also did portraits of friends and of people whose faces I was drawn to. The scales of these paintings, or sometimes drawings, were much smaller – you know, more intimate.'

Extinguishing his cigarette, he sat up in his armchair, expectantly watching the old man remove our glasses and replace them with fresh ones. The old man wiped crumbs of ash from the coffee table with a damp cloth, and, once he had confiscated the bursting ashtray and replaced it with a spotless one, lightly brushed off the remains of more from the armchair, as if to methodically erase traces of harm Lucian had been inflicting upon himself.

'You see, I've always been terribly fascinated by faces. The energy people's eyes project.'

I sensed the old man discreetly edging away from us.

'I wanted to bring out the flawed humanity of my subjects – the sorrows, insecurities and fears that they conceal,' he said with some intensity, as if still haunted by the same yearning. Lifting his glass towards me, and prompting me to do the same, he said, 'Cheers!' in a melancholic, unexcited tone, insinuating the bitter disillusionment of wasted years – of a passion not persevered with. The crisp sound of our glasses colliding accentuated the almost eerie stillness around us.

'To think you've understood the truth in someone is highly gratifying, even if all you've really achieved is capturing glimpses of their outlook in a particular phase of their lives – bound to shift over time. Having children, getting married, experiencing professional failure or success, ageing, divorce, losing a loved one, battling terminal illness, loneliness, coping with betrayal, or not coping at all. Both my abstract paintings and my portraits became part of my practice. They were investigations into the human mind and soul, and fed each other. I regarded my abstract compositions as self-portraits – a window into my world, so to speak.'

'Do you still paint sometimes?' I asked. I very much wished for him to respond affirmatively.

'No, do you?' he answered rather swiftly.

'Very rarely. Every few months I will come back home with the desire to paint. But I never seem to find the end results satisfactory.'

He raised his eyebrows.

'Making art – it's the outcome of an ongoing dialogue you have with yourself. Each painting is a response to the previous one you did and to whatever subconscious tangle of neuroses is occupying your mind at the time. If you stop then decide to return to it after a long gap, by then that dialogue is interrupted. You've moved on. You have different influences in your life, your mind has shifted to other concerns. It goes without saying, it's exceptionally hard to get the momentum back, to be able to revive a broken dialogue.'

He clasped his hands together, tightening the grip in one hand, caused the fingers in the opposite hand to point upwards. He exhaled through his nose, closely monitoring my eyes to gauge how well I understood what he had said.

'What's worse, though, is the complete shutdown. When you keep finding yourself slouched before an empty canvas or a blank sheet of paper with nothing left to say.'

He set aside the toothpick inside his martini glass which was attached to another colossal green olive, his gaze fixed on the base of his glass. He dropped his head backwards and drank a good portion, as if to drown restive thoughts of the incapacitated artist still roaming inside him – the unsettled, forlorn apparition subsisting alongside his functional self.

'Well, anyway,' he remarked, lifting his eyebrows in defeated acceptance, 'It is what it is.' He landed a gentle slap on his thigh, illustrating the presently unresolvable nature of his relationship with painting; he had set forth all there was to say. As if entertaining an amusing thought in his head, he let out a faint chuckle through his nose, his distant gaze directed to the floor. I watched him pensively pinch his bottom lip – then he turned to me with newly ignited intrigue, as if I had just voiced an opinion which had altered his mood.

'You must show me your paintings one day,' he said, wagging the short end of the pale turquoise foulard wrapped around his neck, as if dangling a string before a frisky kitten – playful, even if his faint glare insinuated that he hadn't yet fully recovered from venturing into the past, of reminding himself of what could have been. Eventually his face lit up again, and he placed the same end of the crumpled foulard between his lips. Suddenly amused by his own behaviour, he dropped his head backwards, and let out an earnest guffaw.

'Most of my work is back in Istanbul, but I think I have one or two paintings on paper I can show you here,' I responded, feeling equally baffled and amused by his excessive exuberance, and barely able to hear my own words through his roaring laughter. Soon enough I was laughing alongside him at the absurdity of laughter itself. I imagined his footsteps on the parquet floor of my small living room – where a sofa took most of the available space – picturing him gazing at one of *my* paintings. Right next to it was a window through which, each spring, one could admire cherry blossoms adorning both sides of an otherwise unassuming North London street. Though his spur-of-the-moment request might never materialise other than in my thoughts.

Watching him wipe away the moisture at the corners of his eyes, I realised that the somewhat bewildered, dishevelled expression his unexpected surge of laughter had left him with seemed far more genuine than the behaviour that had provoked it.

11

'My collection is downstairs.'

I followed him past the fireplace, then through a door, which had until then been disguised by the oak-panelled walls. He opened the door. 'Watch the threshold,' he said, pointing at the raised wooden plank which separated the parquet floor of the reception room from the eroded white stone floor of the other section of the house.

I followed him down a dim, narrow spiral staircase without a bannister, my fingers wandering over the rough surface of the wall for guidance. The overlapping echoes of our footsteps crowded my compromised perception, my footsteps landing a little more carelessly each time, as I considered others, now long deceased, who had also once walked down this stairway. One day Lucian and I would also be added to that intangible list, stored inside the infinite memory of the unfathomable universe. Before we reached the bottom of the staircase (and as I continued to examine the outline of his unruly hair, deriving an illicit gratification from observing him without his aware-ness) I listened to him say, his voice reverberating as if we were walking through a tunnel or a cave, 'This staircase used to lead to a small wine cellar, until he decided to add some further square footage, like every other filthy-rich, greedy bugger who

owns an A-list London property does these days. It's the easiest
of investments.'

He stopped and turned his head; we got a passing glimpse
of each other's shadowy faces.

'And, might I add, an ingenious way to make your neighbours' lives a living hell.'

I paused in the doorway and noticed barely distinguishable
silhouettes of picture frames progressing into oblivion. I felt the
air's slight sting on my eyes as I stared into the impermeable
darkness ahead, its uninterrupted consistency partially quieting
the clatter generated by a day's worth of internal anguish and
external stimulus. I played back his last remarks. I had uncon-
sciously formed a near-abstract yet imposing conception of a
person who inhabited this house, from Lucian's descriptions,
and from passing observations I'd made – precious ornaments
on pristine surfaces, unusually spacious, subtly incensed interiors embellished with carefully selected antique furnishings
and works of art; a house inhabited at irregular intervals for
short periods of time, maintained by live-in staff, deprived of the
informalities of day-to-day life and therefore the unassuming
charm brought on by habitual negligence.

'Hang on a minute,' I heard him say.

The soles of his shoes scraped along the floor, piercing the
silent darkness to which I had quickly, easily adapted. I heard
his breathing, caught disjointed glimpses of his shadowy frame
as he seemed to stretch his body towards me, my state of anxious arousal rapidly shifting towards unease, even fear. I had
repeatedly imagined his attempts to make a pass at me, hooked
on the momentary high it gave me – as if it were a television
screen in the background that projected the same hypnotic

scene over and over again – until I had gorged myself on the relentless repetition.

I heard the clicking of several switches beside me, and bright rays of light drenched my field of vision. I desperately covered my eyes and pulled my head to one side. The stinging residue of white light in my eyes began to weaken; it became less luminous, taking on a pinker hue as I pressed my palms against my eyelids. I felt a reassuring warmth from the sound of his footsteps, shuffling round the room, not dissimilar to the random sounds of daily life that came through my bedroom window on mornings I could afford to remain in bed, and when I hadn't yet been roused by the immediacy of a new day. A passing moped's rumbling engine, a man's acute yell or whistle, or the periodic beating of a hammer from a nearby construction site would caress my half-conscious senses and accompany me in and out of exceptionally vivid dreams. I would switch between losing all corporeal awareness and feeling the bliss of indolence in my flesh and joints. My body would merge with the mattress and become one.

Hearing him approach me, I half opened my eyes, feeling distant from the situation, out of place within the white cube of space, its impersonal, bare existence interrupted by an aged wooden table kept bare and positioned at the centre of the room. Rows of small photographs in identical wooden frames ran along the middle of the walls, resembling a wooden railway leading to nowhere.

'Are you all right?' he asked courteously. He attentively placed a hand on my lower arm, then released his light grip when he saw me react to it.

'The lights seemed very bright at first.'

Glancing around, I could just about identify some of the small, solitary silhouettes of human forms in the faded black and white photographs nearest to me.

I recalled Lucian's words: *It's a photography collection with a few other bits and pieces. Mostly late nineteenth century... they're unlike anything you've seen so far.* I wondered what made these photographs so unusual. Perhaps it was a quirk marvelled at by vintage photography enthusiasts, a subtle feature that could easily go undetected.

Lucian brought his hands together, as if to perform a soundless clap, and kept them braced until he spoke – a gesture that emphasised his weight of experience over mine.

'When photography was invented in the nineteenth century, it became a crucial tool for doctors and surgeons. For the first time, they were able to keep a visual record of illnesses and use this to teach medical students. It became easier to follow a patient's progress, to diagnose an ailment. This was an absolute breakthrough in the medical field. What you will now witness in this room are records of malignant diseases and incapacitating war wounds, of extraordinarily rare birth defects,' he explained.

The beat of my pulse in my ears filled some of the uncomfortable silence as I timidly approached the photographs. I felt the windowless, low-ceilinged space bear down oppressively. A part of me wished I had never accepted the offer to view his collection, and that I somehow possessed the gift to reverse the course of events of the day, so we could find ourselves at an ordinary, dimly lit bar surrounded by the protective umbrella of faceless people.

I couldn't bear to observe any of the framed photos; instead I stared into the immediate space before me. Even so, I caught glimpses of deformed faces and body parts. Of young boys and men with missing limbs and exposed stumps. The faded black and white imagery had the yellow tint of decay and death. Knowing their subjects had once led unjustly tormented lives further heightened their ominous effect. I imagined the restive spirits of these people floating in an eternal, dimensionless abyss; I feared they could easily be beckoned into mortal territory by one's unintended, fleeting interest.

'I started collecting these pictures back when I was living in New York.'

I was glad he was standing behind me, at a distance, and not right beside me.

I set my eyes on a photograph of a boy, his slightly ajar mouth and the stunned look in his eyes possibly caused by the unanticipated, commanding flash of the camera. It had given him an endearingly muddled expression. He appeared to be ten or eleven – a child soldier, a war veteran, miraculously spared, yet violated. His trousers were folded up to his knees to reveal a shapeless stump. I rested my eyes on the discoloured oval border of the photograph and observed a pale brown line unevenly running along its frail surface. The elegantly printed wording was incomprehensible to me at first, though I gathered that it must be the photographer's name and the address of his studio in Philadelphia. It was in that clarifying moment that my heart began to pound, this time abrasively, against my windpipe, and a slight bitterness appeared on my tongue and then disappeared at the instant I sensed it. I came to admit to myself what I had acknowledged but attempted to disregard: the true function of the wooden table at the centre of the room. A seemingly insignificant piece of old furniture, it had multiple overlapping lines engraved on its battered surface and a rusty draining hole at its centre. I now dared to imagine gory emulsions from decomposing corpses running into a vertical structure beneath the table, intended to merge with an underground sewage system.

'It took me over ten years to compile this very rare collection of photographs,' I heard him say, like a proud father. 'Most of these images were taken inside photographers' studios with the same props and backgrounds used in traditional portraits. That's why the patients' poses were always staged and formal. Regardless of their subject matter, the photographers' primary concerns were *always* artistic.'

I noticed the boy had been made to awkwardly rest his arm against an ornate circular side table that appeared taller than usual next to his prepubescent stature. Behind him, the thick, cascading drapery covered up a section of the bare, stained wall. Yet Lucian's bid to divert my attention to the compositional properties of the picture did not prevent me from questioning the intention behind his efforts in creating such a spine-chilling space, and whether this evidenced a highly disturbed mind which revelled in the sufferings of others, or whether it reflected an unconventional effort to contain one's existential angst by deliberately exposing oneself to the grisly realities of human tragedy.

I was startled by the clarity of my voice against the dense stillness of the room as I asked, 'What drew you to them?'

'At first, it was the intense discomfort they sparked in me. And, after some time, it was their odd, lyrical beauty, I think.'

I deliberately brought back to mind his earlier guffaws, to push away the insidious fear that whispered that Lucian had brought me down to this secluded underground room – where one's desperate cries for help would be muted by the surrounding layers of concrete and earth – so as to inflict some harm upon me.

One of the photos was of an upright figure of a young woman, unclad apart from a pair of unflattering black hold-ups loosely clinging to her malnourished thighs. I felt unsettled by the ambiguity of her bushy genitalia, and how her nakedness and rare condition contrasted with her regal pose and knowing stare.

'Why do you keep them here?'

'Because, as you can imagine,' he said, heading towards me, that familiar teasing smirk in his eyes rapidly replaced by seriousness, 'They're not the easiest images to live with.'

As he now stood beside me, he gazed at the very photograph I was unable to move away from. Such an action would be too transparent in its intent. Nor could I bring myself to look back at it. I was afraid any acknowledgment of my interest could encourage him to talk about hermaphroditism. I wished desperately to prevent this; the young woman's protruding clitoris, large enough to resemble a miniature penis, had already brought to the surface feelings of deep shame. The crude exposure of sexuality, when I stumbled upon it in the company of a man, could provoke this in me.

'A couple of years ago I purchased the flat above my gallery, where I live now. It was actually intended as a showroom for second-hand dealings and an extra storage space for artworks. I also planned to permanently showcase these photographs in its reception room along with the autopsy table.' He briefly turned his head towards it, then continued. 'It's an early twentieth-century piece, which I bought in Paris after extensive bargaining with a dodgy dealer specialising in antique medical equipment. I am fully aware it is not to everybody's taste. But certain things changed in my life, as they often tend to do. As they say: if you want to make God laugh, tell him about your plans.'

'What was it that changed in your life?'

'Oh.' He hesitated. 'My wife reckoned she'd had enough of me and decided to give me the boot. Our divorce was finalised last month.'

I had assumed he was too cynical, and too much of a free spirit, to have abided by the social ritual of marriage – yet now I could see how his fervent zeal, his impulsive demeanour might have made him susceptible to the utopian promise of everlasting love.

'How long were you married?'

'Seven years... You too will learn one day that nothing in this life is permanent,' he added, not with gloom but with a stoic acceptance.

'Will your collection always remain here, then?'

'Who knows? I hope not. Actually, I'd like to exhibit it at the gallery one day.' He looked up, the reignited sarcastic glimmer in his eyes out of sync with the earnestness in his voice. 'Something like a summer show would be ideal, don't you think?'

I nodded before moving on to the next photograph, continuing to sense his enquiring eyes on me – as if his question had been more than a casual query about the right timing for an exhibition that was perhaps destined to never take place.

'This one never ceases to amaze me,' he said, and we paused. 'It's the first piece I ever bought in New York. I had the most excruciating hangover on the day, so bad I called in sick. It wasn't till the afternoon that I could bring myself to leave my flat and get myself a cup of coffee somewhere. It was below zero. The entire city had been covered in thick snow while I'd been hibernating. It was kind of magical and surreal. As I tramped through it, I bumped into an old school friend from London I hadn't seen for years. After that, I walked around aimlessly in SoHo until my knuckles and toes became numb. I saw a small, unassuming gallery selling old photographs and dived in to warm myself up. And while casually rummaging around inside, I came across this photo: it's what's known as a parasitic twin.'

He paused to see if I knew what the term meant.

'Very rarely, a twin embryo fails to separate fully inside the uterus and one embryo develops at the expense of the other. In her case, the legs of her underdeveloped conjoined twin remained attached to her pelvis throughout her presumably short life.'

I felt I was leering at the girl's bare, prepubescent flesh, which presented itself as a human puzzle of intermingled limbs I was unable to unravel. I was silently ashamed by the sense of relief I desperately clung to – rapidly weakened by the vulnerability of human health, the frightful obscurity of fate, the inevitability of one's own demise. I observed her pretty ringlets, decorated with short ribbons – that I imagined in a muted shade of pastel pink – and the crotchety, defiant stare, which gave her child's face the unsettling bearing of a grown-up. That face reflected the prejudice she would've had to endure. This led me to revisit the humiliation, sorrow and bottled-up rage I had experienced in the past, while watching Black actors on TV portray victims of racial hatred. Given how very little tolerance people *still* harboured towards otherness, I felt disheartened for humanity's future.

Feeling out of sync with the present, I stretched my hand out to balance myself, then rested my forehead against my palm and closed my eyes.

III

'Ada, are you sure you're feeling okay?'

I only looked up at him when his hand clutched my shoulder reassuringly. Sensing the rumblings of my stomach, hoping they were inaudible to him and that they would not linger, I very much regretted not having eaten properly prior to seeing him. At the time, my overpowering anticipation of our nearing encounter had hindered my appetite. I should never have declined his initial suggestion to have a bite somewhere. I wondered whether the untouched bowl of Japanese crackers would still be up there waiting for me upon our return.

'I'm all right, just a little lightheaded,' I said, an embarrassed smile forming on my lips.

'Would you like to take a seat somewhere?' he asked, pausing to examine my face with a look of genuine concern. Yet I continued to suspect that the attentive, firm grip on my shoulder was just an excuse to prolong his physical contact with me, a preliminary step to a set goal.

I noticed the autopsy table was the only place available for me to sit on or lean against.

'By all means, be my guest,' he muttered drily, gesturing towards the table. He giggled and I joined in tensely.

'No, I think I'm better off where I am,' I responded, trying to keep up the appearance of amusement – the comical absurdity of the situation overridden by hounding unease of the table.

He glanced meaningfully at me – then, seeming to hesitate, he retreated, casting his eyes away from me, as if he couldn't seem to find the right phrase to express a pressing thought or to follow through a daring move. He looked up and gazed dreamily towards the low ceiling, tapping two fingers against his stubbled chin.

'You know what's quite peculiar? It feels like you remind me of a girl I once knew but can no longer remember.'

I was intrigued by the possibility of sharing a close resemblance to an anonymous stranger – and yet discouraged by the idea that the impression I had so far made had been previously realised by someone else.

'When you get to my age, you get quite a few of those. People you know at different intervals randomly slip away, as if they had never existed, and unless you run into them again somewhere – or they try to befriend you on Facebook – their memory, along with the experiences you once shared, are lost forever.'

I listened to him with interest. 'I don't see how I could ever forget a person I once knew.'

'Oh, you say that now, but just wait and see,' he answered swiftly with donnish confidence, shaking his index finger at me as if to warn me of the calamities of ageing. He finally released his hold on my shoulder, then subtly moved a step closer. 'Your memories as a teenager, as a young adult are destined to fade away with each passing year. One day even things you're convinced you can still remember will be filled with gaps and misleading discrepancies. A bit like key events from your childhood. In about twenty years there's a considerable chance you'll fail to remember the pallid geeks you went to school with, or some of the people you once hung out or even slept with.'

I was unsure whether to regard his reference to my potential sexual encounters as a cheap ploy to steer my thoughts into the realm of sex, or as an involuntary remark triggered by his own personal experiences – presumably filled with an abundance of steamy escapades. Or perhaps it was a bit of both.

'You're probably right,' I reluctantly replied. I fell short of the years of experience he had to his advantage.

'Oh, I'm always right!' He replied half-jokingly, with a casual confidence that seemed to suggest this was a catchphrase he often employed. 'You must promise me one thing, though.'

'What?' Feeling cornered by his proximity and piercing attention, I briefly looked away.

'Never to forget this night,' he whispered, leaning towards my ear before he caressed my flaming cheek with the back of his hand, cautiously monitoring my unresponsive stance. Heat intensified between my legs as he began lightly tracing my face with his knuckles. 'Better now?'

Unsure if it was a genuine query or an indirect request to take things a step further, I nodded back vaguely, drawn inwards by self-preservation as well as self-doubt – yet at the same moment lured by the uncontrollable attraction I felt towards him. I interrupted his steady movement; the bony, indented back of his hand was alien to me at first as I softly ran my lips over his knuckles, the heat of my breath merging with the scent of his skin – oddly enhanced with the faint trace of tobacco – while I attempted to ignore my mounting trepidation about where our actions were bound to lead, and if I would cope.

His hand lightly gripped my chin, as if to familiarise himself with the contours of my face. I found myself impulsively placing a kiss on his palm.

'You seem so closed up,' he said softly.

'It's not completely by choice,' I responded, the slight strain in my vocal cords towards the end of my sentence daring me to give in, to surrender to a tearful breakdown. But I managed to maintain a collected front, even as I tried to deflect the anxiety attacks that could randomly afflict me. These days, they weren't always prompted by the still raw and painfully vivid recollections of the fourteen-hour captivity I had endured in Istanbul, but – rather annoyingly – by the anguish of possibly triggering an attack. Added to this were the smothering nightmares that made me dread closing my eyes each night, and often deprived me of a good night's sleep. These nightmares captured moments from the abuse and intimidation I had experienced at the hands of several policemen; their arbitrary, ruthless conduct seeming to have shattered – perhaps irredeemably – the equilibrium and unsuspecting trust for others which sensible, loving parenting and an agreeable social environment had allowed me to cultivate.

An almost undetectable amount of moisture released itself under my eyelids before I returned to the arousing effect of his commanding touch.

'What do you mean?' he whispered – but without real curiosity about what my answer might be. He seemed determined not to allow anything to water down the mounting intensity between us.

As if temporarily regressing to adolescence – reluctant to own up to my inadequacies – I shrugged and rolled my eyes at him, smiling, and put on an insincere, lighthearted demeanour. I wished to make believe my previous utterances had carried no significant weight – while trying to ignore the transitory unease of self-betrayal.

Like the texture of his knuckles, so did the supple softness of his lips feel unexpectedly alien to me at first. It had been over two years since I had gotten this close to someone. I had envisioned this scene so eagerly that my imaginings had replaced the tactile sensation of a kiss with something fictitious and unattainable. Yet, before I knew it, I was smitten by the reality of our touch, by the raw sensuality one can never actually recreate in one's mind. Lucian's entire being was channelled through his mouth alone. Little by little it loosened the stiff knot formed inside me.

Soon our exploratory pecks gave way to deeper motion, demonstrative of the uncontainable lust we shared. And just before our mouths slipped away from each other's, I instinctively bit his bottom lip, a playful act that unleashed his unrestrained side.

He grabbed at my thighs and hips, then clutched my hair with one hand – perhaps too passionately, as the uncomfortable tension at their roots brought unwanted flashbacks of Istanbul, and of being brusquely pulled by the hair and the collar of my stretched-out T-shirt, revealing good portions of my bra and bare shoulder. It took me back to that moment – reminding me of the shock, which had taken me away from the immediate chaos around me. Just minutes before, the sudden transition from festivity to fear had seemed spectacularly unreal – and the adrenaline-instigated shield of tingling numbness had temporarily blunted my sense of pain, relieving me from the initially unbearable strain at the roots of my hair, the excruciating burning sensation in my eyes, nostrils and throat, and the physical agony from the impact on my limbs and hips as I was dragged along the uneven surface of a concrete floor. I desperately tried to maintain some dignity, struggling to keep my feet on the ground, then almost immediately surrendered to the unyielding iron strength of the man I could not altogether see – though I could already recognise his voice amidst the commotion of other distressed and crude human voices, having absorbed the distinct timbre of his haunting, venomous voice that carried a trace of a rural dialect. He kept directing, in a deadly calm voice, unrepeatable words of abuse at me – some of which I had not heard until then but could guess the meaning of. The repulsive stench of sweat soaked through his dark uniform, which carried a whiff of spicy kebab; his profanity-laden remarks, his brutish handling, my pathetic weakness all engulfed me with repulsion and profound disgrace, while the chilling obscurity of what was about to happen left me gasping for air. To prevent myself from slipping into a state of delirium, I continued to recite the same lines over and over internally: *I haven't technically broken the law. All I have done is challenge authority by not abandoning my intention to save Gezi Park from destruction. Therefore I should be free to go, for I haven't technically broken any law – all I have done is stand up to authority by not abandoning my participation in the joint attempt to save Gezi Park. For that reason I must be free to go...*

Even then I could guess, mainly through terrible accounts of what others had suffered at their hands, that one's constitutional right as a peaceful protestor had very little weight when one was caught meddling on the wrong side of the fence. In a country heavily dependent on patriarchal intimidation and oppression, the sight of a policeman often prompted feelings of unease – even amongst law-abiding citizens leading unobtrusive lives.

Like a camera accidentally left open, recording critical footage through an unsteady, constantly shifting viewfinder, I picked up images of a small group of protestors, all young men – who like me had had the misfortune of being unexpectedly hunted down by a patrolling police squad. They were begging, or demanding, to be let loose, one with tears streaming down his face, another bellowing hysterical gibberish. They were callously manhandled, as I had been – as if we were a bunch of inanimate objects all being hauled to a specific spot to be bulldozed, prior to the destruction of the noble trees of Gezi Park.

Only a few attempted to resist, but they were immediately brought to submission by the swift implementation of *defence tactics* I had watched being performed on TV. When I sensed the rough tarmac against one of my damp cheeks, I realised I was also being made to join the growing line of helplessly exposed protestors – to lie face down on the ground before being handcuffed. Meanwhile, we all bore witness to a stubby man being gradually beaten into mute capitulation by the heavy blows of batons, kicks, and punches, leaving his swelling, expressionless face a shade of red too bright to resemble blood. As I was being shoved into the stiflingly hot police van (where I would experience my breasts being messily fondled, and the painful insertion of a finger into my vagina through my light summer trousers), a large dog with a visible ribcage, flabby teats and multiple healed wounds caught my attention.

I watched her carry out a series of dull movements – scratching her ear with her back leg, stretching her front legs then sitting up straight – in between displays of growing restlessness, as she observed the pandemonium from between two parked cars. I was trying desperately to hold onto a fragment of everyday Istanbulian street life, and the warmth channelled through the soulful eyes of a stray dog who had been through it all.

LUCIAN

I

SHE WAS RIGHT IN FRONT of you in a slow-moving queue. Now that you were finally being served, and she was also standing by another cashier, you could examine her from a distance. Her tank top revealed the faint outlines of her nipples. She was wearing an unbuttoned cardigan over it; the front of her very short denim skirt crinkled up like the folds of an accordion.

It was late August. Although it was technically still summer, the weather outside was overcast and chilly. You hadn't expected your local supermarket to be so busy. You'd thought most of the residents would still be away trying to catch the sun elsewhere before life resumed. Her legs were tanned and bore a few light bruises. She was wearing a pair of minimal flip-flops. She appeared as if she had got back from somewhere festive and hot, and hadn't switched modes yet.

When you left home, Tabitha had been hanging out with your son and daughter in the kitchen, schoolbooks scattered across the kitchen table. She had always been better at helping them with their homework. She was more patient and far better at explaining things. She got a kick out of solving maths equations, reading long assignments and approaching each given task systematically. You had always been too unfocused to excel at anything at school apart from art. You had spent most of your formative years, until uni, living in a bubble of absurd thoughts, creating short, callow sketches inside your head to pass the time – and if that didn't help, fantasising about girls, and sometimes teachers, you lusted after. Education still turned you off. The last thing you wished to do was to pass on your attitude to your children. Tabitha reckoned this was yet another excuse to abstain from taking further responsibility. She had a point.

The woman's heels were a little unclean. Her brown tresses had been tied back into a messy bundle. Her Roman nose suited her. When she caught you slyly examining her, self-awareness lit up her face. She seemed like someone who was used to getting male attention, and who enjoyed it.

As you had entered the kitchen, you had pulled faces at your children. This had immediately caused them to lose their concentration and start misbehaving. Then you had gone straight for one of the cupboards.

'If you want to make yourself useful, we've run out of cat food,' Tabitha had said sternly, just as you were heading towards the living room, gobbling up a handful of salty cashews. You nearly tripped over your son's plastic toys, and reluctantly turned towards the front door of the house. It was tough, being treated like an unwelcome guest in your home. You could barely stand the contempt she showed you. Like her, you were counting the days until the movers turned up. You had promised her you would change over and over. This time, you would stop the drugs and the heavy boozing for good and become a much better version of yourself. But she was not having any of it. She had already managed to cleanse you out of her system.

You left the shop carrying two cans of premium cat food in a big plastic bag. You were heading home on your usual path, and it just so happened that the young woman who had caught your attention earlier was walking in front of you, heading in the same direction. You acknowledged a group of pigeons pecking away at half a baguette some slothful idiot had dropped on the pavement. The streets were much less populated than usual, but there were still a few touristy types prancing about, pointlessly taking pictures of places they could easily access on Google Earth. The roads looked more littered than usual. London could be such a dump. You observed the young woman's footsteps, the swaying of her boyish hips. When you caught up with her you asked, glancing at the full shopping bags she had in each hand, 'How many are you planning to have round for supper tonight?'

She looked up, widening her eyes, acting as if she was surprised you had spoken to her. And maybe you had genuinely surprised her. In London, apart from loonies and the homeless, people tended to avoid interaction with strangers at all costs.

'Sorry?' She smiled, squinting her eyes dreamily at you.

You both stopped at the zebra crossing. You pointed towards her bags and repeated your question. Her smile widened. She had nice teeth.

'For no one!' she replied, emitting a timid yet flirtatious aura. Her strong accent was likely Hispanic.

'Really? Yet your bags appear *awfully* full.'

You were both strolling over the zebra crossing with unhurried steps. You heard a release of compressed air when a gigantic lorry halted at the junction of a nearby roundabout. You never could understand how they managed to drive those fuckers. Just then, you noticed the guy inside the grey Audi – still waiting for you – give you an annoyed stare.

'It's what I normally buy when I go to the supermarket.'

'Then you must have a *very large* appetite.'

She gave you a look, smiling, understanding the innuendo in your remark without being disturbed by it.

'What about you?'

You lifted the bag up in the air. 'Cat food. Somebody needs to feed the blooming cat. Otherwise he will cease to exist.'

Even the cat had been ignoring you since you started sleeping in the study on a blow-up bed. Or perhaps it was that he was in the habit of lying next to Tabitha in bed while she drafted her stories. You hardly ever saw him, except in the mornings, when he cried in his brassy voice and rubbed himself against any available legs, demanding to be fed. It was crazy, but you had always been a little jealous of the cat.

'Are you married?'

Only a woman who either lacked social etiquette, or one who didn't ponder the moral implications of the answer, would ask that of a man she had met in the street mere moments ago.

'Oh, only on paper.' You immediately regretted your response; it made you look like a total dick. 'Actually, we are about to be separated. I'm moving out somewhere next Sunday.'

'Where to?'

'Fitzrovia.'

She knitted her eyebrows together, clueless. You could tell it was the first time she had heard of the place. She probably hadn't been living here long enough – or, like the majority of foreigners, had a very partial experience of the city. It was quite a surreal moment for you; you were passing your house, like some stranger who had no ties to the place or the people occupying it. You glanced at your pine green front door. Tabitha could be on her way out with the kids – it was unlikely, but it could happen. You tried to imagine her fury, spotting you with some random woman, and how she would barely be able to maintain an unaffected front. The sweet taste of reprisal cheered you up a little.

'What about you? Are you married, or living with someone?'

She laughed. 'Me? *No!* I live with my mother.' She seemed embarrassed.

'There's absolutely nothing wrong with that.'

She then unexpectedly stopped and extended her hand. 'Carmela. And you?'

'Lucian. What a beautiful name. And it suits you,' you said, believing your own flattery as you shook her slender hand.

'You think?' she asked, still laughing lightheartedly as you carried on walking.

'Carmela, there's absolutely nothing wrong with living with your mother. I used to live with my mother. Well, I suppose everyone does at one point. Actually, if I could, I wouldn't mind moving in with her right now.'

'Really?'

'Oh yes, particularly under the current circumstances.'

You both laughed at your situation; the mutual attraction you instantly developed made you laugh at anything and everything.

'May I carry one of your bags?'

'No, it's OK!'

'Really?'

She thought about it for about three seconds and handed you one. As your fingers touched again, you briefly stared into each other's eyes. Just then, out of nowhere, a grey squirrel came running out in front of you. It ran frantically before you from one side of the pavement to the other, then quickly climbed up the trunk of the next tree. She laughed heartily, as if it was the funniest thing she'd ever seen.

As you reached the end of your street and turned the corner, she said, 'Whereabouts do you live?'

'Relatively close by. And you?'

'I live on this street,' she said, as two teenagers in hoodies rode past on the pavement, showing off agile manoeuvres on their bikes.

'Really? Where?' You wondered why you'd never come across her before. After all, you were practically neighbours.

She pointed towards the council tower-block further ahead. You passed by the ugly building at least twice a day: in the mornings on your way to the Tube, and in the evenings on your way back home. On some evenings, when you happened to walk by its high walls, you would catch the heavy smell of spliff and hear youngsters laughing inside its obscured garden.

'Do you like your neighbours?' you asked, looking up at the abundance of flats, which were probably a third of the typical rent in your trendy, expensive neighbourhood.

'They're OK. I don't really know them.'

At the front gate of her building, you stared and smiled at each other as if to raise the pivotal question: *what now?* You thought about asking for her number, but something prevented you from acting upon the impulse. You were attracted to her, but, on a deeper level, were too depressed and cynical to take initiative. And there was something about her. Perhaps it was her overt friendliness that had put you off.

'Here,' you said, offering her heavy shopping bag back. She extended her hand; you briefly held onto and massaged her thumb and index finger before handing the bag back to her.

'You're naughty.'

'I'm sorry,' you said, glancing towards your feet while not feeling particularly apologetic.

She came towards you, lifted herself up on her toes, and landed a leisurely, moist kiss on your lower jaw, which immediately gave you goosebumps and stimulated blood flow to your penis. She moved away rather comically, in a hurry, as if slightly nervous to receive an over-enthusiastic reaction. You couldn't help but smile.

'Good luck with the move next week.'

'Thanks.'

She flung the gate open, headed towards the entrance to the building. You glanced down to see how visible your hard-on was under your trousers. It was pretty obvious.

Just as you were about to leave, she came back towards you.

'Do you want to come inside?'

The building was cool and damp and reeked with an odd, sour stench. You turned into a small hallway and passed by the two sets of lifts. Vandals had scribbled illegible words onto their silver aluminium exterior. You were as quiet as you would've been following a dealer on the way to his hidden stash. You were heading towards a tired-looking red door at the end of the small hallway. Some other frustrated punk had scraped *Get Out* on it.

You pushed open the door for her and followed her into the stairway. When the door shut behind you, a clamour travelled through the building; all the doors on connecting floors had opened slightly and then loudly slammed against their frames. Soft daylight came through a large panel of frosted glass which followed the straight, cemented staircase, eventually leading to a landing with a second set of stairs.

She knelt down to place her heavy bags against the wall. As one of the bags slouched over and opened up, you noticed a packet of tiger prawns, lemons, and recognised a pint of semi-skimmed milk by its green label.

You approached each other and without forewarning, began to gorge yourselves on each other's lips. Your fingers had let go of the plastic bag; the sound it made as it hit the ground had made both of you smile as you sucked on her small, lively tongue. You brusquely lifted her tank top and the wired bra she had underneath, and lightly bit the ends of her large, dark nipples, which made her softly mumble something melodic and incomprehensible. You suddenly sensed a draught on your bare ankles and stopped what you were doing. The red door behind you tremored lightly. It had opened and closed in on itself, and variations of its kinesis had repeated throughout the building. The front door of the building had slammed closed and someone's footsteps were progressing towards you.

'Don't worry,' she whispered, pressing her palm to your cheek affectionately. 'No one ever takes the stairs. Really. They're all too lazy.'

You kept still, looking into her fierce eyes and feeling her warm breath on your lips, listening to the galloping coming from the lift shaft behind the wall. *What am I doing here? This is crazy!* You heard footsteps enter the lift, and as the lift took off you sighed with relief.

You went down on your knees and shoved the moistened string of her underwear to one side. The tip of your tongue plunged into the space between her bushy slit, like it had done countless times before with other women, repeatedly stroking the area until you could identify her clit among the befuddling, small folds of soft skin. She tasted salty and slightly sour. Her breaths were audible and intermittent. She pulled at your hair erratically. She pressed her fingers all over your skull, your face, kneading at your skin, as if it were a rough piece of clay she was trying to shape.

'I want you inside me,' you heard her demand breathlessly. You stood up and watched her lift up her skirt so it sat on her small waist like the ridiculously massive eighties belt Madonna used to wear. She took off her small cardigan and laid it across the floor, then knelt on all fours. She rested her hands and elbows against the second step of the hard-edged staircase.

Your fingers shook while you tried to unzip your trousers quickly, blindly fumbling inside your boxer shorts before you took your erect knob into the open air. You were certain you didn't have a condom on you (it wasn't an item you remembered to carry with you when visiting the local supermarket) and you had no desire to rummage through your pockets for one. You were in an anarchic mood. You couldn't care less about the consequence of your little escapade. It was all about living in the moment. At the same time, the danger of being caught remained an immediate threat.

She coiled her back, the way you saw your cat often do when it needed a good stretch. You parted her legs to make room for yours. Soon, you started to focus less on the just-bearable discomfort of the concrete floor against your wobbly kneecaps as you glided again and again through her tight moistness. Just then, it felt strangely like it wasn't the first time you were shagging her; the smell of her skin and her low groans brought back intimacies with other women you thought you had long forgotten.

You took your throbbing cock out of her then began to tease her expectant opening with its swollen tip before inserting it abruptly into her a couple of times. You planned to repeat the joyous act until its predictability caused it to eventually lose some of its appeal. Yet, suddenly, you heard loud reverberations coming from high above: what sounded like a sequence of doors banging against their frames, one after the other, until you heard the door at the end of the staircase before you open slightly, then slam angrily against its frame, followed by the red door beside you, which mimicked the action with less intensity. You sensed the suction of air on your knees.

'Don't worry. Someone's probably taken the stairs to get to one of the flats on the next floor,' she whispered, out of breath, and you really wanted to believe her. You tried to evaluate the accuracy of what she had said as you lightly bit and sucked the skin on the back of her sun-kissed shoulder. It bore no bikini strap marks, only a faint tattoo of Tweety. Attempting to regain your previous fervour, you thrust into her one more time, though with considerably less determination and enthusiasm than before. You heard again the sequence of banging doors repeat itself throughout the beastly building, progressively travelling towards you – this time accompanied by the roaring echoes of male voices. For a while you detached yourself from the peril heading your way. You kept thrusting into her harder and harder, your sweaty skin gliding against hers, as if it no longer made any difference what you were thrusting yourself against.

All of a sudden, you stopped – as if the warning signals being issued by your brain had finally grabbed your attention. She started thrusting herself back and forth, rotating her narrow hips like a highly skilled salsa dancer. Maybe one of the boisterous chaps galloping down the staircase – by now merely a floor above your heads, and seconds away from running into your semi-clad, entangled bodies – was a current or an ex-boyfriend of hers, and you had foolishly placed yourself in the middle of a twisted revenge plot. Or maybe she was just into getting caught.

You pulled away while she still vigorously pushed herself against you, and you had to gently shove her to one side to stand up. You were in the process of clumsily doing up your fly as you dashed out of the tall building.

You ran as fast as you could, which wasn't that fast at all. You probably hadn't run anywhere for at least ten years. Being a heavy smoker didn't help, and you never knew how to position your arms when you ran. If you were in some sort of a rush, you preferred to walk briskly instead. You happened to be one of those physically blessed people who are naturally lean, so you never could understand the point of running as a form of exercise – or exercise itself, for that matter.

You didn't look back to see if you were being pursued. No one shouted after you. Nor did you hear footsteps behind you. Yet you continued with your pathetic run.

You were gasping for air by the time you threw yourself into the house. After you shut the door behind you, you peeked through the peephole while trying to catch your breath, intermittently wiping off the sweat dripping down your temples. As soon as you turned around, your soon-to-be-ex-wife's ghostly, silent presence startled the shit out of you.

'Where's the cat food?' she asked, fed up. It was hard to believe how the same voice had once been girly and playful, employed to tease and seduce you. She eyed you up and down with a disapproving and curious look.

'Shit!' you said, slapping your palm against your sweaty forehead. You pictured the cans of overpriced cat food still sitting at the bottom of the staircase. The thought that they might still be where you had abandoned them made you feel especially uncomfortable. In your mind, they appeared like evidence left behind at the scene of a crime. You pictured Carmela picking the bag of cat food off the floor after lowering and straightening her absurdly short skirt, pushing her large, erect nipples – that had appeared at one point during your romp like the unevenly bulging small antennae of a Martian – back into her bra, and adjusting her tank top and her messed-up hair. Knowing from being married to one that cat owners took every small opportunity to mention their furry loved ones, you guessed she didn't own a cat. She'd probably end up giving the cat food away to a friend. She was bound to know someone with a cat.

II

Among the many women who have graced your life, however briefly, Carmela and Ada are at different ends of the spectrum. Compared to an impulsive, ready-and-waiting broad like Carmela, Ada has been less approachable. Yet, despite this, you are still surprised when you finally pluck up the courage and make your move. Although she loosens up rather quickly at first, in a matter of seconds she displays an obvious change of heart. She pushes you away, shouting at you to get off her, as if she has suddenly woken from sleep to find you on top of her, molesting her.

You apologise several times, despite not being entirely sure what you've done to deserve such hostility; deep down, you feel pretty aggravated.

The burning rage in her eyes is quickly replaced by a confused, sorrowful look, as if she has two conflicting sides battling it out inside her. You cautiously take a step forward and reach out to caress her cheek – but she immediately withdraws, as if she can't stand your touch.

'Just leave me alone!' she growls. Seconds later, appearing embarrassed by her reaction, she covers her face with her hands, says, 'I'm really sorry,' and storms out of the room.

Suddenly feeling profoundly tired by it all, as if the entire day's exhaustion has finally dumped its heavy load on you, you sigh and rub your face with one hand, overhearing her rushed footsteps up the stairs.

Well, *that* worked rather brilliantly, don't you think? You grin clownishly to yourself. Trying to see the funny side of things is a survival mechanism. Even at your mother's funeral, struggling to keep it together, you amused yourself with the occasional clumsiness with which the gloomy ceremony had been handled.

You come across your own reflection in the glass of one of the photographs lined up on the wall, and make a half-hearted attempt to straighten your mess of hair. You kneel down to collect your foulard; your head pulses with an excruciating pain, as if someone has quickly inserted and removed a long, fine needle into your skull.

You walk around inside the basement room – moving about in an unhurried manner, switching off lights, attempting to check your email even though you know the room has no internet coverage – in some childish attempt to prove to yourself that you haven't been affected by Ada's erratic behaviour. As if you couldn't care less whether she is still going to be there when you eventually make it upstairs.

When you walk up to the reception room, you find her standing there, playing with her phone.

'I don't know what to say,' she mutters, barely able to look you in the eye.

'You don't have to explain yourself if you don't feel like it.' Frustrated as you are, you have no intention of making her feel any worse.

After a short silence, she says, 'What's the closest Tube station?'

'It's a bit of a schlep from here. Let me call you an Uber instead.'

You really don't want her to leave. Regardless of the *scene* she's made, you still fancy her. You are often drawn to offbeat, unstable types most men would run a mile from.

At least in principle, you don't mind dealing with the emotional baggage such women lug around, since you secretly strive for high drama, and their complex hang-ups make you forget yours.

You also don't want her to leave because you don't feel like being on your own. You feel vulnerable and lonely – and any company feels better than no company. Since the decree absolute came through your letterbox, just like any other boring government document you would normally defer looking at, your worsening hangovers have deepened the grief you suffered having lost Tabitha, the family life you had with her and your adorable kids – and even *that cat*. You try to fend off new shades of gloom you haven't experienced since the death of your mother by indulging in more booze and narcotics. You know it is a vicious cycle, but have neither the will or the intention to stop yourself.

In the distance, you hear Everard's approaching footsteps. The professionalism with which he administers his shitty job, day in and day out, creates the illusion that the menial duties it involves are much more pressing and complex than they are. Yet, without admitting it to yourself, you envy him his blind dedication and sense of purpose.

'But, before you go, why don't we sit down and have one more drink?' you propose, upbeat, as if what has just happened is already history to you. 'I'm feeling quite peckish, aren't you? I can ask Everard to prepare us something to eat.'

She shrugs indecisively.

'And, as you can see, Rex is quite a serious art collector. Most of his collection is in New York and in LA, but this house also displays a good chunk of his eclectic taste: Abstract

Expressionist paintings, Aboriginal sculptures, Renaissance drawings, some wonderful late Impressionist works and what-not – none are as creepy as my little assembly downstairs, and worth that multiple times over. If you like, I can walk you through his collection. And then I can call you an Uber, in, shall we say, forty-five minutes?'

'I don't know. I really feel bad for—'

'Well, let's not leave things on a bad note. You know, George Eliot once lived in this house.' You eagerly point this out to seal the deal, while acknowledging she might not have an inkling of who George Eliot was. Yet it seems to do the trick – or perhaps it is because, like you, she isn't quite ready to call it a night.

Everard dutifully appears next to you. You ask him to open a chilled bottle of Riesling. You also ask him if he can prepare you some food.

'We don't have much time. Something not too fussy,' you emphasise, before he heads off, his new task in hand, towards the large kitchen fitted with stainless steel cabinets. It is as pro-fessionally equipped as a restaurant's, but very seldom used at capacity. You grab the bowl of Japanese crackers off the coffee table and offer her some, after greedily scooping yourself a generous amount to assuage your own hunger.

You feel newly energised, having been granted a second chance with her. You excitedly walk her up to the small pas-sageway which connects the double reception to the grand foyer. It has beautifully detailed preliminary drawings by Dürer and Raphael hanging on its walls. The two of you once again plunge into the subject of making art.

'I never used to do preliminary drawing for my paintings. I *did* sketch still-life compositions though. I got into the habit while preparing for an art degree I in the end realised I didn't want to do. The more I drew, though, the more innovative and fluid I became as a painter,' she explains.

'Wasn't it Van Gogh who once said drawing is the backbone of painting? I did endless sketches of my friends. If I were still making art today, I would ask you to sit still somewhere just so I could fill a page with a close-up of your remarkable face.'

Lowering her eyes, she says, 'I'm not sure I would be a good sitter. I probably would find it very difficult to stay still.' Then, glancing back at the finely detailed study of a hand, she confesses: 'It's so well-executed, yet it doesn't move me in the same way some contemporary works do.'

'It's probably because perfecting the drawing of a hand is less of an artistic concern for you.'

You enter the drawing room, decorated in mid-century furniture. You walk her through the large abstract expressionist canvasses Rex acquired through his chief art advisor, a pompous, very goal-orientated young bloke based in New York. He sources many pieces for Rex, mainly by bidding on his behalf at evening sales, or from dealers like Quinn, who make the greater part of their profit by facilitating secondary sales of very rare and highly sought-after works by artists (alive or dead) who have somehow *made it*.

Soon Everard appears, bearing a massive silver tray in the shaky grasp of his rheumatoid hands. One by one, he lays down wine and water glasses, plates and silver cutlery, an oval plate with carefully stacked sandwiches on it, a jug of water, a slender ice-cold bottle of Riesling, and two white napkins which have been immaculately ironed, probably by his wife Leslie. Leslie must be holed up in their self-contained flat, hoping you will bugger off so poor Everard can come and watch a bit of telly with her. Apart from overseeing the maintenance of the property while Rex is away, Leslie and Everard dedicate their time to the local Anglican church. Leslie sings in the church choir and volunteers at many of its events, as well as occasionally knocking on her wealthy neighbours' doors to raise money on behalf of the church. Everard undertakes the seasonal trimming of the neat hedges that border the church's small garden, mows its small lawn and tends to its rose bushes.

The last time you were in church – one of the rare occasions you've attended – was about two months ago, for your half-brother's wedding. You absolutely despise weddings, particularly big ones. You consider them a great waste of the couple's savings and other people's time.

You wouldn't be so spiteful about the whole affair if they weren't so bloody long. At forty-three, you neither have the patience nor the gift of time to endure nearly a day's long torture consisting of endless ceremonial gibberish, followed by drinks on a soggy lawn, and an unbearably tedious dinner inside an either cold and damp or stiflingly hot marquee – where, possibly due to an undisclosed grudge the bride or the groom bears against you, or out of sheer bad karma, you're almost always made to sit next to some unattractive, self-obsessed bird who decides to confide the fine details of her miserable life to you after knocking down a few glasses of passable wine. Right down to the *who said what exactly* in past conversations with apparently appalling exes. You're left having to console them for what feels like hours, fully aware you would immediately cross to the other side of the road if you ever happened to see them walking towards you. And, eventually, after the bride and groom perform their first dance to the beat of some cheesy track (and expect others to rush to join them on the dance floor, so as not to appear like self-applauding monkeys), you end up feeling obliged to ask these women up for a dance, just so you no longer have to listen to their repetitive, self-pitying chatter.

You were slightly more accommodating about Tristan's big day, on the basis that he is the only half-sibling of your father's emotionally scarred progeny with whom you've been able to maintain a genuine, loving relationship. Once you set yourself down, you glanced uninterestedly at the leaflet you were handed at the entrance of the church by the best man, who was wearing a tense smile on his face. The ceremony consisted of an introduction made by the priest, followed by a hymn, and then two short yet nauseatingly sappy poems about eternal love, read aloud by the best man and then by the bride's sister, followed by the exchanging of vows, followed by another hymn, followed by the signing of the register, and brought to an end by a recital of 'Ave Maria'. *Jesus, how cringe-making!* you couldn't help but think. At least it was short. Tristan is too considerate to have a hundred-odd people locked up for longer than an hour (particularly when it turned out to be an unusually sunny autumn's day) to celebrate the fact that he has found someone who appears to have the patience to put up with his gruelling stutter.

By the time the bride and groom exchanged their vows, your arse was already in extreme discomfort, flattened like a pancake from sitting on one of those rock-hard wooden benches you reckoned had the power to obliterate the slightest interest in Christian redemption. Each time the crowd rose from their seats – joyously flexing their rear muscles, making some effort to sing in key but failing – you glanced around, trying to spot a pretty face from under the vision-obstructing barricade of flowered or feathered wide-brimmed hats. Then, at the very end of the service, when a chubby young blonde woman stood up in the balcony and started serenading the crowd in a remarkably soothing, clear voice, you were unexpectedly moved. To that day, you had never heard someone singing 'Ave Maria' so beautifully – a piece of popular classical music you normally consider overrated, if not in bad taste. Her voice penetrated the great wall of cynicism you reserve for traditional weddings.

You sat back and closed your eyes. A few times, when you came close to crying, you conjured up the image of a greyhound with trembling back legs humping another. A distasteful intervention – but, in any case, it relieved you of the public humiliation of shedding a few tears in front of a crowd.

Due to the menial duties necessary to keep the enormous house in tiptop condition during Rex's long absences, Everard and Leslie are the two people most regularly subjected to your collection in the basement. A sucker for anything edgy and unusual, Rex was smitten by your uncanny assembly the minute he laid eyes on it. He insisted on buying the entire collection from you – offering nearly twice what it was worth. You turned him down, but finally gave in when he suggested exhibiting it at Cheyne Walk. It is a compromise for him as much as it was for you – men like Rex always prefer to *own* things rather than having provisional access to them.

Whatever Leslie and Everard think of you, it can't be good. Especially since you've formed the habit of using Rex's London headquarters – at his repeated insistence that *You should make the most of it* – as a shagger's retreat.

'It will give them something to do,' Rex argues. Yet when you get to see Everard or Leslie, they often imply they can barely cope with the number of errands they need to run to maintain such a huge house. You find it amusing how people can have such a relative take on things.

You turn up at Rex's mansion with a different girl on your arm each time and drink up an impressive amount of his nearly infinite booze supply, before leaving bodily fluids on the bed-sheets, sometimes alongside other relics of an excessive night, for Everard and Leslie to clean up. But then again, they're pretty used to that kind of stuff with Rex.

Rex's generosity is a means of controlling and owning people – but, you reckon, as you've selflessly lent your collection to be displayed for an unlimited period in his house, you're sort of on equal terms. If you don't include the numerous times he's picked up the tab for your meals. But Rex is the sort of guy who always will pick up the tab – he won't have it any other way.

After you both devour your briny tuna sandwiches and refresh your glasses with the divinely aromatic white wine, you rest your back against your chair and light yourself a cigarette. It is then that she asks you how old you are. You try to delay your answer by directing the same question at her. When you admit your age to her, just about twice hers, she seems unmoved. You want to tell her that it doesn't seem that long ago that you were as young as she is now. Twenty-one years have passed in the blink of an eye. Yet you don't know how to phrase this fact without sounding boringly middle-aged.

'I think it's best I leave now,' she mutters, having quickly glanced at her watch and noticed the time. You can't tell if she feels obliged to stick to what you agreed or whether she actually is ready to leave.

'Really? I haven't shown you the rest of the art, yet.'

She shrugs, then stands up.

'Hang on a minute. Let me at least order you that cab.'

Of course you still don't want her to leave, but you can no longer think of anything else to say to convince her. Also, you feel that if you insist once more, she might regard you as a disingenuous tactician who never really means what he says.

On your screen, a local map appears, Ubers travelling up and down the embankment like busy insects. You ask her for her postcode. You tap it into your phone, with at least the reassurance that you now know where she lives, then reluctantly press enter.

'A car will arrive in exactly two minutes,' you say, annoyed by the app's efficiency.

She thanks you in a timid, over-polite manner, as if your gentlemanly deed has embarrassed her more than anything. By the time you are both in the cloakroom and you are holding up her coat for her, a second alert goes off on your phone. The bloody car is already here.

The damp cold gushes in as soon as you open the front door. She turns around as she comes out onto the porch; her quick movement, and the light breeze in the air, briefly sets her hair in motion.

'Thank you for everything,' she says again in her polite voice, which is less restrained this time. Her fragility moves you.

'Really? You mean it wasn't all that bad?' you ask half-jokingly, to tease her a little, while looking for reassurance, or for any sign that might alter the course of things.

'No, of course it wasn't,' she responds shyly, dropping her gaze.

'Let me walk you out.'

Even though she insists you don't have to, you say you feel like getting some fresh air. You close the front door and walk out with her. It has stopped raining and the air is infused with the smell of wet soil. Along with a few other large townhouses, the house is on a small side street, parallel to yet partly insulated from the embankment's noisy traffic by large bushes and a couple of pine trees. There is a red Peugeot parked on the road behind your car. You can vaguely make out the dark silhouette of the driver inside. When you reach the end of the short patio and pass through the tall, narrow fence gate, which makes its usual squealing sound, you stop.

She turns, and this time looks candidly into your eyes.

'Well...' she says, and sighs, appearing to be lost for words. In the background you can hear wet tyres travelling along the embankment. The moment feels special – yet on some other level you know it is just another evening.

You can't hold yourself back any longer.

'I really think you ought to stay.'

At first she stares at you in astonishment, then inquisitively, like she is trying to makes sense of it all. She pauses for a moment to think it through. Yet she remains hesitant, unable to make up her mind about whether to go or stay.

'Do you have something urgent to do that cannot possibly wait until tomorrow?'

She smiles as if you have caught her off guard, then shakes her head.

'Then why leave now? It's only nine o'clock, for crying out loud. Let's just hang out, talk and get to know each other. I can always order you another Uber when you're properly bored of me.'

She turns her head around towards the stationary Peugeot and asks, 'But what about him?'

You go and speak to the driver. He doesn't seem particularly glad about being sent off, but remains poker-faced throughout your short interaction all the same. He probably doesn't want to receive a poor rating – these days it is all about ratings.

On your way back to the house, Ada blithely goes on about how absurd it all was. Despite two attempts, she *still* hasn't managed to leave. She jokingly says that it is as if she has been cursed by a spell that prevents her from leaving.

You respond, 'It's probably because your heart was never in it.'

She smiles, but then pauses and gives you this self-conscious look, as if your words have revealed the plain truth.

III

'You can take your drink with you, if you wish,' you say, just before you begin your ascent of the grand oak staircase – that, with the smallest shifting of your weight, creaks, snaps and shudders like a seaborne sailboat. In a bid to get properly hammered, you downed two glasses of wine in several gulps after arriving back in the house. Climbing the stairs now, you can barely feel your limbs. At times you feel weightless, like a ball of energy gaily cruising through the air.

You don't think she is as wasted as you are. You look at her, your eyes stinging as if alcohol is evaporating through them. She is animatedly explaining something to you. *What's the point of all this? Why can't we just shag?* you think. Why can't people just get on with things? But you know only too well through personal experience the hesitations and boundaries one can inflict upon oneself. Once you reach a certain peak in your inebriation you are able to see life more plainly, with clearly defined margins. It makes you feel more seasoned and resilient for having endured the troubles you have – issues most would regard as first-world problems, but then, each to their own.

Blissfully unaware of your lustful stare, Ada is busily explaining something to you.

'...it doesn't have a mirror inside to create the illusion of space, nor does it have glass on its door for you to be able to see out. And it breaks down, every six months or so.'

'Goodness me, how appalling.'

You realise you have no idea what she is going on about. You hold on to the handrail tightly to support your dwindling sense of balance. You think for a few seconds, glancing upwards at the walls covered in faded pastoral murals of the most exquisite type. *But of course!* you respond inside your head, pleased you haven't experienced one of your mini-blackouts, as you continue – slightly out of breath – to climb the many steps of the staircase. She is referring to the decrepit elevator in the building of her top-floor family flat in Istanbul. Apparently neither she nor her parents ever used it. Since you returned to the house, she has become surprisingly chatty.

She's mostly been speaking about her life back in Istanbul. After a long break, her father is preparing for his next show. Her mother is a professor of English Literature. Ada is an only child, but she has plenty of cousins. She keeps referring to Istanbul like she is desperately missing it. You can't understand why she continues to remain in London if she is this homesick, particularly since her degree has come to an end. Or why she doesn't just hop on a plane and go there for a fortnight to get it out of her system. Nor can you fathom why anyone would be so attached to a place. You have never been devoted to London – yet, besides a brief fling with New York, you have lived here all your life. It wasn't a conscious decision on your part, it just happened that way. You do appreciate London's upbeat energy and cultural diversity, but these days you are somewhat fed up with it. The city reminds you of your two biggest failures: your failed artistic career and, more recently, the turbulent ending of your marriage. You often feel like running off somewhere: moving to Dorset and living in a derelict farmhouse, away from the superficiality of the art scene and the drug-taking it condones. But the countryside gives you cabin fever.

You're about two-thirds of the way up the curved majestic staircase, yet the weariness of your footsteps make it feel as if you are climbing a descending escalator. Once, recently, when you were pissed as a newt and in the company of some other young woman – encouraged by her, and eager to demonstrate your limber moves – you courageously slid down the polished banister from the first landing. You reached the bottom in no time, skidded, and tore the crotch of your trousers. And, amidst all this, from sheer shock, a fart stealthily slipped through – one that sounded similar to the party horns your kids used to return home with. You couldn't join her in her laughter; you were in too much agony.

'This way,' you say, making a serious effort not to stagger, as you finally reach the first floor. You guide her to the end of a softly lit corridor, then stroll into Rex's stately bedroom as if it's your own. The dimmer lights have been turned to their lowest setting. Rex's favourite Diptyque candle is burning slowly on the mantelpiece of a small fireplace no longer in use. You wander up to his king-size canopy bed, higher than most beds and apparently the same make as the Queen's. You switch on the three spotlights, aimed at each individual part of a triptych, and theatrically exclaim, 'Ta-daa!'

Different takes of the artist's self-violated, close-up face come forward on a stark black background.

You know she is impressed – she has to be. If there is one thing of Rex's of which you are shamefully envious, it has to be the Bacon. You explain to her how Rex, who can smell a good opportunity from a mile away, acquired the piece years ago from a desperate business associate – who, having become insolvent, opted to settle a portion of his debt to Rex with this three-panelled wonder. Rex could now easily quadruple the nominal sum he paid for it at an auction or a private sale. Though you doubt he has any intention – or need, for that matter – to sell this significant piece of art by one of Britain's finest. It never ceases to draw you in with its dark quest into the human psyche and its painterly brilliance.

'A couple of times, he's lent it to museums.'

The room is rotating around you, a phenomenon that often reminds you of a DJ scratching a record. Whenever you experience it you play the sound effects in your head. You sense the cumbrous weight of intoxication settle inside you like a heavy anchor. You could easily pass out on the bed. But, just then, you catch an affectionate glance from her. The next thing you know, she is pressing her palm against your cheek. You become alert and turned on. You are ready to snog her, but something is holding you back. Then you remember.

'Oh shit!'

'What is it?' she asks. She continues to rotate with the room whenever you disengage your gaze from her.

'Listen, maybe we should first jointly sign a piece of paper which lays out what I'm allowed to do to you,' you say, slurring your words (knowing it isn't a good look) while trying exceptionally hard to stay still and not be affected by the constant spinning.

You make her giggle. There is some soft commotion between you. By the time you realise what is happening, your trousers have already been unzipped and have dropped to your ankles.

'Are you sure we shouldn't discuss things before we carry on...' you gab, not really meaning your words. You joyously sense her sweet, succulent kisses on your lips and her light caresses over your penis through the top of the pricey boxer shorts Tabitha bought you one Christmas. Tabitha has a thing for giving her closest family members underwear for Christmas; she can't bear the thought of buying gifts that never get used. You used to appreciate her no-frills attitude.

Without warning, Ada slips from your arms. You see her a few steps away from you; she is bending over, balanced on one foot, trying to remove one of her ankle boots. The room is still spinning, and so is she, as you watch her discard most of her clothes. Soon, she is in her plain beige underwear. You are finding it immensely difficult to keep your eyes open. Through your increasingly narrow vision, you observe her bare, shapely long legs; her breasts, plump and ready to spill out of the tight grasp of her wired bra. Her smooth olive skin looks warm and luminous as honey under the soft light.

You hesitantly take one step forward towards her, then another, like someone attempting to walk again for the first time after a paralysing ski accident. You attempt to release your feet from the restricting entanglement of your trousers – and trip and land on your face. The sudden impact is painful and disorientating, like an unexpected, hard slap to the face. Your head throbs as your cheek presses itself against the soft fibres of the cream carpet. You are able to detect minute particles between the woven fabric the powerful suction of Leslie's vacuum cleaner hasn't managed to pick up. Too pissed to lift yourself, you lie there, still. She immediately rushes over.

'Are you all right?' she asks with a genuinely worried look that is just about able to hide her bemusement. You both explode into laughter. You roll over onto your back, then to your side, and then to your back again, holding your stomach, struggling with the sharp cramps that each guffaw brings, while you keep hearing her, and occasionally see her bending over to cope with her sweet, hysterical giggles. Towards the end, your guffaws lose their clarity and fizzle into weak, irregular shrieks.

An attack of the giggles is something you have inherited from your mother and your equally charmingly insane aunt and grandparents. For this reason you can't help but be instinctively drawn to anyone you can get into an unprompted laughing fit with.

Your emotional outburst has sobered you up a little. Ada lends you a hand, and with your joint efforts, you lift yourself off the floor. You sit on the bed and wipe away the tears still trickling down the side of your eyes. You remove your trousers, still wrapped around your feet like a pair of ankle cuffs. You glance at the Bacon – the potent imagery screaming out of each canvas feels too much to take in. You lean over and switch off the spotlights.

After you pour her a glass of water from the water jar on the bedside table, you pour some for yourself, and drink it up heartily. As soon as she sits beside you, you kiss her; in the background, you can hear the rain begin to lightly patter as you hungrily devour her lips. Yet, this time, you can recognise her tensing up again – and knowing you have to, you pull back.

She sighs and drops her shoulders, discouraged.

'Do you want to talk about it?'

You realise you are back at square one.

You are fed up with being jerked around like this. Having come to terms with the fact that you might not be getting laid after all, you say, 'We don't have do this, you know? We can stop.'

Her eyes well a little; you pat her lightly on the shoulder. You are unsure whether she has got a bit sentimental after a few drinks too many, or if she suffers from an emotional barrier that can't be eliminated by any amount of booze.

'Ada, what do you want us to do?'

Eyeing you, she responds, 'I want to be with you. I want us to have sex.'

You rub your eyes and faintly chuckle. 'But do you? *Really?*'

'I – do!' Glancing away, she adds, 'But...'

'But what?'

'Never mind,' she mumbles, like she is too embarrassed to come out with it.

Then all of sudden it dawns on you.

'Would you rather be in charge?' you suggest.

She nods – her gaze quickly escaping yours.

She removes the foulard from around your neck, and helps you take off your jacket and shirt before you lie down on the bed. For a moment, you feel like you are in one of those dodgy Thai massage parlours a permanently depressed, frequently single art dealer friend of yours – who annually vacations in Thailand and, word has it, had an affair with his Thai cleaner – once dragged you to. English repression, combined with the detached pretentiousness of the London art world, can harbour some of the most spectacularly odd and troublesome characters.

Heavy raindrops, hastened by the forceful wind, start tapping against the windows. You watch how her breasts tilt and alter their shape as she bends this way and that, planting sensuous kisses across your body, until you close your eyes and leave yourself completely in her hands. She digs her hand into your boxer shorts and asks if you have any protection. You tell her, breathing heavily, to open the second drawer of Rex's bedside table – which is full of condoms, as well as lubrication, and just about any sex toy you can think of.

She has you sit up on the bed. She starts to shiver uncontrollably and embraces you more tightly, her breaths hastening with the gradual progress she makes. Like she is able to reach that cusp between pleasure and pain each time she lowers herself further onto you. She lets out a moment's high-pitched cry when at last she has you all the way inside her. She holds you tightly. After a few more cautious movements, she begins to loosen up. She breathlessly whispers into your ear, 'I've been thinking of this moment the entire day.'

Deeply aroused by her confession, you reply, 'That makes two of us,' then passionately kiss her.

As she lifts herself onto her knees, you gently suck her soft nipples, one at a time. You lick her navel, lying on your back while she again takes you inside her, your movements carried out in effortless synchrony. You growl like a wounded animal when she has you enter her all the way in one swift go. You cup her buttocks, encouraging her to go faster and faster before restricting her movements so she is thrusting herself only as far as the tip of your knob. After she does this several more times, you come joyously, groaning with all your might.

She drops down beside you. You both lie there on the bed for some time, her head resting on your shoulder, your arm around her, your bodies still perspiring, trying to catch your breath.

When she lifts her head and declares it is time for her to head home, you still don't want her to leave. But, this time, you don't interfere.

By the time an alert notifies you that the driver will be here in three minutes, she is already zipping up her ankle boots. She walks up to you, runs her fingers through your hair, and says, 'Thank you for everything,' like you have done her some kind of huge favour. You hold on to her arm.

'It's so nice and warm under the sheets. Cuddle up with me for a little bit.'

She sighs and rolls her eyes at you, as if she has no intention of falling into the same trap for the third time. Then a second alert goes off on your phone.

'Your designated driver seems to be stuck on the Royal Hospital Road for some reason. He might be running late. You needn't rush.'

'Goodnight, Lucian,' she says. It is the first time she has addressed you by your name.

'Let me walk you down,' you offer, despite feeling totally knackered and ready to drift off.

'No, it's OK, you *really* shouldn't,' she insists; you like her even more for it.

With your last bit of strength, you lift your torso off the bed, pull her closer, and give her a peck on the lips. As she approaches the door, you ask her to switch off the lights, and then – she is gone.

I V

Hearing voices in the foyer, you open your eyes. You aren't sure if you have been sleeping. You hear someone climb the stairs and walk through the corridor. Then the door swings wide open.

'Well, hello!' Rex says.

The light reflects off his bald head. He switches on the bedroom lights, walks up to the bed, and shuts the half-open drawer of the bedside table. You are surprised to see him; though you know he arrived in London early this afternoon, he told you over the phone that he had no intention of being back home before eleven. You don't know what time it is, and you aren't sure how long it has been since Ada left.

'You're using up all my condoms.'

'Someone has to,' you mumble, feeling completely exhausted and trying to adjust to the brightness.

He grimaces and says, 'You call that having sex? It suffocates my penis. How can you stand wearing one?'

Lifting yourself up a little, you rest your back against the two pillows you prop up against the headrest, and then say, 'It's too high a price to pay.'

'They're nearly seven pounds a packet; at this rate you're going to make me go bankrupt, you son of a bitch.' His devilish eyes twinkle with affection.

'Aren't you afraid of catching something?'

'I'm fifty-eight fucking years old. What difference does it make if I catch something?'

You guess he does have a point. With the new medicine around, these days one has better life expectancy with HIV than with diabetes.

'What if you passed it on to someone?'

'Nonsense! I'm pure as a baby's bum!'

'You could get someone knocked up.'

'Me? Get someone *pregnant*? That would be nice,' he responds. He starts rubbing his hand over one of his nipples through his shirt and says, 'You know, I've been sort of feeling broody lately.'

You lever yourself out of the bed and head to the bathroom, reminding yourself that it is pointless attempting to change Rex's opinion on anything. He is ultimately an old buffoon, too set in his ways to ever consider someone else's sensible viewpoint. The expensive condom supply by his bedside is a simple plot. According to Rex, women are more likely to have unprotected sex with him if they are under the illusion that he is *mostly* careful.

You leave the door open behind you, walk over the lukewarm marble, and grab one of the bathrobes that hangs on a hook inside the bathroom, putting it on without tying it up at the front. You stand before the basin and turn on the taps.

'I gather tonight wasn't so entertaining,' you say as you begin rinsing your face with icy water.

'Nah... it was full of geriatrics.'

Rex flew in from New York this afternoon to attend a black-tie private musical event at the Barbican, alongside one of his biggest investors who was hosting his own table at the event.

'I thought I was going to pass out from boredom.'

'How did you escape?' you ask, before wiping your face on the hand towel.

He sits on the untidy bed. 'I told him I was suffering from a gastric attack.'

'Do you think he believed you?'

'What's not to believe,' he says, stroking his enormous belly clockwise. It looks odd next to his otherwise lean and long-limbed physique.

You walk out of the bathroom. His gaze follows your partially visible penis; Rex's twisted sense of humour is mostly devised to cause psychological discomfort in others.

'I gather you've had company. Did you make sure to kick her out before I came?'

'No, she left of her own accord, actually.'

'Funny, I ran into her on my way in. She seemed nice.'

Trying not to look surprised, you respond, 'Yes, she is nice,' wondering how long it has *really* been since Ada has left – coming to the slow realisation that you have probably dozed off for only a few minutes.

'I even invited her back in to join us for a drink.'

'What was her response?' you ask uncomfortably.

'She gave me this very peculiar look, as if I had asked her for a threesome.'

171

'She was reading your filthy mind!'

'You reckon?'

You go to retrieve your clothes off the floor. He gets up and strolls towards you.

'Even so, we had a nice little chat. She told me she's from Istanbul. She told me the two of you met at the Fair. She also complained that you were a lousy lay.'

'Go fuck yourself!' you snap coolly. You know he is only trying to stir you up – but still.

Your hostility can have consequences. And you guess right. In one swift motion, he grabs you by the neck and pulls you down. You struggle to free yourself from his strong grip, grabbing the wooden pole of the bed. He is a few inches taller than you and, despite his age, strong as a bull.

He eventually lets go. For him it is nothing but a bit of harmless playfighting. Sauntering towards the door of the bedroom, he says, 'I asked Everard to prepare us some vodka martinis. Come and join me in the study when you're ready.'

Jesus fucking Christ! you think to yourself as you pull up your boxer shorts. All you really want is to get home and go to bed.

'Perfect. I'll be down in a minute,' you respond, trying to sound keen. You have just shagged someone in his bed. The least you can do is join him for a drink.

ADA

I

I ENTER MY FLAT, bearing fresh physical traces of the evening (the crotch of my briefs still slightly damp, a low burning ache between my legs, a tingling sensation on my swollen mouth), and aim straight for the storage cupboard where I dump all sorts of things I can't find a more dignified, purposeful place for, including my painting equipment. When I fled back to London, a Turkish art-collector friend of my father had generously proposed I stay at the one-bedroom flat he had bought for short breaks with his wife several years ago – but also as a hedge, in case Turkey should one day completely spiral out of control and become uninhabitable for anyone who wanted to live under a secular democracy. He had insisted I could stay here without paying rent, and for as long as I wished, provided I took care of the council tax and other bills: a thoughtful, kind gesture towards me and my family, but also a defiant act in the face of the outrage he had felt during the Gezi Park protests – particularly at the unjust, brutal killings of innocent protestors.

The urge to paint came upon me as I was being driven through heavy rain, inside an overheated car that reeked of the sugary smell of air-freshener, by a man I would not recognise if he were to knock on my front door at this moment. The car went along a route I didn't follow. I was preoccupied, replaying the events of the evening, all the while sensing Lucian's smell on me – as I still can now.

I put the kettle on and select a jazz album on Spotify. I quickly cover a small vacant area in the living room with pages of an old newspaper I keep for such moments, which seldom occur. Mostly, these happen when I'm inspired by someone's company – an artist or an individual who absorbs life with flair – or by a uniquely inspiring movie. Sometimes it's just the changing weather that drags out the artist in me. On this occasion it's my head-on sexual encounter with Lucian, which has brought my extended period of celibacy to an end.

The intensely loud whistle of the kettle interrupts light notes of improvisation from the solo jazz piano recording. I rush to the kitchen to make myself a strong black coffee; I need to avert the impending exhaustion (after the alcohol and a long, busy day) that can very quickly destroy the mental clarity and the spark of excited energy I currently have.

I glance out of the kitchen window with a burning hot mug of coffee in my hand, its steam rising to my face, and notice the narrow back of an animal trotting down the pavement opposite, towards the far end of the otherwise empty street. At first, I think it's a cat – but then, becoming aware of its larger frame and huge, lush tail, I realise it is in fact a fox. Part of me wants to leave my flat, rush down the boxy stair-case, go outside, and cautiously approach the solitary animal;

I have never seen a fox up close, nor have I seen one from my window until now – as much as I have occasionally looked out for them when I hear their tortured calls in the middle of the night. I swallow a mouthful of steaming hot coffee without flinching, and derive joy from the metallic bitterness it leaves in my mouth, as I watch the fox pause, then turn around and canter in my direction.

As if sensing it's being watched, it stops in front of my building – a sombre brick Georgian townhouse converted into small flats. I can just about make out its close-set eyes as it inspects the area and gives me a view of its pointy muzzle, before it slips back into the dark shadows and disappears for good, probably seeking its usual route through adjacent back-yards to its hidden den. I think of the many times I've been stirred from my light, skittish sleep by the foxes' high-pitched shrieks, which resemble the desperate cries of something, *someone* being subjected to an intolerable kind of agony – the uncanniness causes me to revisit the long, harrowing night of my detention. It's triggered in me an irrational fear of the night, of the unimaginable menace it might bring again, as I lie in a foetal position in my oppressive bed. I listen to my loud heartbeats and to the ear-numbing timbre of silence, now and then drifting off, only to wake abruptly, shivering, wedded to this anxiety that sometimes lasts till dawn. Only then does my irrational fear gradually lift – my bed becoming cosy again, my surroundings familiar and safe – as I sense the sky gradually lighten through the thick, drawn curtains.

I kneel on the floor and start to turn the stiff pages of the A3 pad I had bought when I first arrived in London, glancing through several other attempts – each one reminding me of the phase I was in at the time, and the particular mood that had instigated each self-doubting effort to paint something different. Before this can dampen my current determination, I turn to a clean page. Brushes in various sizes, an old spatula I use to scrape off paint and sometimes to make impromptu insertions with, a glass of clear water, a stained tea cloth, a bottle of linseed oil, a bottle of turpentine, all rest nearby. I unlock and open the square vintage conductor's case – purchased on a weekend visit to Camden Market – filled with a disorderly mixture of tubes, acrylics and oils, as well as a few colours of glossy nail varnish I sometimes apply to a small area of my paintings at the very end; a subtle, feminine finishing touch. I reach out and trace my hands over the absorbent surface of the bare paper, getting light goosebumps, and taking deep, meditative breaths; it's a ritual that brings me a little closer to the tactile reality of the material. When I paint, I start by rendering certain structural aspects of an existing *thing* I have pictured in my mind, then, in the spur of the moment, fill in the gaps with patterns picked up from elsewhere. I love exploring the textural, the structural. The thingness of things.

I am a colourist, like my father. I love experimenting with deep blues and purples, with pastel pinks and greens, rich reds and bright yellows. It's the intricate balance and contrast between colours and textures that makes the composition stand out. Autobiographical details are hidden within my paintings. I liken them to dreams. They are attempts to create new narratives from whatever my subconscious throws at me: haunting curiosities, recent observations and recurring motifs – fraught with meaning I am unable to decode – that I for some reason keep returning to.

II

The artistic training I received alongside my father at his studio, since I was old enough to hold a paintbrush between my fingers, was deliberately relaxed and undemanding. My father believed in cultivating the imagination before anything else, and chose to teach me what I wished to know and what I *had to* know – such as the fundamental techniques for acrylics and oils. Like most parents, he wanted to encourage in his child what he had been deprived of, blaming the traditional, strict art training he received from a young age for his continuing inability to create spontaneous paintings. Instead his large canvases relied on a rigid methodology he had developed over time.

During my final years in Istanbul, while I was still in high school, I used to spend my free time painting at my father's studio in his silent company, as he worked on a single painting for days, sometimes weeks. I had hoped to acquire the patience and perseverance that came to him so instinctively. The rest of the time, I'd live inside epic novels I devoured in a matter of days; I would happily lose myself with fictional characters whose intricate lives I'd get wrapped up in but would soon forget. I still managed to be an above-average student with impressive grades, and – amidst the chaotic immaturity of the private high school – I was a student most teachers took a liking to; they valued my shy, respectful personality that did not scramble to fit in. With my closest friend Elif, I created a niche, an alternative existence within the clamorous classroom, withdrawing from our peers, whom we found pretentious and lacking in substance and integrity. Their jokes were banal and forced, their pursuits and hang-ups the reckonings of feeble minds. We did not hate them, nor did we pity them – we just categorised them as *the others*; people of a radically different mindset from ours. We knew we could never belong, even if we tried.

I towered over Elif; the visual oddity of our union silently amused me every time we walked side by side down the loud school corridors, and out to the small treeless schoolyard.

Each year, after returning from our summer vacations – with our contrasting dark tans and sun-bleached hair – to a new classroom, we would spend most of our time obsessing over older boys we had met or watched in awe from afar, holidaying in laid-back coastal towns where our families owned summer houses. The still-dizzying memories of their enigmatic demeanour and muscular torsos would keep alive our fragile hope of a passionate fling the following summer, when we expected to be more daring and provocative. These fantasies made the long school year ahead, and the company of those we never felt comfortable with, more tolerable.

With the support of her parents – who watched her with wonder while she played lengthy classical pieces they admitted were beyond their musical grasp – Elif was eagerly being groomed for the rigorous, confined life of a concert pianist. But she also could picture herself one day composing musical scores for movies, and her time away from school was spent in front of her baby grand piano – which her father had bought for her after she had won Best Stage Performance, aged fourteen, at the annual International Young Talent Music Competition in Istanbul. Most of her days were taken up by piano lessons, practising, and composing short pieces she wished to someday adapt to an orchestral format. She would play these for me on my weekend visits to her family flat, where the sounds of a football match on TV, and the occasional glimpse of her mother shelling beans in the kitchen, affirmed that – apart from the striking presence of Elif's baby grand piano – theirs was a typical Turkish household.

In the last year of high school, Elif began preparing for the higher education examination in April – which we all needed to sit – and for the conservatoire's piano exam in the summer. While an air of staidness hung over the most carefree spirits in our class, I had little ambition to begin priming myself for the still-distant exams. Even so, at my father's request, in late autumn I was ushered by an artist friend of his – a short, middle-aged romantic who liked wearing berets and painting pictures of bicycles – into the weekend studio of Oğuz Bey. I was expected to dedicate each Saturday afternoon to learning how to draw still-life arrangements and various objects and instruments. It was intended as a groundwork for the talent exam of the painting department at Mimar Sinan Fine Arts University. My father, with the somewhat subjective viewpoint of a former graduate, had deemed it the best place in Turkey one could study fine arts, despite voicing his concern that the quality of the teaching, along with the student environment, had deteriorated since his time.

On my first visit to his studio, Oğuz Bey – a recently retired professor from Mimar Sinan – placed three dazzlingly green, sour-looking apples on an earthy raw linen cloth laid on a table. He then left my side without saying much, as if further direction would have ruined the point of the seemingly straightforward exercise. Having always relied on leftover impressions of things and my imagination to execute a painting, this was to be my first attempt to sketch an object from real life. I had secretly fretted about this moment (which I knew had to occur once I approached painting as a serious career path), worried I would be unable to develop the skills to capture fine details of a real-life object – a crucial, if basic, prerequisite for any practising professional artist. My father, on the other hand, was confident: as someone who was already observant and creatively sensitive towards her surroundings, I was bound to possess the skills required to be good at still-life drawing.

I sat on a wooden stool, nervously glancing at the pad I had been made to prop up flimsily, at a twenty-degree angle, on an easel – a piece of equipment I had never opted to use until then, having found its rigid, upright formality too restraining.

A part of me wanted to quietly abscond and do something much less demanding and more fun for the rest of the afternoon – but, aware that this was not an option, I pressed down warily. The pencil's hard, octagonal edges felt uncomfortable against my self-doubting fingers; I drew a weak, streaky curve of a line, intended as an outline of one of the apples.

Glancing at my watch I suddenly realised, in a state of near-disbelief, that forty minutes had flown by since Oğuz Bey had left me to my own devices. Through the partially open double-doors, this smaller room expanded into the main studio, where the rest of his weekend students – mostly housewives who wished to reinvigorate their stagnant lives with a new purpose – were painting silently. Their assignment was a still-life composition consisting of an antique-looking brass jug and some giant quinces in a glass bowl, placed upon a pedestal covered in ample folds of satin.

Tugging my sleeves up to my elbows, I sensed the gentle warmth of the sun, as I kept applying faint lines that hardly had an impact on what was already there. Noticing Oğuz Bey's skeletal silhouette approaching, I caught sight of slow-moving particles in the air, glinting in the sun. I briefly entertained the idea that the entire universe was just as temporary, a thought that momentarily diminished the dread of the scrutiny I was about to face.

'How have we been doing?' Oğuz Bey asked. He spoke in a considerate yet authoritative tone, with the laid-back poise of someone used to inspecting others' work. He directed his attention to my sketch.

'Not great.'

'But *why?*'

'My sketch is too small in relation to the paper. It looks a bit ridiculous, I think.'

His eyes went back and forth between my drawing and the still-life composition.

'The position of the apples among the folds of the material, the spatial relationship between each component...' he loosely interlaced his hairy fingers. 'You must be very sharp-eyed; you've been able to portray this very accurately.'

'Really?'

My confidence thriving after Oğuz Bey's comment, I began to share my father's point of view.

'If I were you,' Oğuz Bey continued, 'I wouldn't beat myself up for not getting the scale of your composition right this time. You must understand that these things only get better with repetition. For the next still life, you will consider this aspect of your drawing before you begin. My only criticism would be that your lines are a little too faint. They demonstrate a lack of courage. Don't be afraid to press harder with your pencil; remember, mistakes can always be erased.'

I watched him leave the room at a determined pace. I listened to his steps retreating down the small, dim corridor to the dark entrance of the flat – large enough to house a small family, and tucked away from Üsküdar's chaos and noise pollution.

From that day on, each Saturday I watched the early afternoon sun refract through the net curtains and heard the glass door that jolted and squeaked each time it opened on to an empty concrete balcony – where I witnessed Oğuz Bey having his cigarette breaks. He would gaze at the obtrusively close apartment buildings on the opposite side of the narrow street, their faded fronts smudged with soot. Some flats had exterior clotheslines – exposing rumpled-up laundry and Turkish flags hung during national celebrations but left attached for weeks, sometimes months. As if such a gesture could mend the widening cracks of a crumbling society, or reinforce a unity long forgotten.

The building was perched at the top of a remote street so steep that, commuting there in the winter months, I sometimes had to take a brief cab ride from the port right to the front door of the liftless building. When the temperatures occasionally dropped below zero, a hazardous layer of frost coated the road's time-worn cobblestone surface.

On that first visit, Oğuz Bey energetically returned to the room, an umbrella in one hand, and a confident, daring expression in his dark eyes that temporarily lightened his withered complexion. This was a look he usually had, I would learn, when he came up with challenging new assignments for his students. Such moments were the highlights of his teaching, as he tried to kill time by organising his already tidy studio while treading softly around his students, silently absorbed in their work for hours on end. Or he would go into his study – leaving the door open to remain available to students – to make small alterations to his nauseatingly colourful, abstract canvases. His paintings, executed in a futuristic style, were exhibited at second-rate galleries with deceptively exclusive atmospheres. Or he might light another cigarette out on the bare balcony and ruminate over issues in his seemingly uniform personal life – the details of which he refrained from confiding to any of his students.

'Even though it's deemed bad luck to open one indoors,' he remarked with smiling eyes, and opened the umbrella. Its tent-like cover briefly created the illusion that it took up a large section of the room. He left it on the floor at a distance from me.

'Oh no,' I let slip, immediately regretting being so transparent to someone I barely knew – someone considerably older and more senior.

'If I thought it was too much of a stretch, I wouldn't place it in front of you.'

Invigorated, I gazed back at the umbrella – this time setting aside its obvious utility and considering only its distinctive design and structure.

Sighing deeply, my anguish rapidly replaced by some enthusiasm, I responded, 'I'll try,' while considering how I could realistically portray the integral relationship between the umbrella's rounded exterior vault and its concave interior in a two-dimensional medium. Its tiered metal ribs that evoked the jointed legs of long-legged spiders I stumbled upon at our summer house, when they crept unannounced from the dark. And, finally, the wooden cane of the umbrella, which met the taut canopy at a sharp angle.

Despite her intense schedule – perhaps subconsciously reacting against it – Elif had met someone online, on a popular dating site she had signed up to with no serious intentions, mostly out of boredom and frustration at her unchangingly stolid lifestyle. She had been secretly meeting up with a young man named Burçak, roughly three years older than her. In her words, he was *hot, but a bit of a layabout.* She met him mainly on Saturday afternoons (telling her parents she was meeting up with me), following the weekly two-hour piano lessons she received from Ayşe Hanım – a humpbacked, never-been-married old lady, long retired from her brief moment of vague recognition as a concert pianist. According to Elif, she adorned her basement flat with many framed photographs, nearly all of them ancient or touched-up self-portraits that bore very little resemblance to her present self.

As a safety measure, Elif had initially met Burçak at an always-crowded café in Taksim Square. By a curious twist of fate, roughly a year and a half down the line, when I had returned from London, the venue would be a frequent backdrop in our lives. Elif and I – reunited after being apart for almost a year – would be side by side at the Gezi Park protests, boisterously chanting along to euphoric slogans – until, rather too quickly, our voices would become hoarse. We, along with millions of others, had seemingly been summoned by a greater force to the streets of Istanbul to retort against the intolerance, cruelty and greed so openly being practised.

It was the very end of spring. As soon as the challenging first year of my degree had come to an end, and after Gezi Park and Taksim Square had been seized by the people, I was returning to Istanbul to begin my summer holiday. Back in London I had watched, in total shock and heightened joy, endless international news coverage; late in the evenings, too intrigued to fall asleep, I had become hooked on live footage, streamed by anonymous protestors fleeing quickly advancing police forces, my laptop the only source of light in my bedroom. Fretting for their safety, I shed tears, wishing I could somehow be teleported there that night to join their noble cause and march with them through familiar locations. Loud blasts would sometimes resound at close range, the chaos captured and amplified through wobbly recordings. Cheerful crowds carried floating banners, defiantly saunter-ing along major high streets across Istanbul; cars in traffic persistently sounded their horns in support; a huge group of people, young and old, whistled, clapped, and shouted all at once, 'the government must resign!' The footage had trans-formed places I had known since childhood simultaneously into a war zone and a carnival, a spectacle I never imagined I would witness.

I hadn't been quite sure, after landing at Atatürk Airport – noticeably more hectic than usual – whether the tension and excitement I sensed around me was real, or generated by my alertness, which interpreted anything out of the ordinary as a possible side-effect of the ongoing protests. By the time I reached my neighbourhood, I knew it was the former. The protests had completely altered the place's mood, demonstrating how a city's established image could be modified overnight. As it was a weekday, and during daytime, the protests were confined to Taksim Square; elsewhere, as much as people tried to carry on with their lives, they were consumed by what was taking place in the heart of the city.

I arrived at Gezi Park in the early evening, having agreed to meet Elif there. By then, against her parents' stern objections, she had already disappeared into the crowds, as if the inextinguishable blaze of mutiny, having seeped into her bloodstream, had bestowed upon her a willpower no longer impaired by sentimental misgivings. A year and a half after the episode with Burçak, she had at last risen against the control exercised upon her by her seemingly modern, ultra-secular parents, who wished to preserve the precious hymen she, by that time, no longer possessed intact.

When I reached the grounds of Gezi Park sometime after the sun had set, I was mesmerised by the friendly, unpretentious vibe. Since the demonstrations had begun, it had quickly transformed into a communal habitat with round-the-clock residents, and into a regular haunt for other devoted protestors who – due to work, school or family – couldn't afford to guard the trees all the time. People constantly flowed through the grounds, traversing the park day or night – some to glimpse what the fuss was all about; others to experience, if briefly, the unprecedented phenomenon that had shaken the country to its foundations. People lay across blankets on the dried-out lawn, a drink in one hand and a cigarette in the other, as if they were relaxing in their backyards. Bare-footed yoga enthusiasts concentrated on carrying out poses on their colourful mats, their heads tilted towards the darkening sky as the horizon accentuated the dusky silhouettes of trees and the skyline of towering hotels and apartment blocks ahead, making them appear like flat, cut-out shapes in a shadow play. The overlapping calls from nearby minaret tops were still fresh in my mind; a group of Muslim men crouched, putting their shoes back on, after performing their evening prayers. Further along, a woman addressed an audience through a scratchy microphone, passionately accentuating the word *resistance*; a handful of Kurds with smiling faces and determined glances formed a circle, trying to dance the *halay* in an absurdly small area; somewhere in the distance a group of voices, accompanied by an amateur guitarist, sang 'Ciao Bella' in a somewhat unsynchronised effort: an anthem for Turkey's disillusioned leftists, their morale suddenly boosted. Fascinated and baffled by the polyphonic occurrences, and encountering such varied segments of the population for once acting peacefully towards a common purpose, I had suddenly picked up faint, drifting fragments of music I vaguely recognised. Without knowing what it actually was, I kept trying to answer its call, occasionally squeezing through throngs of people to get closer to it. The music was intermittently muffled by other sounds, and I doubted I was getting any closer to it at all.

Moments before I lifted myself on my toes to see through the small, keen audience, I had finally recognised the solo piano piece – it was being played by none other than Elif, a knowledge that had perhaps resided in me all along, but which I had overlooked, my attention seduced by the vibrancy around me. The short piece in which she was absorbed, once considered radical for its experimental approach to form and rhythm, was one she knew inside out, possibly because it reflected her creative tendencies so well. Carefully pacing herself, she moved her slender fingers with fluid ease over the keys of the portable keyboard she had brought to the park that day, along with an enormous backpack with her essentials. Kaan, her boyfriend of six months (a conservatoire drop-out turned professional keyboardist, music producer and DJ) had helped her carry it from her family home – a place she would never return to again.

I I I

A year and a half prior to that crucial period – that would shape our lives in ways neither of us would imagine, and, in my case, would ever want – in general terms, Elif and I were not all that different from other teenage girls on the delicate threshold of adulthood. As if to distract ourselves from more pressing issues, we speculated about boys we were obsessively attracted to, but were not sufficiently in love with, at times plotting risky sexual escapades that proved more gratifying within our imaginations, all the while harbouring frustration heightened by fluctuating hormones and the burden of parental expectations.

During one of our lunch breaks, on a sleep-inducing blustery day, we were cramped with other pupils inside the airless cafeteria, waiting our turn in a long, disorganised queue extending in all directions, surrounded by individuals we would never really get to know. Elif had uttered in my ear, melancholia in her striking olive-green eyes, 'To me he's nobody and conveniently forgettable,' referring to Burçak, who – with his unspectacular life and his naively well-intentioned responses to her difficult behaviour – took up the largest part of our conversations in those days. Behind Elif's mask of indifference was a volatile inwardness. She tended to get her fixes from trials of the self she impulsively chose to perform with the obsessive commitment of a performance artist.

'I told him to find somewhere more private next time,' she said. She almost immediately averted her gaze, as if she didn't feel the need to dwell on the obvious. She frequently referred to her virginity as an irritating scab she had wished to pick off prior to finishing high school – this was less of a goal for me at the time; possibly because it had never been an aspect of myself I had been pressured to preserve.

'We couldn't do it,' she reluctantly confessed the following Monday, angrily unfastening the leather straps of her canvas bag and discarding her notebook and pen onto her desk before letting the nearly empty bag collapse limply onto the floor. As I stood beside her, concealing her noticeably troubled presence from the rest of the class, I watched her nihilistic mood briefly turn to annoyance as she looked up to acknowledge one of our class's most popular yet most obnoxious characters strutting by us with his usual air of played-up arrogance – weakly supported by his relatively appealing looks – en route to his designated place in the back row (where, during breaks, he would aggressively thrust himself against his desk in a spontaneous display of unruly male desire). Other students were settling in, occasionally passing derogatory remarks about each other that were intended to be funny but hardly ever were.

'But how come?' I asked, stumped by her statement. Perhaps Burçak had failed to find them a suitable place to go. Still, I was happy and relieved to see my closest friend before me at last – despite how frail she appeared, her tiny shoulders slumped.

I had spent the latter half of the weekend increasingly worried for her well-being, and curious whether she had achieved what she had set out to do – she hadn't answered any of my calls or text messages since Saturday afternoon.

I discreetly observed her unbrushed hair, messily gathered at the top with an elastic band.

'We tried for nearly two hours and we just couldn't do it,' she muttered with a lifeless gaze.

'So you *did* actually get to meet him on Saturday.'

She nodded, restlessly pulling at her sleeves – as if unbearably constrained by the compliance the garment signified.

'We met at Taksim at the usual spot. Then he took me to his dead great-aunt's flat in Şişli.'

I silently nodded. The impulse to openly express my thoughts – here, on his choice of location – was suppressed by the dreadful mood she was in, along with the particular subtlety required by the delicate topic of one's first sexual experience.

'Someone needed to see if everything was OK in the flat, and he volunteered. No one had been back there since the day her cleaner found her dead in bed.'

I noticed a slight swelling to her eyelids, and wondered – I had yet to witness her cry – why the incident had caused her so much grief.

'Don't worry, we didn't try it in her bed,' she added; a trace of humour momentarily replaced the gloom in her eyes, as she considered the quasi-comical distastefulness of the set-up.

'I'm glad to hear. But *why* couldn't you do it?'

If they had tried, I couldn't quite understand what hurdles there could have been; at the time I considered intercourse to be a fairly straightforward undertaking.

'I don't know exactly,' she replied, arching her shoulders and tilting herself infinitesimally away from me; her body seemed to close into itself. After a long pause, she tactfully lowered her voice. 'It just wouldn't go in,' she admitted. 'I suppose the problem was him,' she said shyly, looking the other way, while I carefully observed her – not used to seeing her tackle the subject of sex with such coyness.

'I see!' I eventually remarked, having come to a clearer understanding of what had gone wrong between them.

She nodded.

'Maybe he couldn't handle the pressure of being your first?'

'No, it wasn't that. It was *her*.'

'What do you mean?'

'His mood shifted the moment we arrived. He got all tense and weird. He rushed off, saying he had some things to do around the house, as if they were the main reason we were there. I waited around for a bit, assuming he was going to be back at any time. Then I started looking for him. The flat wasn't huge, but it had a very convoluted layout, with rooms connected in odd ways and several closed balconies – and there were piles of clutter everywhere. I heard him lock himself in one of the loos. He was easily in there for twenty minutes. God knows what he was up to. Once he came out, he vanished again. Eventually I found him on a balcony next to some parched plants with a watering can in his hand. By this point, I was furious. I told him I'd had enough, that I was getting the hell out of there. I don't think he knew, before dragging me there, how uncomfortable he was going to feel.'

'But you stayed.'

'He insisted. He said he was going to make it up to me. Then he took me to her living room,' she muttered, lowering her head, glancing around watchfully to see if anyone had heard; she could easily imagine how our rowdy classmates would torment her the rest of the school year with shoddy, unimaginative comments that revealed the small-minded sexism of a society we – as young women – never felt fully attuned to.

'He seemed emotionally disconnected,' she confided almost inaudibly. In order not to miss any of her subsequent revelations, I had snuggled beside her, perching myself uncomfortably on her chair. She picked up her pen and started scribbling, perhaps to dissociate herself from the still fresh and unsettling memory. 'His kisses were short and timid. He didn't even bother to use his tongue. His hands were all sweaty. The thick carpet beneath us gave us carpet burns. We weren't even allowed to use the sofas.' Her eyes locked on the fierce star she had sketched; she kept going over it with her pen, pressing into the paper.

'Will you see him again?'

She paused, and then retorted: 'I don't know, and I don't care!' She seemed so distant from her usual coolheaded self. She slumped over her desk, burying her head in her arms. Sensing inquiring heads turning in our direction, I knelt and protectively wrapped my arm around her. Not used to such physical contact with her, I was surprised at how slight she felt.

'Please, please don't cry,' I whispered in her ear – sensing her silent sobs through her lightly tremoring back. I couldn't bear to see her in such agony – even if I had yet to fully understand its underlying reason – especially while surrounded by those who often regressed into a collective mindset of seeking to exploit others at their weakest.

'What's wrong with her?' the girl seated behind us – keen to be let in on the story – leaned forward to enquire. I briefly turned and shrugged – not taking any notice of her seemingly genuine look of concern – to imply that I was as clueless as she was.

'Baby, come over this way, I'll give you something *big* that will make you forget all your troubles!' shouted the guy in the very back row. His lewd suggestion was immediately met with shy giggles, then roaring applause and a few sharp whistles as more of them joined in, striking their palms against their desks as if demanding he enact his promise there and then.

To fend off the growing attention, Elif lifted her head. Facing the wall, she discreetly wiped away her tears with the ends of her sleeves, as if methodically dressing a wound, before turning to me.

'My parents know everything.'

I stared at her.

'How did they—'

'I was running late in the morning and forgot to sign out of my email.'

I remembered our brazenly outspoken, excessively detailed gab on the topic – all stored in her chat history. And presumably read several times by her parents. I whispered back, 'How did they react?', dreading her answer.

'Predictably.'

I nodded, sensing the surge of anger behind her emotionless front.

'When I got home, they sat me down to talk, but things got out of hand pretty quickly.' She sighed deeply. 'My father, he lashed out at me the minute I began to explain myself,' she whispered in a soft, fragile voice.

When I visited her in her family flat, Elif's father would affectionately wind his daughter up with banal one-liners we would react to dismissively. Yet we shot wide smiles at each other, triggered not by her father's cringeworthy jokes, but by the cartoonish poses the three of us struck in this moment – as if assuming roles in a comedy routine. How could the same father justify resorting to physical intimidation and violence, all in the name of imposing his way of life – while in complete denial over his adolescent daughter's natural instinct to explore her sexuality?

'He hit me wherever his blows could reach. My mother kept yelling at him to stop as she tried to come between us. It's surprising no one called the cops on us.'

'I'm *so* sorry, Elif.'

She briefly looked up at me to acknowledge my words, her usual, refreshingly offbeat energy no longer there, as if it had been drained out of her by desperation that left her skin a pallid yellow.

'Maybe if your mother had warned you beforehand...' I mumbled hesitantly.

Elif threw me an exhausted glance, shrugging off what I had thoughtlessly proposed. When her daughter's chastity was at stake, her mother's viewpoint was identical to her father's.

'Straight after school she's taking me to her gyno.'

At last the biology teacher entered the classroom, striding towards his desk holding exam papers. I stood up, sensing the discreet motion of students returning to their seats. Elif's words had brought to the foreground of my awareness the shame of objectification I could all too easily relate to.

Nevertheless I cautiously kneeled again and whispered in her ear, 'What for?'

THE FUGITIVE OF GEZI PARK

'To make sure I've remained unspoiled. I told them nothing happened, but they no longer believe a word I say.'

I glanced back at her with pity.

'They confiscated my mobile and laptop. I'm not allowed to leave the house unless one of them is with me.'

A fighter at heart, Elif would swiftly rise above the intolerable despair and fury of the incident; it would prove an unmendable rupture of trust in her relationship with her parents. A year and a half later, against their wishes, Elif would sneak out to join the intensifying protests outside, knowing she might never return home again. And despite the disruption of my arrest, Elif and Kaan would stay on at Gezi Park until that Saturday night, when an army of riot police, backed by water cannon, would flock into the square one last time, spewing litres of water mixed with tear gas. They would be targeting the crowd with rubber bullets and teargas canisters – including the many families who, beguiled by the happy-go-lucky ambiance, had turned up at the park with their kids for a pleasant evening outing. In a single effort they would wipe out our paradise of communal solidarity, along with any shreds of hope for our country's future.

The next day, over the phone, Elif would explain how their eyes and throats burned in agony from the teargas. Kaan attempted to shield her from the rubber bullets and gas capsules. Hundreds of other protestors, caught off guard and frantically looking for an escape route, trampled others to dodge the swinging batons. Elif and Kaan would eventually reach the nearby Divan Hotel, its lobby a pandemonium of angry cries and helpless sobs.

She told me how there were people throwing up. Some were brought in unconscious, some drenched in blood. The entrance of the hotel was continually bombarded with teargas; it had become the enemy base. They thought they'd never get out of there. Inside the lobby, they could barely see. Everyone had to keep their gas masks on. Things had evolved so quickly Elif and Kaan hadn't had a chance to grab theirs from the tent. The hotel management handed out gas masks to those who didn't have one. They tried to help everyone as much possible, Elif said. 'Late in the night, a few conspirators started to spread the rumour that there was an angry mob gathering outside, preparing to set the hotel on fire and burn us alive, like they tried to do with Madımak, and it caught on with the rest,' she said in the hyperawake voice of someone kept up all night.

Afterwards, Elif bore a few weeks on a thin mattress in the very narrow space of a classmate's bedroom – making polite conversation in the mornings with her chatty parents – while Kaan moved out of his family flat, packing up all his music equipment, and renting a place he could afford close to the underground club he DJ'd at, in the upmarket district of Cihangir. Then they moved into a one-bedroom flat in Tarlabaşı, in one of the less derelict, just-about-habitable nineteenth-century Levantine buildings on the ever-hectic boulevard – a road surviving from the Ottoman era, pragmatically widened into a dual carriageway in 1983 by bulldozing over three hundred less fortunate historical buildings.

These days Tarlabaşı was mostly occupied by struggling immigrants: Romani, Africans, Kurds, Syrians – some of whom had escaped purges elsewhere – as well as prostitutes, squatters, drug addicts and other marginalised subgroups, their risky daily dealings regularly spawning noisy arguments that escalated into violence, suppressed by patrolling police squads.

'I couldn't sleep again. I'm woken nearly every night by an incident, whether it's drunks smashing bottles on each other's heads or sex workers being beaten up by their clients – or, mind you, sometimes it's the other way around. Whatever it is, the racket just won't stop! I find it's harder to cope on nights when Kaan is out working. He doesn't like it either. He says coming across small units of policemen gathered here and there on his way home gives him the creeps. I worry that, because of his tattoos and unusual look, they will pull him aside and take him in. We're starting to regret we ever moved here,' Elif told me barely a fortnight into their stay. I heard cabinets being opened and shut in the background, along with the overexcited meows of the two kittens she had adopted on a whim, snatching them off the kerb as they hungrily devoured some greasy scraps left behind on a newspaper by one of Istanbul's dedicated animal lovers – mostly people with limited means who went out of their way to provide for the city's endlessly expanding cat and dog population.

Later, after they had lived there for a couple of years, the vicinity's nightly disruptions diminished to tiny nudges against the edges of her sleep, often seeping in and enhancing the narratives of her fantastic dreams. She had adjusted to the startlingly sudden, frantic shrieks, the drunken scuffles and manic police sirens, the same way some people learnt to sleep through the sporadic barking of a neighbour's dog. Occasionally, the gruesome – possibly overstated, if not fabricated – details of a recent outrageous nightly episode, passed on to her by a neighbour or a local shop owner – which she had comfort-ably slept through – would prompt her to declare her intent to move out as soon as their lease came to an end. It was an ultimatum she hadn't followed through so far. She gave private piano lessons to supplement their rent. Tarlabaşı's disobedient, wounded charm – qualities she too possessed – had already won her over.

However, roughly a year and a half before that pivotal moment in Elif's life – when the defiant spirit of Gezi had given her that final push to set herself free from the tyranny of parental control – Elif had already overcome self-pity, less than a month after her father had beaten her. Rather than be defeated by the additional restrictions – making her daily routine resemble that of someone under house arrest, which her parents were single-mindedly convinced she would benefit from in the long term – she had found escape from its grimness by composing a series of nocturnes. I would eventually listen to them on our lunch breaks, on recordings she made on her mobile phone. By late April, she'd finally been allowed to have her mobile back, the first concession after she'd obtained an impressively high score at the university entry examinations.

Meanwhile, I had been continuing to attend my weekly drawing lessons at Oğuz Bey's studio. Initially, I had looked forward to each lesson. Yet, as weeks passed by and doubts about what I *really* wanted to do with my life set in, I became less eager to turn up.

'If you carry on like this, you will have no problem entering Mimar Sinan,' Oğuz Bey had whispered encouragingly into my ear one Saturday. He was looking at a drawing of mine that was finally coming together. Until that moment, I had been too immersed in executing it to pause and question whether it was, in fact, any good.

I smiled cautiously back at him, torn between priding myself on the good progress I had made in life drawing, and embarrassment at my perpetual contemplation over when and with what plausible-sounding explanation I could finally drop from his weekly lessons – particularly when he was standing beside me, praising my work. By then, the thought of not following the route designated for me had been strengthening day by day, eventually forming into a solid conviction I knew I would eventually have to admit to my parents. I didn't know how I would bear witnessing the disillusionment this was bound to cause in my father, who regarded me as his prodigy. Yet it was an event I had begun to anticipate; I was more troubled by the disingenuousness of hiding what I wanted to do with my life from the two people who mattered the most to me. And I was eager to obtain their consent and support.

The passion I had previously harboured for painting hadn't altogether disappeared, of course, but it had taken a back seat – as the urge to explore independence, other career options and ways of being had galvanised in me new lines of thought. The desire to make art, like any other strong inclination, would remain inside me, though dormant. It was a pursuit I knew I was young enough to walk away from, and one I could always return to, perhaps with the focus and determination I currently lacked.

It had been in the middle of breakfast on an unrushed Sunday morning, a snowed-in Istanbul visible through every window frame, that my parents raised the question of the distant summer ahead. They were considering the number of flights they needed to book back and forth from our summer house in Bodrum to Istanbul. Then they brought up Mimar Sinan's talent exam for the painting department, to be held in the summer – so I finally plucked up the courage to say what I had been carefully devising for some time.

'I no longer want to enter my name for the exam,' I calmly declared, surprised by how easy it was to voice it at last.

I tended to become more anxious than a given situation warranted – a quality, Marlene had pointed out, that was also connected to my creativity. According to her, it granted me the ability to imagine the disappointments and misfortunes I could face, with an insight which seemed brutally realistic but was often exaggerated. Regardless of the secure upbringing I had experienced with my unusually open-minded but equally over-sensitive parents, who from the beginning had encouraged me to communicate my thoughts freely and speak up to authority, I was one of those people who placed too much emphasis on other people's thoughts, and who suffered from an easily affected (or some would argue weak) bearing towards unpredictability.

Turning towards my father, I said, 'I'm not sure I want to become an artist, like you. Maybe one day, I will – but right now, I want to try other things.' I paused to observe the impact of my revelation on both of them, while experiencing its heightened effects on myself. I was in a state of sheer excitement – finally having let the cat out of the bag – but also of anguish.

My father subtly nodded his head, unreadable; perhaps he had prepared himself for such a moment, having already sensed the change in me over the last few months; my visits to his studio had become less frequent.

My mother seemed not to be looking at me, but somehow gazing through me, as she slipped into deeper thought.

'I would like to do a degree in History of Art.'

My father lifted his eyebrows in acknowledgement, then glanced away evasively – before returning, as if nothing had happened, to the fixed rituals of his breakfast. Reaching over to seize a generous pinch of red pepper flakes, he sprinkled it over the feta cheese on his plate. He ate it with half a *simit*, a quartered tomato and a small sliced-up cucumber – a breakfast he alternated with a boiled egg, a handful of black olives and wholemeal toast.

'Tijen also did a degree in History of Art, didn't she?' my mother pointed out – an open-minded response that implied she wasn't taking any sides.

I joyfully responded, 'Who knows where it will take me?'

My father sat back in his chair, before dryly commenting, 'Donald Judd studied History of Art before channelling his energy into making art,' perhaps to reassure himself that I could, after a brief detour, return to the path I was destined for.

'Especially these days, very few end up having a career in what they specialised in at university,' my mother said, stirring her tea, its layered aroma, a mixture of native and English blends, boosted by the tiny crescent of lemon that swirled manically around on its surface. The crystals of melting sugar and tea leaves which normally settled on the base had risen inside the tulip-shaped tea glass, caught up in a small vortex her quick action had generated. She lifted the glass by its slender midsection and took a cautious sip from it.

'But, of course, it will be an altogether different experience to study History of Art at Mimar Sinan. If that's where you intend to do it, of course,' my father pointed out after some consideration, this time with a hint of annoyance.

'I'm not sure I want to go to university here,' I nervously admitted, aware that as their only child my sudden bid to live abroad was likely to be the most taxing part of my request – my breakaway had been envisioned as a distant, gradual event expected to take place in my mid- to late twenties.

'Where would you rather be?' my mother, leaning forward, had asked.

'London,' I responded hesitantly – fearing that the location, so far from Istanbul, and the remarkable cost, would instantly confirm my selfishness.

My presence felt almost invasive as they exchanged a series of restrained glances. My mother finally put an end to the extended silence by saying, 'Well, if you're really serious, I'm sure we can think about it.'

She'd always been a keen advocate of breaking out of one's comfort zone, but the calm expression she subsequently adopted didn't entirely hide her motherly anguish.

'By all means... if you're serious... yes... I'm sure we can consider it,' my father responded, while his hands made a series of awkward, fidgety gestures.

'I know it's a lot to ask.'

As if to grant himself some latitude, and perhaps also to witness the snow's present splendour before the bright morning sun and streaming traffic transformed it into a brown slush, my father looked outside. The stillness enveloping us was broken by a few distant vehicle horns.

'So London, ha?' he muttered.

'I just want to experience life abroad for a few years. I think I would benefit from trying it on my own and being exposed to a completely new culture,' I eagerly explained – and, as I did so, I acknowledged the soundness of my decision.

I V

An incoming message interrupts the moment.

I've been completely engrossed in painting. What I have been spontaneously creating has pulled me in, as if it's an opening to another dimension consisting only of enticing fumes, runny, viscid colours, evolving textures and shapes – excluding my awareness of anything and everything else. It's been a while since the album I put on came to its end – at the beginning, the music contributed to the stream of ideas. Yet the clarity of the airy silence prompted me to make a rapid succession of bold decisions.

I lean forward and grab my phone. The message reads: *Fancy joining me on a studio visit tomorrow night? Lx.*

I giggle to myself, tensing my shoulders and raising them to contain my exuberance. I cover my face with both hands, suddenly embarrassed – as if, his teasing eyes gleaming in amusement, he's able to see my reaction. The gesture takes me back to more carefree times in Istanbul. Glancing at the paint smeared randomly over my fingers, seeping deep into my cuticles, I reminisce over how Elif and I would share, in guarded whispers, salaciously detailed accounts of what we wished to do to boys we had hardly exchanged any words with, already seduced by their dizzying pull.

When, in one of our most recent sessions, I had mentioned the occasional flush of desire inside me – an urge not aimed at anyone in particular but towards the act of sex itself – Marlene had responded, smiling, 'Sexual desire is one of the most fundamental indications of one's attachment to life.'

I cherish the excitement Lucian ignites in me; my desperate

bid to avoid any form of close interaction with any man who has indicated the slightest hint of desire for me has, for the past two years, felt like a solidified state of neurosis, a testimony to the death of my libido along with my trust in men – aspects of me I could never believe would show signs of resurrection. But I'm fully aware I have a long way to go.

I imagine Lucian just a few steps behind me as I carefully lift my drying painting off the floor and rest it against a wall – not solely as someone I have become deeply attracted to, but also as a creative, intuitive individual to whom I can easily divulge what I have been trying to attain. With a sense of achievement I haven't experienced for a long time, moved by catharsis, I sigh a deep sigh, taking a step back.

I observe my painting affectionately, wishing I could have my parents beside me in this moment – aware that the photo I will take in broad daylight and send to them will not mirror the experience of a physical encounter with it.

At the centre of the page stands an upright configuration made up of different fragments of varioud objects (some painted flatly, others possessing the optical illusion of depth). The flat portrayal of the hatchback of a yellow car with rust on some corners also appears as it is: like smudges of earth-coloured paint on a bright yellow plane. At the very top is a swirling marble statue of the head of a man with lush, unruly hair; at the bottom left, there is a small set of keys – as similar as my memory permits to the ones that unlock the top drawer of my desk at the Fair – dangling tenuously from a thin iron pole. Beneath it, a little saucer, drenched in an abstraction of electric blue and hot pink. The odd sculptural arrangement is pulled together by various shapes and planes that also resemble mass-produced industrial plastic set on a plinth, the speckled concrete texture of the plinth adding to the tension between the various elements of the composition.

It's a loose attempt at exploring notions of abstraction and figuration, flatness and depth, surface and texture, and memory-instigated fictive narratives: themes I have played with in the past, though never so extensively in a single painting. Making art has felt like a state of mind I could no longer connect with, whereas now my mind is thriving with new ideas. In Lucian's words, this could be the start of an internal dialogue which, if pursued, could lead to a series of new paintings, and these paintings could steer me towards new artistic concerns and quests – and possibly to areas I never imagined I could venture into.

LUCIAN

I

'I DON'T BELIEVE I've been informed of the exact financial agreement that exists between you and Ms Compton.'

He leaned forward on his chair, crossing his pasty hands together on the table before resting his frosty blue eyes upon you. They appeared massive under those magnifying lenses he wore, like a pair of depthless fish eyes.

'Nor have I,' you said, to be funny, but he appeared unmoved. You tried to picture his lousy suburban life. The froufrou, outdated décor inside his house. At the end of each day, wearing his old-man slippers, he most likely retreated to the living room to watch telly. He'd keenly tune into *University Challenge* with his equally humourless wife – slightly chubby, with a boxy, rigid hairstyle akin to a Lego woman's – who did greasy Sunday roasts and overly sweet sponge cakes for the extended family. You imagined him diligently shining his car, tidying up the leaves in his driveway with a leaf blower, if he wasn't attending to the vegetables he cultivated in the greenhouse, or mending something in his man-cave. You found the boring, conventional life you assumed he had sickeningly oppressive. You felt happy not to be in his shoes.

'Well,' you said, straightening your back, attempting to appear as sombre as him, 'Eloise earns a monthly salary, and in addition to that, she receives a percentage from any work she sells.'

'And what percentage might that be?'

Jesus, you thought, then scratched your head. The previous night's drinking with Rex was still lingering inside you. Luckily the evening hadn't metamorphosed into one of your wild nights; Rex's efforts to find some last-minute company hadn't led anywhere.

'If she makes a sale, she gets ten per cent of the profit I make from the artwork.'

'I see. Are these earnings meant to be paid to her at the end of each month along with her salary, or in some separate arrangement?'

You defensively took a deep breath. You couldn't stand the interrogation. Especially since you were mostly clueless about your own finances. You had resisted evolving into a properly functioning grown-up, into someone who was in control and aware of his own dealings. You just didn't have a capacity for such things, keeping track of sums and figures. Instead of trying, you have altogether refrained from such basic responsibilities, expecting others to do your work. You act as if you're still a teenager living at home, or that self-absorbed artist you once were, content with existing in some delusional bubble.

'Looking at your company bank statements, I haven't discovered any separate, regular payments made to Ms Compton apart from her salary – which, as you also very kindly pointed out, she receives on a monthly basis.'

Your last accountant couldn't take it. Having found more straightforward clients to assist, he took off eighteen months ago.

All of a sudden, feeling hot, you discard your jacket. A craving for nicotine passes through your mind. Then you remember your loose financial arrangement with Eloise.

'No. As odd as this may sound to you, to this day I haven't paid her a penny for her sale-related earnings. Whenever I bring it up she insists I needn't rush. I guess money isn't a motivating factor for some people.'

Looking unimpressed by your answer, he nodded. You were two different species of the human race, operating in very different modes. It was unlikely he could make sense of your choices.

'Of course, I intend to pay her what she has rightfully earned. Eloise is an exceptionally devoted employee; I'm very lucky to have her.'

'He that trusts much, obliges much.'

Annoyed, you looked up and directed him a quizzical glance.

'Mr Huxley, it shows on your company bank records that eighteen months ago you authorised Ms Compton direct access to the account.'

'That sounds about right. I promoted her to gallery manager. I no longer had an accountant in charge of paying people's monthly salaries, so I gave her the task,' you dully explained, doubtful this was going to lead to anything meaningful.

'Have you been keeping track of your business account in these past eighteen months?'

'Not religiously, no,' you said, fiddling with the tip of one of your slightly overgrown nails.

You really couldn't care less; you pictured the unopened bank statements you occasionally came across. Recognising their uniform envelopes, you never bothered to open them. You hadn't a clue what eventually became of them. Did they get filed? Were they accumulated somewhere in their unopened state, or even chucked out?

'You have also authorised an expense account for Ms Compton. Have you been monitoring her spending, Mr Huxley?'

Oh, Jesus Christ! Here we go again. The grilling. You felt like you were seated before the school headmaster. Your impulse to act up was naturally rekindled.

'*Nope.* Running a gallery is a multifaceted venture, *Clive.* I have exceptionally close ties with my artists. Not only do I assist them in their quests to create something profoundly unique and enduring, I practically run their lives for them. I work night and day to promote their artistic vision. I arrange solo shows at the most esteemed public spaces, at established, trendy galleries across the globe. I sell their brilliant photography to rock stars and movie legends – so they get to hang on the right walls. I make sure the shows they put on at my gallery get extensive coverage in the *Guardian*'s and *FT*'s art sections, and in leading art magazines, so they get the right kind of exposure. So they are regarded as hip and as hugely significant and influential. These things just don't happen overnight. It takes months, even years, of dedicated input. You have to understand it's impossible for me to do what I'm doing, and be expected to play detective. That's why I've hired you.'

You sounded like a complete tosser, when the fellow was merely trying to do his job. The overstated, boastful drivel – this wasn't you.

Exhausted, you leaned back on the chair and dropped your shoulders. You wished you could have postponed the meeting. Be somewhere else. Then you remembered Ada. Your mood eased up a bit. You were glad you were going to see her tonight.

'Very well,' he responded, not letting his professionalism slip. 'Then should I assume you might not be aware that the credit limit of the company card under her name has been very generously set up to your company's credit limit of thirty thousand pounds?'

'Blimey! That's awfully nice of me.' You pulled your face into an exaggerated expression and giggled nervously. You had a vague recollection of signing some standard bank forms.

'Well, the young lady has nearly reached that limit.'

You felt like you had just been stabbed in the chest. 'What?'

'I'm afraid so.'

He paused and tilted his head downwards, looking over his glasses straight into your eyes. 'This is merely the tip of the iceberg.'

You gestured for him to carry on.

'You have three huge in-trays full of outstanding invoices. I spent most of the previous week on the phone chasing after your clients. It turns out Ms Compton gave them huge, false discounts. Many of the two separate invoices she had to prepare for each sold item – one for the gallery's own records and the other for the client – don't match. Every single client I have spoken to was very surprised to hear from me. They naturally assumed they had paid the full amount of the artwork they acquired from you months ago.'

'Fuck!' You shifted uncomfortably in your chair, trying to come to terms with it. For a moment, your father's response when you had told him you were opening up a gallery echoed in your mind, like an obvious prognosis you had ignored.

Someone like you should never attempt to manage a business on their own.

Your accountant sighed, then added, with a pitying look on his face, 'I'm afraid the unpaid deficit this has left behind not only amounts to many thousands of pounds, but also puts your company's finances in an inextricable mess.'

You couldn't believe this was happening to you. 'But why would she do something like that?'

He shrugged.

You could feel your pulse inside your throat; you began frenziedly shaking your legs. You hungrily bit chunks from the skin around your nails. Until now, you had been turning a complete blind-eye to your misgivings about Eloise. Yet deep down, you knew she was a crowd pleaser, a fucked-up megalomaniac. You pictured her Instagram account, filled with her sexed-up selfies. You visualised her desperate, slutty dance moves at art events that had shifted to the dance floor. She was a manipulator. No, worse – she was a liar! You remembered how the Turner prize nominee Nigel Tyler, a close friend of hers, had come to you to complain that she was telling everyone he had gifted her a massive painting when he never had.

Eloise had a talent for making people feel special. That's why clients loved her. That's why Nigel was still her friend. One of your most important clients had once told you he thought she was full of shit – but he still called her up when he felt like acquiring another photograph for one of his many homes. She knew how to sugar-coat everything. She could sell anything to anyone.

Surely that was a remarkable gift. Or was it, in fact, the seamless workings of a con artist? She could probably convince people a close-up photo of a cat licking its butthole was cutting-edge photography. That was the kind of persuasive power she had. You knew all of this, yet you still entrusted her with your finances. You needed someone to run the business, do the legwork, while you got high and did all the fun stuff. It was convenient for you to fall under her spell. And so you happily provided her with an entry pass into the highly exclusive art world, and the platform from which she would dazzle collectors, become best buddies with artists and toffee-nosed curators. All this, when she was just a provincial English girl with a second-rate university degree – but smart and sassy, and adamant to up her game.

Her sisterly, tactile ways had easily won you over. Her bossiness and professional attitude had given you the illusion she was competent. Though you had sensed she was a backstabbing bitch from the way she slandered the other girls in the gallery. You ignored the warning bells when her old landlord from Norwich tracked her down and called the gallery one day to reclaim the three months' rent she hadn't paid before vanishing. You chose to believe her – that it was a total misunderstanding – when, in hindsight, to deceive, steal and run was her normal behaviour. All along, you had been under the delusion you were a great team, and that she had your back no matter what. What a complete idiot you had been.

'There's one more thing,' Clive said. He rested himself against his chair and adjusted his tie. 'Looking at your company's more recent transactions, I came across a few substantial payments made to a Blue Seahorse Limited based in Guernsey. I did some research, and the company is under Ms Compton's name.'

'What makes her think she could get away with something like that?'

You already sort of knew the answer. She probably assumed – since you had your head so high up your arse – she could take the socks from off your feet, and you would never notice.

He shrugged, then said, 'Maybe she's got it all carefully figured out. Or maybe she's in some delusional state. Who knows? In my thirty-five years in this profession, I've pretty much seen it all.'

You were destroyed. You were furious. You felt like leaping out of your chair and kicking something, anything, but you remained still. What disturbed you the most was that, at the very back of your mind, you had suspected Eloise could get up to something like this. It was a rational suspicion that you had gagged before it had evolved into a proper thought, the way you always declined to open your monthly bank statements. Instead of listening to your gut, you had chosen to look the other way.

Like the way you remained silent when you watched Rex insult and try to break down the young pretty things he pulled every quasi-chivalrous tactic to lure into his web. You couldn't admit it, but you felt pathetic and dishonourable for not coming to their defence. Deep down, you felt nearly as vile as him for not having the decency, for once in your life, to voice your disapproval to his face. For all he knew, you couldn't care less – and, considering the slight, nervous smile appearing on the side of your lips each time, he was probably under the illusion that you found his despicable behaviour entertaining. You looked up to Rex and were afraid to disappoint him, to lose his friendship. Just as you were afraid of finding out what lay in those bloody statements. You thought that if you didn't face up to what was inside those sealed envelopes, if you refrained from thinking about their looming reality, they would somehow disappear altogether.

That had also been your strategy with Tabitha. You had refused to own up to your hunch that she was having an affair with her former history lecturer. After many years, out of the blue, Oliver had reached out to her through her publishers. In his brief but friendly email, he had written that he just wished to say 'hi' and was also wondering whether they could meet for coffee so he could run a few things by her – get her opinion on some plot ideas; he was writing a period novel. *No one would want to publish it. But still, it would be nice to catch up after all these years*, he had written.

At first Tabitha was reluctant to meet up. She didn't see the point of it. He had never been a friend. He would probably attempt to shag her again, and she no longer had the patience to be subjected to such nuisance. In your relationship, neither of you (at least on the surface) had any issue sharing details of past flings. Tabitha had given you a full account of their history. She had harboured a small crush on Oliver in the third year of uni, when she had taken up history. Unlike her other male lecturers, he was dashing and young, with Hugh Grant-like floppy hair. Keen to find out whether he was straight – and, if so, available and interested – she would occasionally throw him meaningful glances while tolerating his colourless lectures about the Reformation.

Her efforts had eventually paid off. One day, in the middle of a student–tutor meeting in his tight corner office, he had declared, after a long, charged pause, that he was terribly attracted to her. The bold declaration, which could easily have seen him barred from academic life, had been followed by drinks at a pub in Bloomsbury, and had ended with a drunken snog by a bus stop. The whole thing had very quickly fizzled out; Tabitha had realised she didn't properly fancy him. For her, their *thing* had been nothing other than an exercise in seduction, a brief quest into realising her fantasy of having sex with a lecturer – which, she would find, wasn't that difficult to achieve.

About a fortnight after the email through her publishers, Tabitha had a change of heart. She thought it would be impolite not to offer to help. She was married with kids, and he had probably settled down in a similar domestic arrangement. There was no harm in meeting for a quick coffee somewhere central. She already knew he wasn't the type to pester her. The few close friends she had at uni had all moved abroad to pursue different paths. Although she heard from them occasionally, it had been ages since she had last seen any of them. It would be nice to encounter someone from that period of her life. She was curious to find out what he had been up to, if he had changed at all, and how.

It turned out Oliver was still teaching at the same university, but had recently become a professor, and regularly taught as a visiting senior lecturer at other universities across Europe. Such frequent travel had its consequences, of course. He had unintentionally fathered a son in Amsterdam with one of his ex-students. These days, he made monthly trips there to visit the toddler and the mother of his child, whom he claimed he maintained an open relationship with.

He had written several books and plenty of scholarly articles on political thought during the Modern Era; the backdrop to his still-in-progress historical fiction was the revolutions of 1848. He reckoned times of drastic social change were a perfect setting for a period saga.

You and Tabitha both had several friends of the opposite sex (some of them long-term exes) – quite a few of whom you got together with along with spouses, others whom you met up with separately – so initially you saw no reason to interfere when they started seeing each other every month or so.

And besides, you had no right to. You didn't own Tabitha; she didn't own you. The freedom you granted each other from day one had been cultivated by a mutual understanding that neither of you would ever cheat. Yet, however hard you tried to hide your actions from her, over your seven-year marriage your recurring drug- and alcohol-fuelled escapades had gradually but steadily corroded her already fragile trust in you. By the time Oliver came into the picture, Tabitha had completely lost her confidence in you and your marriage. She no longer believed you would give up the heavy partying, or that you were able to keep your pants on once you got as high and hammered as you did.

And she hadn't been entirely wrong. One time you'd lapsed and snogged this hot crazy chick inside a dark bathroom at Rex's. The next time, when she threw herself at you again, you had given in a bit more, intimating you could go along with a blowjob. But she had refused and insisted she wanted you inside her. You had walked off, incredibly regretful the next day of your near-miss, of having almost breached the pledge you had made to Tabitha, but also the promise you had made to yourself to never be unfaithful. At the time, you had still been deeply in love with your wife. You believed in your unity and couldn't imagine life without her. Even though her mood swings and the unnecessarily strict attitude she could sometimes adopt were difficult to handle, Tabitha was the kindest person you knew. As much as you admired her artistic, rebellious soul and her sense of humour, it was the real compassion she could harbour towards just about anyone that had ultimately won you over.

You knew that if you broke your pledge and let your high libido run loose, you could easily see yourself bonking every bird you found moderately attractive. You couldn't live like that and stay married. Still, you had cheated on Tabitha by lying to her, by denying what you got up to, letting her down over and over with your excessive partying. You had promised her countless times – right up to the day of your marriage, and then every time your regular relapses set off new disputes between you – that you were going to do away with the drugs and the mindless drinking for good. Each time, you had meant what you had said, and on a few rare occasions you had miraculously managed to turn down a night of excess. But on the whole, you hadn't kept your word to her. In fact, all these years, you had laid the groundwork for her to be unfaithful to you.

She had sat you down one evening after putting the kids to bed and bluntly opened up to you about her affair with Oliver. Tabitha was not one to mince her words. She said the affair had developed very organically; she referred to it as something that was meant to be, although she no longer believed any relationship could last forever.

'Everything has a sell-by date.'

11

You emerged into a bustling, crowded main street in Soho. It was around five thirty, but the late autumn sky had already turned pitch-black. Touristy types were wandering about, cafés and bars were packed with people, and restaurants were getting busier by the minute. You walked amongst the hustle, feeling beaten up, miserable and out of place. The divorce and now this: the life you had set up for yourself was crumbling into pieces, as if it had always been a forced endeavour, never meant to stand the test of time.

You watched the people around you. You found it odd that everyone else seemed to be getting on with their business as if nothing had changed. You couldn't acknowledge that what had happened to you was a mere speck in the grand scheme of things. You couldn't see that this too would pass.

You thought of calling Tabitha, but you couldn't do it. Considering the seriousness of your troubles, you knew she would listen and show you some sympathy. But the insurmountable hostility between you prevented you from making the call. You had to accept she was no longer a partner, a close friend. What if you called your half-brother Tristan, who looked up to you and regarded you as some big shot in the art world? Or Rex? He was most likely at home, on a conference call to LA or New York – if he wasn't already getting drunk with some movie-star wannabes or another sleazy film producer like himself at Claridge's Bar. You could hop in a cab, join him, and spew every revolting detail of what had happened to you. What if you rang Quinn instead? As someone in the same profession, but savvier and more accomplished, he could give you crucial advice about what steps to take next – how to fix it. The names of a few other friends cropped up in your mind, but you couldn't bring yourself to dial their numbers. No man with half a wit could get himself into such a mess. You were too embarrassed to disclose to any of them how devastatingly you had cocked things up.

So you called Andy, your dealer. Andy sounded chirpy, as always. He asked you whether you wanted *the usual*. You said yes. Andy lived in a flat somewhere in Notting Hill. He asked you to meet him in front of the Electric Cinema in half an hour. You hailed the empty black cab driving towards you.

When you got there, you saw him standing under the gentle rain with his hood on, slouching, his hands hidden inside the deep pockets of the black anorak he always wore. As the cab came to a halt, you fumbled with your loose coins, dropped some on the floor, then settled the fare with a scrunched-up note you found in one of your pockets. Amidst all this you noticed Andy rocking his body from side to side, as he always did, occasionally monitoring his surroundings. Andy was a good guy. Over the years you had gotten to know him, his earnest nature, combined with his seemingly trivial existence, had made you feel pity for him. You suspected he was some years older than you. His limp and slightly hunched back gave the impression he was schlepping along in the body of a pensioner. Though, quite refreshingly, he had the mental makeup of a boy of thirteen.

'It's good to see you, Lucian,' he said, greeting you cheer-fully in falsetto, and with a loose handshake, while he subtly passed over the merchandise. You asked him if he had time for a drink. He nodded keenly. You weren't generally in the habit of inviting him for anything other than a cigarette. You mostly met at your gallery, usually on the day of an opening or before any other night you'd be gearing yourself up to go completely off the rails. After being greeted by one of the girls at the front desk, he would be sent to your office. You would chat for ten minutes or so. He usually made observations or asked basic questions about the new exhibition on display, or asked after Tabitha and the kids like a close family friend, although he had never met them. For some reason, you always were slightly worried Andy would outstay his welcome – even if he never had so far – possibly because you always, come rain or shine, suggested having a 'quick fag' in front of the gallery before sending him off.

Andy excitedly suggested going to his local pub. The two of you headed towards Ladbroke Grove, and eventually entered a tatty pub, at a street corner, mostly inhabited by rough, working-class types.

Andy said, limping slightly ahead of you, 'You know, there was an article in the *Evening Standard* about the Fair yesterday and it made me think of you. I thought to myself, he's probably there.'

'You thought right,' you responded after a deep, troubled sigh.

You had forgotten about the bloody Fair. Tomorrow was its last day. Were you even planning to make an appearance? Since leaving the accountant's office, your mind had kept running ruthless revenge plots against Eloise which you already knew you would never follow through on.

You were going to hire some thugs to terrorise her. You were hoping Pawel might know a gang of Poles who could do the job. If not, you were sure Rex, through one of his dodgy business associates, could help you liaise with those sorts of people. East End thugs or Russian gangsters operating underground in London. You could have Eloise raped and tortured and have one of her hands amputated. Wasn't that the penalty for stealing in Saudi Arabia?

You had a meeting at noon the next day with a solicitor your accountant had referred you to. Over the phone, he had firmly advised you not to take any drastic action, legal or otherwise, against Eloise – apart from calling your bank immediately to freeze your business account along with the credit card under her name. He had urged you to be very discreet and not to do anything you might regret until you had a chance to properly discuss your options with him.

If you did decide to go to the Fair in the morning, was there any way you could act normal in front of Eloise? And, if so, could it end up being your most convincing performance to date?

'Let's grab those two,' you said, pointing at a couple of stools by the bar, miraculously still empty.

'It must be really exciting, the Fair. All those collectors, those wealthy people, those trendy, famous artists. Are there any pretty girls?' Andy eagerly asked as soon as you both sat down.

'Yes, plenty.'

'Do you ever get to meet any of them?'

'Sometimes, if I get lucky,' you replied, thinking of Ada. Earlier today, at the Fair, you had gone near Quinn's booth. You had positioned yourself at the corner of the booth it faced, out of Quinn's field of vision. Luckily, he had been too preoccupied with clients to catch a glimpse of you. You had watched Ada for a while. Just like the very first time you had laid eyes on her, she was seated behind the desk, typing something up on her laptop.

You're looking terribly busy. Why not lift your head for a moment and look around? you had texted. With voyeuristic pleasure, you had watched the shift in her expression as she got hold of her phone and immediately looked up. Once her feline eyes had tracked you down, you had stared and smiled at each other. You had wiggled your fingers at her before taking off.

The prospect of seeing her again was the only thing that let you set aside the legal and financial nightmare that was about to take over your life. Despite your shock and disillusionment, you were still looking forward to seeing her.

'I've always had a better knack for chasing pussy than selling photography,' you admitted.

Wearing a coy grin on his face, Andy flashed his eyes at you, like an adolescent boy simultaneously embarrassed and aroused by any sexual comment made in his presence.

'Why don't you come to the Fair tomorrow? I can arrange a collector's pass so you don't have to pay at the entrance.'

'Really?' he said, his droopy eyes widening with excitement.

'By all means.'

'I'd love to come, Lucian. Even if I don't get to meet any of the pretty girls, I can look at all the art, though I doubt that I'd understand much of it.'

'Nor do the rest, Andy, nor do the rest,' you mumbled, at the same time signalling to grab the elusive barman's attention.

He had a pen tucked behind his ear and was chewing gum. Soon he came over, took your orders, then served you your drinks.

'I think I've got myself into a very deep puddle. No, it's more like a very deep pit,' you said, feeling the malty bitterness of the stout that had streamed down your throat moments ago. Andy gave you a vacant stare and took a gulp from his pint. He turned around briefly to glance at the silent game of football on the TV. A few people sat quietly in front of the small set, eyes glued to the screen. You took a sip from the short glass of neat bourbon and then tapped it against the counter.

'The gallery is in big trouble.'

'I'm really sorry to hear that, Lucian. I really am,' he said, sweeping a few leftover crumbs on his side of the counter with slightly trembling fingers.

'Good old Eloise has been cleaning me out, right under my nose. Can you fucking believe it?'

Andy nodded. He often chatted with Eloise and the other girls when he came to visit you at the gallery.

'I believed in her, I trusted her. I was a complete idiot,' you said, resting your elbow on the counter, then rubbing your face with one hand. 'I was naive. I let it happen. It's all my fault and now I'm completely *fucked*!'

You looked over at Andy. He said nothing.

'She forged invoices and stole thousands off me. The gallery is in huge debt.'

Andy just nodded at you, then began drawing lines with his finger in the condensation on the outside of his pint glass. It was like talking to a wall.

'For heaven's sake! Have you not heard a single word?'

You sensed a few heads turning in your direction. Andy hid his head inside his zipped-up anorak.

'I'm *really* sorry,' you said. 'It's just...'

He nodded. 'I'm really sorry too, Lucian. It's awful you're having such a bad time. I just don't know what to say. I don't understand much about business and stuff,' he responded, his falsetto deprived of its usual vigour and cheerfulness.

You looked out through the windows. There was a crowd of smokers accumulating outside the pub. You were so fucking confused. You didn't know who to feel more pity for – yourself or Andy.

'Listen, I don't expect you to give me any financial or legal advice...' You were about to say *I just need to talk to a friend* – but Andy wasn't your friend. He was your drug dealer and, worse, a fucking retard. 'I'm sorry; I shouldn't have reacted like that. It so happens I'm having an exceptionally bad day.'

'It's OK, Lucian,' he answered, nodding his head again.

Attempting to take a few deep breaths, you found you couldn't inhale properly for a moment. You pushed your fingers into the centre of your ribcage.

'Are you all right, Lucian?'

You told yourself to snap out of it, then knocked back the entire bourbon. 'I've genuinely made a huge mess of things. In the past I was so scared of failing that I used to give up on things, give up on myself. Now that I've finally buggered up in such a massive way it's almost a fucking relief.'

Andy nodded.

'Who knows? Maybe I should close the gallery and start all over again.'

'So you'll open a new gallery?'

'What? No, no, I doubt that I'll be doing that again. I've figured out that, like you, I'm not particularly good at the business side of things.'

'I guess it's not everybody's cup of tea, is it?'

'No, I don't believe it is.'

'What will you do next, then, Lucian?'

You didn't know how to respond. You told Andy you were going to nip downstairs to the loo to powder your nose.

You locked yourself into the only cubicle in the men's toilet and took out the small, neatly sealed sack. You drew a long thick line of white powder across the toilet lid. Then, just as you knelt down, holding a shortened straw between your fingertips, you remembered how edgy it could make you feel, particularly if you were in a bad mood, and not sufficiently drunk. If you met up with Ada in such a state, you would be unable to connect with her on any level. At this point you couldn't tell if what you had could become anything more than a fling. All you were certain of was that you didn't want to jeopardise your chance with her. Particularly after what you had been through with Tabitha. You couldn't bear the thought of your life being a series of identical cock-ups. Although you had hit bottom, a little voice inside you said you were better than that, and you wished to believe it.

In a gesture of brusque resolve, you wiped the line of coke away with the side of your hand and remained there on your knees, watching the white powder immediately descend.

'Merry fucking Christmas,' you whispered, before flushing the loo and rushing back upstairs.

'I don't think I'm in the right frame of mind for this.'

You ducked your fist inside Andy's pocket. As your fingers let go of the small, rectangular thing you understood why he favoured keeping his anorak on at all times; it was hosting a handsome quantity of identical little packets.

'You can keep it aside for me, can't you?' At that point you were unable to admit to yourself that as soon as the restlessness and boredom set in again, you'd be eagerly dialling his number.

He nodded obediently.

You took a fifty-pound note out of your wallet. He didn't refuse it when you slipped it tactfully into his hand.

'I'm too wired as it is. If you're not in a good place in your head, that stuff can take you to the sewers.'

Andy claimed never to touch drugs, so you weren't entirely sure if he was able to personally relate to your concerns.

You stayed at the pub for another ten minutes or so. It was Andy who did most of the talking. He talked about a couple of birds that had recently made a nest on a sheltered spot on his roof. Apparently, these days he spent the mornings monitoring their actions from his top-floor bedroom window. Just to appear interested, you asked him what species they were.

'They're just birds,' he responded.

Parting with Andy, you were hit by a profound sadness. Unloved, abandoned and stabbed in the back – you had no one to turn to. You had never felt this lonely. What had you done to end up in such a lousy, miserable place? The little sense of purpose you had had been snatched from right under your feet. You were in freefall, desperately searching for something to cling to.

As you turned into an affluent part of Notting Hill with its multicoloured houses, you nearly slipped on something soft.

When you looked back and saw the trodden pile of mustard-yellow dog shit some dog owner hadn't bothered to pick up, you started laughing hysterically at yourself. You laughed but also wept, rapidly switching between the two states until you were mostly weeping.

You tried to wash off the gooey remnants stuck to the side of your shoe in a small puddle of rainwater, then lit yourself a cigarette. You were a survivor. The ardour to carry on, however faint, was still inside you. It had kept you going despite your insecurities and limitations. Everything you had embarked on you had done so with some level of earnest passion and commitment. That's why (apart from your fucking father) others had believed in you, even if you never fully believed in yourself. That's why Tabitha had agreed to marry you, why your artists looked up to you, and why your gallery had gained its place in the London art scene as a respectable and relevant venue for art photography, though it had just been properly proven that you had absolutely no fucking clue how to run a business.

You walked back to the main road that ran uphill. It buzzed with cars. Was there any point pouring some of your inheritance dosh that lived in a Swiss bank account into the gallery's account, if things got to that? You felt you had had enough, and saw little sense in trying to salvage something that had so hopelessly failed. Knowing how difficult it was to gain a living from one's art, to be taken seriously as an artist, you were devoted to promoting your artists, building them the career you never had.

Engaging in in-depth dialogues about art, with artists or clients, took you back to your student years at the RCA – a time in your life when you finally felt *in your element*, and making art was all that ever mattered. But, apart from that, the gallery was a half-hearted venture for you. It had been kickstarted as a futile attempt to gain your egotistical, narrow-minded father's approval – when the only thing that would've satisfied his expectations would have been for you to prove your loyalty by working under him. Or, if not that, going for a more traditional, solid profession: becoming a barrister, or a doctor, or even an accountant. It had been four and a half years since he had passed on, and you still continued to foster the scrutiny and disapproval with which he used to observe your every action.

Your phone rang just as you climbed into the back of a cab. Dog-tired, you reluctantly picked up the phone.

'What ya doing?'

You sighed and looked out of the window.

'I'm in a cab.'

'Where you heading?'

You had given the driver the address moments ago, but still you had to remind yourself.

'Camden Town. To Ed's for a studio visit.'

Ironically, this had been an engagement you had been anticipating for days.

'Ooh, nice. How's he been?'

You sensed a bit of an echo in Rex's voice. You wondered whether he was perched on the loo.

'I'll soon find out.'

After a long pause, he asked, 'What ya wearing?' in a silly, flirty tone. It was obvious he was stoned and bored out of his brain.

'Cut it out.' You sounded beat, unamused, even to your own ears.

There was another long pause.

'It feels like you don't wanna talk to me – I can hang up, ya know.'

You rolled your eyes.

'Where are you?' you asked, hoping to veer him off the needy-annoying talk, but he was too sharp and headstrong to be led anywhere.

'I'm at home. *All by myself.* Apparently, no one wants to talk to me tonight; not even you, my one and only true friend – it's a catastrophe!'

You heard panting and hiccups. At first, you couldn't figure out what was happening. Then you realised he was pretend-sobbing again. It was as annoying as the one other time you had been subjected to it. You sighed. You cringed. This was the last thing you needed.

'I thought you had plans for tonight,' you mumbled, while he carried on sobbing unconvincingly.

'It's been cancelled,' he eventually responded in a whiny, childlike voice. There was something profoundly disturbing about an old man pretending to cry like an infant. It carried a sexual connotation you couldn't put your finger on. You looked out of the window, this time able to recognise the part of London you happened to be passing through. Rex had probably spent the whole afternoon on conference calls, smoking pot inside his unventilated study.

'What's the occasion for your visit?' he asked, reverting to his normal manner of speech. You were glad the nonsense was over.

'He's going to show me his latest work.'

'Yippy yoo... the golden goose has *finally* laid his egg. Can I come?'

'If you like.'

As much as you refused to admit it to yourself, you always felt a hint of privilege when Rex accompanied you somewhere. After all, his arthouse movies had been the backdrop to your youth – and, during your years as a university student, part of the cultural heritage that had defined the period. It was very difficult for you to separate the seriously flawed individual from the creative visionary whose cinematic achievements were bound to go down in history.

And besides, you were sure Ed wouldn't mind. They had already met once at one of your gallery dinners. You knew Ed would be flattered to show his new collection to the likes of Rex. You couldn't think of anyone, really, who would turn down the opportunity to get to know someone like him.

'I'm expected for supper. I'm sure Ed could produce an extra plate—'

'I'm full as a barrel. I'll come by a bit later. I've already eaten everything there is to eat inside my fridge. I'm contemplating throwing up.'

'Oh—'

He hung up.

There was congestion through Marylebone. The driver was bored and tried to start up a conversation. Met by your grunts and silent nods, he quickly gave up.

You googled your gallery's name and glanced at the images that came up. Installation shots from shows, pictures of yourself with artists at openings. You even came across a couple of pictures of fucking Eloise latching onto some collectors and brazenly pouting at the camera. What kind of false reality did these images represent? Success? Longevity? By the time you arrived at Ed's front door, you were questioning what the hell you were doing there.

III

'Lucian.'

'It's about time, you old queen!'

Ambling through his front door, you briefly stopped in your tracks to give his hand an earnest shake. Ed is your most prized artist. He could easily ditch you tomorrow and go with one of the corporate biggies in Mayfair. Some of these had branched out by acquiring a second gallery in an edgier (and less expensive) part of town. A warehouse-like venue where they could organise more ambitious exhibitions that could just about compete with well-funded public exhibitions. Some had even opened galleries or acquired viewing rooms at prime locations in New York, Hong Kong, and Zurich, just to prove they could – and to reach out to A-list clients overseas. You are certain they have approached him behind your back multiple times with lucrative offers. But, having endured being treated as nothing more than a very profitable commodity, Ed has stayed loyal to you so far. To have him on board since the early beginnings of your gallery has been a great boost to your confidence and your gallery's profile.

With you, he has the advantage of being treated as an individual. Of getting to have the final say. Sometimes he works as long as a year on a single photograph, finely manipulating the image with digital technology's latest tricks, to configure further ties between painting and photography.

Straight after his last exhibition in 2013, consisting merely of three massive aerial shots of English fields, brutally photoshopped to resemble Mondrian's abstractions, he had vanished for about six months. Next, you heard through a mutual artist friend that he had checked into a meditation retreat in Cambodia, trying to delve into his own truth. Upon his return, he looked fit and revitalised. Wearing eye-catching string bracelets around his thin wrist, he had dropped by the gallery and talked – in a roundabout way, as he tended to do – of his intention to explore new ideas.

'I want to embark upon a routine procedure – something we've become immune to the reality of – and turn it into a visual spectacle.'

For ages, you hadn't heard from him – until a few days ago, when he had called to say he had a new series of photographs he wanted to show you.

'My, you look like you've had a rough one. Is everything alright?'

'Never been better!' you responded, defensively jaunty.

He paused to observe you again, then, drawing a little closer, he added, 'She's downstairs in the kitchen. Very lovely girl indeed.'

He went off and shut the front door, then asked if you would like a drink.

'I'll have what you're having,' you answered, squeezing yourself past his enormous bike, which leaned at a wide angle against the wall. Keen to get to her, you carried on down the long corridor, then down the glass-panelled staircase.

You poked your head quietly through the doorframe. Like the compositions Vermeer had painted, depicting young women performing simple household tasks, you found Ada immersed in setting the table. You watched her carefully fold a paper napkin, then place it beside one of the forks. It took about five seconds for her to sense she was being watched.

'Hi.'

She coyly tensed and raised her shoulders and smiled at you. Everything aside, you were happy to see her again.

The floor-to-ceiling windows were covered in dense steam and the place stank, a fusion of food smells that had combined into one heavy stench. It was only a matter of seconds before your nose was immune to it. You watched her pull out another paper napkin, fold it, and stretch across the table.

'Awfully nice of you to be helping out.'

She shrugged, as if to say it wasn't a big deal, and smiled. All the same, her shy ways couldn't conceal her chirpy mood. You figured she was happy to see you again.

You wrapped your arm around her waist, and pulled her towards you, as if you were about to whisk her off somewhere. Taken aback by your sudden gesture, she let out a light shriek, then laughed briefly at her own reaction. You kissed her lips again and again, deeply inhaling and exhaling between each kiss. You sensed her fingers running through your hair as she eagerly reciprocated. It seemed there were no longer any barriers between you.

'You seem different today,' you whispered into her ear. Your lips embraced one another at short intervals, while her fingers caressed the back of your stiff neck.

'So do you,' she eventually whispered back.

Loosening your grip, you asked, 'Do I? In what way?'

She paused, and then replied, 'I don't know. You look quite tired.'

'Oh, crikey,' you responded, letting go.

'You looked tired yesterday, too, but today you look even...'

'Worse?'

You both chuckled at your lousy state. At her pitiless honesty. Trying to contain a giggle, she added, 'I didn't mean it like that—'

'Yes, you did. You should speak your mind more often. It suits you.'

She smiled.

'And besides, I can live with a little criticism, coming from you,' you said, the arousing memory of your intimacy spontaneously coming to mind.

'What's different about me?' she asked, tilting her head to one side.

'You seem much more open.' You wished you could just rest your head on her shoulder and remain that way for a while. 'I've missed you,' you added, twirling a lock of her curls around your finger.

She caressed your cheek, smiled shyly, then looked away. You wished you could just tell her everything. Just come out with it all. You looked around the spacious open-plan kitchen. The sink and the L-shaped counter were covered with unwashed pots and utensils; bundles of peeled vegetables; scraps of other foods. Ed always took his assignments very seriously.

'What if we never get bored?'

'Of what?' she asked naively.

'Each other.'

She shrugged timidly; her cheeks rapidly caught some colour. You knew you were coming on too strong. Letting go of the strand of hair, you began walking around, opening and slamming cupboard doors in search of anything that resembled an ashtray. You eventually came across an abandoned saucer inside the sink, camouflaged under a fluff of thinly peeled carrot skin. You rested your tired sorry arse on the edge of the sink, crossed your legs and lit up. Then the kitchen door swung wide open, and Ed entered, cradling a bottle of red in each arm.

'Don't smoke in my house.'

'Why? Have you given up?'

He sighed peacefully.

'I'm coming up on my third month.'

'Why did you have to do that?' You weren't even kidding. While you hardly ever paid a visit, Ed's happened to be one of those very rare abodes in which you could leisurely light up whenever, wherever. You were annoyed such precious freedom had now been taken away from you. Particularly on such a day.

'Lucian, darling, it's not only me. The entire world is giving up. Smoking, I'm afraid to say, is a self-degrading, pointless habit only practised by losers who've given up on themselves. You really ought to give it up before it gives you up.'

What the hell for? you thought, then rolled your eyes at him like a teenager. Smoking was something you just *did*. To put you off, a few self-righteous types had pointed out how chain-smoking had struck your beast of a father down at seventy-seven. Fortunately, your response, 'Everyone is eventually going to die of something,' was able to silence the most radical of health fanatics. Truth be told, you would consider it a triumph if you made it to his age. You took one last, deep drag, turned around, and drowned your fag under the running tap.

Ed and Ada went busily back and forth, bringing new things to the table. You pulled out a chair and sat yourself down. You regularly sipped from the large glass of red wine, which had been handed to you, while you talked about how exceptionally well the gallery had been doing at the Fair so far, mainly addressing Ed.

'People keep coming up to me and saying we've got one of the best displays,' you bragged, like an annoyingly cheerful fucker having his moment, desperately trying to keep up appearances, wired and hyper as if you had actually done that line back at the pub. Nervously shaking your legs, running a jittery finger over your greasy forehead, and relentlessly biting the loose skin from your lips, you kept yapping. You were afraid if you slowed down and let down your guard the truth might just slip out, as it tended to with you. There was no way you could reveal how stupidly you had fallen into Eloise's trap (she was practically a child, in Ed's eyes), and had failed the gallery and consequently him. You couldn't do that to the old faggot, to the artist you had never ceased to admire after all these years. His opinion of you mattered too much. You couldn't even begin to imagine how you would look him in the eye once he figured out he had been represented by a sloppy venture destined to go bust and vanish from popular memory.

'When do you intend to take us up to your studio?' you asked, unsure how, in your current state, you were going to hold out for an entire dinner.

Heading towards you, carrying two large plates of steaming beef stew, he said, 'I suggest we eat first.' It sounded a reasonable strategy – except you were pretty certain you couldn't stomach any food. Although you hadn't eaten anything since lunchtime, you sensed a barrier, a blockage, in your gullet.

Ada walked slowly towards you, carefully holding her plate with both hands. After she sat beside you, you looked at the piles of beef stew on everyone's plates. They were very dark, like cow pats, but runnier. You remained at the head of the table as Ed perched himself on the chair opposite her (leaping back to the counter at the very last minute to fetch the salt and pepper). Water was poured into glasses. Side dishes were cordially passed around. Steamed broccoli; roasted, caramel-ised carrots; crispy potatoes roasted in goose fat. To avoid appearing like an ungrateful git you helped yourself to a little of everything. Then you forced a piece of beef into your mouth. Repulsed by its rich aroma, you stopped inhaling through your nose and ended up sucking out all its juices, turning it into an unchewable gob that reminded you of the dense but soggy furballs your cat periodically brought up. You had to wash it down with wine and water after it got stuck halfway down your throat, like an obstinate piece of excrement refusing to be flushed away.

'Mmm,' Ada murmured between bites. 'It's delicious.' She was probably right. Ed was a highly able, dedicated cook who made seasonal jams and jellies and baked his own sourdough bread. If you opened the door to his tall freezer, you would see it packed with containers of homemade stock and apple purée.

'I'm glad to hear that. Do you like to cook, Ada?' he asked, seated in his usual uncompromisingly upright posture.

He had caught her with her mouth full. She covered her mouth demurely while continuing to chew, and shook her head.

'I'm sure you have more exciting things to do with your time,' he said, throwing a moment's teasing glance at you. You

238

realised that, apart from Tabitha, Ada was the first love interest you had invited to Ed's house. The last time you had paid a visit had been over two years ago. When he had asked you over to show you his latest work. At the time, you had been under the delusion you were in a solid relationship, and running a well-functioning, reasonably successful enterprise. What had made you so sure things would just carry on as they were? You wanted to laugh at yourself.

'Why waste your time in the kitchen, when at your age there's a world out there waiting to be explored?'

'Couldn't agree with you more,' you muttered, just to say something. You were starting to find it hard to keep up your high-spirited performance. You had nothing left to brag about. By this time, the shock, devastation and self-blame had completely drained you. The red wine wasn't helping, either. Nor was the exhaustion of the last two days. You felt like curling up in a ball somewhere.

You shoved another piece of beef into your mouth – and this time, without making a song and dance about it, you swallowed. You shoved another piece of meat in, then another. It was just something that had to be done. Then, bypassing the stodgy potatoes, you went for the carrots and the broccoli. You imagined each bulk of improperly chewed food as very visible lumps travelling down your neck. You drank what was left of your wine, not sparing the sediments. Desperate to start a conversation which could develop independently of you, you said, 'Come on! Tell us about Cambodia.'

'Well, all right.'

He talked about his days packed with meditation, yoga and healing sessions, and retreating to silence on a mountaintop.

The idea was to relax into the centre of one's being, to release the heaviness of the past, he explained.

You thought of the irony of all those people – most of them well-off Westerners – travelling as far as they did in a bid to get closer to who they were. For you, it was all hogwash, but Ada seemed intrigued and kept asking him questions. Soon they were having an animated discussion, sometimes finishing each other's sentences. You leaned over and poured more wine, occasionally nodding or making eye contact to appear mildly interested. By the time the topic had been sufficiently exhausted, Ed noticed that your plate was still more than half full.

'Lost your appetite, my dear?'

'Terribly sorry, Ed. I had a very late lunch.'

'I see.'

You rose from your chair and told them you were going out for a fag. You had to get away. As you didn't have a mountaintop to run off to, Ed's back garden would have to do.

'There's homemade apple crumble. Shall we wait for you?'

Too tired to play the game, feeling frail and fed-up, you shook your head.

Gesturing towards the glass door, he said, 'It's unlocked.'

Had it not been for Ada, you would've bailed at this point, saying you were suffering from some intolerable ailment and had to immediately go home and collapse into bed. Or maybe you would've already cancelled the meeting with a short apologetic text. You'd be back at your miserable flat snorting lines and getting pissed on whatever hard liquor helped take the edge off a little. Bourbon? Cognac? Or perhaps absinthe would be more appropriate this time.

When you stepped outside, the biting wind tore through each small opening in your shirt. Hard to bear at first, the cold revived you a little. You stared at the dark bushes at the end of the garden and the neighbouring houses. Only a few had light seeping through their curtained windows. *Other lives,* you said in your head as you lit up. The effect of the nicotine quickly spread, setting your bowels into light motion. Acknowledging that an endless configuration of human situations was happening independently of you made you feel even more desperately alone. Every drag left a sour-bitter taste in your mouth, and scratched a fine spot inside your throat. As with many things, your cigarette had failed to live up to its expectations.

You could no longer find it in yourself to ponder Eloise or the future of the gallery. It was as if you no longer cared. *Just fuck it,* you kept repeating to yourself. *Fuck it!* The anarchist in you thought, *Let it blow up; let it burn into ashes like the Hindenburg!*

Why did you need to validate your existence with achievements and financial success? What was the purpose of trying to prove yourself to anyone? Why did you have to pitch up at some workplace and carry out the same moronic tasks you had been carrying out year after year, like some brainwashed imbecile? It was *fucking madness!* You could get by, somehow, with what you had; earning a living was not a necessity for you. And, given there was a good chance you might have to shell out from your savings to cover the towering deficit – not to mention the massive legal fees the whole saga was bound to generate – it was better you refrained from any business ventures from this point onward. Permanently. You had had enough of trying to be *that* person. *Go fuck yourself!* you kept saying, though you weren't entirely sure whom you were addressing. Maybe anyone who was going to judge you for your massive cock-up, or the system itself, that made institutionalisation mandatory for everyone. *Just do me a favour and go fuck yourself!*

You were ready to pack your bags and take off. *I can live in a beach hut somewhere for the rest of my sodding life*, you reckoned. You knew you had it in you to give it all up. To extract yourself from all those meaningless, constraining social obligations and embrace idleness. That, or to altogether submerge yourself in the deep end of decadence and excess. Either way, you could finally devote yourself to *just living in the moment*. Particularly since it was going to be all over in the blink of an eyelid.

You could occasionally hear their voices. You turned around and saw Ed and Ada seated at the table, digging into their apple crumble. Deep down you knew the truth: no matter how hard one tried to create some sort of self-protective buffer by maintaining close friendships, and having children and life partners, ultimately everyone was on their own.

You snuck back into the warm kitchen, then pulled the sliding glass door shut behind you. You had caught them with their backs turned, carrying some plates over to the sink and chatting. Upon noticing you, Ed made a tongue-in-cheek comment you were too distracted to pay attention to. He had become touchy around the subject of smoking; perhaps he had referred to how you had managed to repress the dense odour of food with the trenchant smell of cigarette smoke (like some very effective skunk). Or perhaps he had said you would rather eat fags than food, or something in that spirit. Ada whispered something back to him, all smiles. Appearing amused by what was going on, you headed towards them.

'Look at *you*,' you remarked.

Ashamed that she'd joined Ed in his bid to take the piss, her gaze immediately escaped yours. She recoiled a little when you put your arm around her shoulders, but, immediately after, she snuggled up against you, resting her head on your chest. Your bodies fit together perfectly, as if they'd been made for it.

'You two make a handsome couple.'

'Easy now,' you said, though you were secretly pleased to hear it. Ada dug her head further into your chest like a restless puppy, skulking behind a curtain of hair.

'How I miss that wonderful buzz of something new, something unpredictable,' Ed added, gazing wistfully at the both of you.

Ed had been facing the world alone for many years – ever since his long-term boyfriend had left him. They had been discussing adoption. It had happened before he'd been introduced to you and had signed to your gallery. Ed had never spoken openly about the relationship and what had gone wrong. Assuming its memory was too painful to revisit, you had never asked. He would only bring up his ex's name very occasionally, referring to incidents that took place while they were still together. At his openings, there was always an entourage of toy boys following him around like a cloud of gnats, hanging on to his every word. He could bag someone the next day, if he weren't so bloody picky. He was in pursuit of the real thing.

'No, no. I haven't entirely lost all hope of finding love again. As they say, anything is possible. Even for a bony, ageing queer like me.'

You all chuckled. After opening another bottle and topping up everybody's wine glass, he led you to his studio on the very top floor. It was equipped with lanky lighting units, shelves of pricey lenses and cameras, and laptops with large hard-drives. Ed explained, walking you across the airy room, that one of the greatest revelations of his Cambodia trip had actually happened on his way back, at Phnom Penh airport, just before he boarded the plane to Bangkok en route to Heathrow.

'I was collecting my stuff from the security conveyer belt, relieved I wasn't going to miss my flight after being dragged through an endlessly long, desperately slow-moving queue.' Lowering his voice, he added, 'As much as the Cambodians are a warm and cheery bunch, I'm afraid efficiency isn't always high on their list.'

Ada gave him a polite smile. You felt sharp as a razor. The restlessness inside you was preventing you from succumbing to the effects of alcohol.

'Just as I was about to run off to find my gate, a vibrantly translucent X-ray on a computer screen grabbed my attention. Of course, I often caught a passing glimpse of these images on my travels. When an item passes through a scanner, what's projected onto the screen is a highly formalised interpretation of the truth. Everything is reduced to its most basic lines and to a very limited, though striking, range of colour – and into something that's strangely appealing to the eye. It's this stripping-back that intrigues me.'

You were curious to see what he had come up with this time. But knowing what you knew and withholding it from Ed made you feel like a fraudster who didn't deserve to be there.

You drank what was left, then put down your stained wine glass next to theirs.

'Right,' said Ed, rubbing his hands together, as if finally prepared to get on with it.

The shrill buzzer took you all by surprise. You glanced at each other.

'Maybe it's a Jehovah's Witness – mind you though, they're never this late. And when they do pitch up, I always say the only religion I might ever convert to one day is veganism, which *immediately* sends them running,' Ed said.

The buzzer rang again, this time more insistently.

'All right, all right,' he said, reluctantly shuffling his feet.

Finally, it hit you. '*Shit.*'

It probably wouldn't have been an issue if you had just remembered to *ask*, as a courtesy. You closed your eyes, covered the side of your face with one hand and rubbed your face, wanting somehow to expunge yourself from the situation. You tiredly admitted, 'It must be Rex.'

Ed looked at you, confused.

'I think I invited him over on my way here,' you mumbled. '*What?*'

From his terse response, you couldn't make out whether he was upset or just very surprised. He very briefly turned towards Ada, as if you were no longer in the room, and remarked, 'Something is up with this one today.'

'I couldn't say no. *I thought* I had already asked you. I don't know how, I must've completely forgotten!' you called out after him apologetically as he left the room, in a weak bid to explain yourself. Moments later, you could hear him in his politest voice, talking on the intercom, buzzing Rex in, then energetically galloping down the stairs to greet him.

Until now, you had always managed to maintain a seamlessly professional front in your dealings with Ed, which had provided the evidence that when you did try your very best, you were highly capable – a point of view that had now been crushed altogether. It felt like the final straw.

Provided you had warmed up your act, you *were* sufficiently able to hide your troubles behind gimmicky self-ridicule. Pretending that it was all a childish game for you, you covered your mouth, pulling a funny face at Ada, and remarked, 'Oops.'

'I don't think he's *that* upset about it, is he?' she asked with a look of concern.

'Beats me,' you replied, raising your eyebrows and shrugging. Even if he was, there wasn't much you could do about it now. She smiled softly, supportively.

'Come over here,' you whispered.

As soon as you took her in your arms, she pressed herself against you and dropped her head on your shoulder, as if she needed the reassurance of your embrace as much as you did. Further consoled by the scent rising from her hair, you closed your eyes, blocking out the occasional noises coming from other parts of the house. You wished you could be transported somewhere, just the two of you.

'This feels so good – so right – doesn't it?' you remarked in a sleepy voice, pressing her further against your chest, as if you were already between the sheets and could drift into sleep. You sensed her nod. When love struck, there was always an element of neediness in you – the need to fill that void present in so many casualties of turbulent parental divorce. This also manifested itself in your strong desire to escape the depressing monotony of day-to-day life, and to devote yourself to the high order of true love – as if it was the only thing that could save you from yourself. You would always plunge into relationships with full force, as if you had absolutely no time to waste.

Despite your cynical approach, when it came to *things that really mattered*, you were an irredeemable romantic at heart, as your dearest Mama had been. You believed in the healing and transforming power of art, as you did in serendipity and people's goodness. It must be why you referred to yourself as a *hopeful pessimist*.

You could no longer ignore the clatter of footsteps ascending the stairs but you continued to embrace each other as if it were just the two of you – you wished you could freeze the moment and remain like that for a while longer.

IV

'Oh my, look at these lovebirds!' you heard Rex say in an unconvincingly exaggerated Southern drawl. He loved doing impersonations of American accents, and didn't give a toss whether he got them right.

You immediately let go of each other. Seeing Rex's bloodshot eyes, you reckoned he must've smoked another spliff while being driven there – as he usually did before he came out to mingle.

'Yes, I know, I've been dying of envy the entire night,' Ed remarked.

'Behave yourselves,' you warned. You enjoyed the humour transmitting among you, but it had also set off an ominous feeling.

'Rich coming from you,' Rex shot back with a toothy grin. He paused and studied Ada with half-open eyes; you felt hers fixed on you. In this awkward moment, you vaguely noticed Ed slip away and head to the other end of the room to start laying things down.

Fuck! What were you thinking? Have you completely lost your fucking mind? Had your world not been completely turned on its head – causing you to suffer what had to be some form of temporary amnesia – there was absolutely no way you would've allowed Rex to tag along when Ada was present.

'I think the two of you have already met,' you said, nervously scratching your head, unable to strategise how to handle the situation. Knowing how Rex could be, there was the potential for the situation to get ugly.

'Of course we have!' the cunning old fox jumped in. Chivalrously bowing before her, he kissed the back of her hand. As the act grew uncomfortably long and intrusive, he watched her growing unease with delight. He leaned over to her and complained, 'You know, he always tries to hide them from me,' as if he was a chummy, avuncular character subtly warning her of the obvious dangers of falling for a guy like you.

'Even the ones you get to meet through me, eh? You ungrateful bastard!' he said, touching your cheek with his fist, as if badgering a spoilt youngster.

Glancing at her, you shook your head several times, letting out a tired sigh, to emphasise that these were the absurd ramblings of an old geezer. Her expression remained deadpan.

'But luckily, *in your case*, he's not so hung up about it,' he said, ogling her from head to toe, deluded enough to believe he might actually have a chance with her. Then he turned to you. Still struggling to lift his heavy eyelids, he said, 'Well, is it a lie?'

You didn't respond. Instead, you observed her. This time you interpreted her impassiveness as a kind of withdrawal from you. Rex's stupid comments were getting to her.

Feeling on edge, you looked away. Ed was carrying a large folder over to the rectangular table at the far end of the room. Rex took a swig from his neat whisky. He was only warming up.

'I'll be flying to your hometown, Cons-tan-ti-no-ple, next week,' he bragged, like the world was his little oyster – which it sort of was.

'What for?' you butted in, a tad envious.

'I'm meeting my author there to go over a few loose ends on the script,' he replied. 'His novel is the basis for my new flick,' he added, this time addressing Ada, in case she hadn't already grasped who he was and what he did for a living. 'He was the Egypt correspondent for the *FT* during the revolts at Tahrir Square, and thus came the inspiration for his novel, la-di-da,' he explained, gesturing in circular motions, bored by the process. Yet you knew he had a lot of hope invested in this new project of his. He thought it would be groundbreaking to make an epic movie about the Arab Spring.

'The world's focal point is shifting away from the West to other parts of the world. Great films reflect the social situations of their era, even if only some succeed in addressing these on a personal level,' he had said once.

What's more, the book had a very unconventional plot. If it could be appropriately transferred to the big screen, he argued, it could open up a whole new era in filmmaking – a potential which, in his words, 'gave him a massive hard-on'.

You knew he hadn't attained this in his professional life for ages. Since making his mark in the nineties, he had become part of the establishment. These days, like everybody else, Rex was producing safe bets that gave him no excitement or pleasure. Nor was an actual hard-on something he could experience naturally; he gave himself penile injections before having intercourse (Viagra could no longer cut it) – the thought made you squirm in terror.

He was planning to partly self-fund the multi-million-dollar movie, deemed by his usual backers a risky project they expected to be unprofitable, if not the biggest flop that year. Rex wanted to be the maverick he once was, someone who could still go against the grain and set trends. For this, he was willing to sacrifice his integrity and reputation, along with a huge chunk of his wealth. It was insane, if not potentially suicidal, from a career perspective, but you knew such ambitious undertakings always required the kind of headstrong determination that could also lead to self-destruction.

'The dude now resides in Cons-tan-ti-no-ple,' he said, referring again to the author, this time in a plausible West Coast accent. He then paused and observed Ada with a chilling stare, causing her to blush instantly. Reverting to a British accent, he defiantly added, with an air that suggested he might have some personal score to settle, 'Or as you lot like to refer to it these days, Istanbul. Though I much prefer the old name. What about *you*?'

She looked helplessly over at you.

'Why don't you tell her what your movie is about,' you suggested, trying to appear casual. He blinked slowly, as if to say, *Well, if I must.*

'The Arab Spring. Do you know what the phrase refers to, my dear?' he asked, leaning over and bringing his stoned face millimetres from hers. She hesitantly took a step backwards and, glancing away, mumbled some half-spoken words.

'C'mon! You're boring us with the interrogation,' you objected.

He smiled at you, completely aware how much his behaviour was getting to you.

'Did you say you're making a movie about the Arab Spring?' Ed shouted across the room. When you looked up, you saw him carefully shifting a large-scale photograph onto the table. Behind him was a folder, open and resting on a desk. On one side of the folder lay a very slim stack of other photographs from the new series. The one at the top was obscured by a thin layer of glassine.

Rex turned around and nodded.

'What an intriguing choice of subject. I'll make sure to pop to the cinemas when it comes out here.'

'We're ready when you are!' you shouted impatiently across the room.

'Nearly there,' Ed replied, preoccupied with adjusting the head of one of the two spotlights positioned over the photograph. He was well aware of the importance of immaculate presentation, after years of having people round for studio visits.

The three of you moved towards him. A near-abstraction of interwoven, translucent hues of electric blue, green and peach leapt out at you from different corners of the large photograph laid lengthwise across the table. A moment of silence followed as you all observed the work.

'It's riveting – but *what is it*?' Rex asked.

Ed smiled, his hands inside the pockets of his jeans. 'The interior of a suitcase.'

'Crikey,' Rex remarked, then took a swig of his whisky.

'Well, that's what it was initially. An X-ray image of a suitcase. Like the ones you get at airport security scanners.'

'Yes, of course. The security check is unquestionably my favourite part of the whole trip. Particularly when I have to be hand-searched!' He held back for a few seconds, inspecting everyone with a naughty grin, before muttering, 'Gives me a *massive* boner every time!'

You and Ed chuckled at his inappropriateness. However tensely, even Ada smiled. He looked back at everyone, poker-faced, as if to suggest he had no idea what the fuss was about. Such gimmickry was typical of Rex. This was him at his very best, you thought – being hilariously vulgar, yet without a hint of malice.

'The suitcase contained a homemade bomb I clumsily tried to put together—'

'*What?*' you blurted, pretending to be more shocked than you were. By now you were used to Ed going to extreme measures to create work that had arrived from what he liked to call *a real place*. 'Where did you learn how to do that?'

He placed his hand on his chest as if reciting Shakespeare. 'Like all aspiring terrorists, from a YouTube video, of course!'

'Trying to get arrested, are we?' you teasingly sniped.

Rolling his eyes dismissively at you, he continued. 'Even if most of us have to hop on a plane on a regular basis—'

'I never really liked flying,' Ada interrupted.

'And you're not the only one! Even when being whisked away to some exotic paradise, one's anticipation is accompanied by an undercurrent of terror. What might happen once the plane is airborne.'

Rex coughed heartily several times. You gave him a few pats on the back as he cleared his airway.

'As Orson Welles once said, *There are only two emotions on a plane: boredom and terror.* I tend to suffer *acutely* from the former.'

'I can totally sympathise,' you said, recalling how you stuffed yourself with bland airline meals just to pass the time.

'But here, I was more interested in delving into the realm of the latter emotion as a collective phenomenon – before my ambitions got hijacked, shall we say, by purely pictorial concerns.'

Ed grinned widely as Ada gave a small chuckle through her nose. Placing the tips of his fingers on the table, right next to the photograph, he added, 'This is why, as a starting point, I tried to create every passenger's worst nightmare, filling a suitcase not only with clothes, toiletries, and the usual stuff people pack when going on holiday, but also with weaponry.'

'Jesus! What else did you have in there?'

'Well, let me think. For this particular one, besides the bomb, there was an automatic rifle—'

'You don't say.'

Glancing at the photograph, Ed replied, 'Well, I do agree that at this stage it's a little hard to detect.' He was amused, if not flattered, by Rex's discombobulation.

Suddenly you were able to pick out some of the electric blue fragments that formed the rifle: its muzzle, its trigger and long barrel. 'I see it as a vibrant rendition of a Cubist painting,' you said.

He looked you in the eye and gave you a discreet nod, trying to play down his contentment. Even a very established artist like Ed carried some real, hidden anxiety about having created work that didn't come across sufficiently.

Feeling Ada's gaze on you, you turned towards her. You looked into each other's eyes and smiled tenderly, as if to say you were happy just to be in each other's company.

Rex mumbled, 'The colours are...' and left it at that, looking like he could do with a lie down.

You leaned over and whispered in his ear, 'You okay, Ty?' An affectionate abbreviation for Tyrannosaurus Rex. He gave you a blank stare and rubbed the tip of his nose a few times. Worried that Ada would understand what was being discussed, you shook your head. You turned away to prevent the silent exchange from going any further. You considered how annoyed he would be if he knew you'd given away the gram of coke you'd paid for.

'The colours are there to implement a very standardised and dull procedure. X-ray scanners identify the density of the objects by colour-coding them. Metals and other inorganic objects come up as blue, organic stuff as orange, and anything in between as green.'

You watched Rex glance at the near-abstraction of overlapping transparencies. You reckoned that in his stoned state, with his sensory perception heightened and susceptible to delusions, he might be able to engineer whole new readings of the composition, none of which were evident to anyone else in the room.

After a while he looked to Ed, squinting a few times, as if he had just woken from a dream.

'It's brilliant – can I buy it?'

Ed crossed his arms, a diplomatic smile on his lips. His gaze slid towards you as he replied, 'I'm afraid you will have to wait for the exhibition.'

You affirmed his comment, performing a series of slow, assertive nods. At this point the guilt and the shame had lost their hard edges. *He'll be all right*, you consoled yourself, observing Ed in brief glimpses when he happened to be looking elsewhere. The plain reality was, you had always needed him more than he needed you. And besides, your collaboration had been dragging on for too long. You no longer had anything new to offer him beyond the stability of a settled, predictable relationship. Changing galleries would do him good, you tried to convince yourself.

'So, when is it?' Rex asked, his eyes more alert than before. It seemed the heaviness of the dope was starting to leave his system.

'God knows!' Looking over at you, he added, 'We haven't gotten around to discussing it yet.'

'Don't worry, I'll make sure to send you an invite,' you promised in your usual sarcastic way, then looked over at Ed; your fingers automatically delved into your pocket and touched your packet of cigarettes. The dishonesty of the moment became too much for you. Struggling to maintain your composure, you placed your hand on Ada's shoulder. 'You know, Ada is also an artist.'

Suddenly all eyes were on her. Smiling uncomfortably, she shook her head and pulled away.

'Why didn't you mention it?' Ed asked.

Shrugging apologetically and shaking her head several times, she stressed, 'I'm really not an artist. I mean, I used to paint, and I still very occasionally do, but—'

'Come on, stop being so modest!' you insisted.

Of course, you could sense she wasn't tolerating being put on the spot well. Even so, you didn't have the nerve to steer the topic away from her. Not when you were on the brink of confessing how you had driven your business into the ground, before breaking down in front of everyone. Like one of those people who collapsed on live television, in front of millions and millions of others. You couldn't be *that* person.

'Ada paints still lifes. What are they called again?' you asked, before remembering the coined term yourself. Your exaggerated exuberance was bordering on hysteria. 'You refer to them as fictitious still lifes, don't you?'

She stayed silent.

'I'd love to see them one day,' Ed remarked cordially.

'Me too!' Rex all too keenly jumped onto the wagon.

She shot you an uneasy glance.

'Hey, she's a total catch!' he added, giving you an impish nudge of the elbow. You noticed her subtly shake her head, as if in her head she was giving Rex, and possibly you, a mouthful. 'Beautiful – and exceptionally talented too, it appears.'

You could sense your temples pulsing. Ed naively said, 'Couldn't agree more.'

Watching Rex leave your side and stride towards her, you tensely scraped your teeth over your upper lip.

'Why do you call them fictitious still lifes?' he asked, as if he was genuinely interested.

Looking guarded, she shrugged and responded, 'It's just what they are.'

You extended your neck, indicating the open folder behind Ed with your chin and almost shouted, 'I'm really dying to see the rest!'

But your remark simply bounced off Rex, who was too preoccupied pursuing his game.

'All in good time,' Ed responded. It seemed – and rightly so – that he felt no commitment to continuing unless all parties were one hundred per cent tuned-in.

By this time Rex had already offered to visit her at her home 'to view her artwork'. He was telling her how he had a good eye for these things. He certainly had some nerve, coming on to her when you were clearly so smitten. Maybe (as ludicrous as this seemed to you) he was trying to compete with you – or it could well be he just didn't respect you enough to abstain from his skirt-chasing, even on this occasion.

He asked her if she would be available some time this coming weekend, before he sodded off to effing Istanbul. This time he had used the name Istanbul; he was currently not in aggravation, but decoy mode. Typical, you thought.

'Maybe,' Ada responded without eagerness.

'Splendid!' Rex declared, turning towards you and winking. Then he took out his massive iPhone. 'What's your number?'

'WILL – YOU – JUST – FUCK – OFF!'

Everyone turned and froze, like time itself had stopped. You had exploded in such fury, juddering on the spot. You had shouted with such might you could still feel a burning inside your throat.

His eyes were now wide. Yet the touch of mockery in his voice when he spoke up revealed he wasn't going to back off so easily.

'I was just asking for her—'

'WILL – YOU – JUST – FUCK – OFF!' you erupted once more, this time ejecting drops of spit in his direction. You tried to catch your breath and to contain your anger, dismissing the questioning glances directed at you. 'I mean, what kind of a friend does that?' you asked in a drained, sad voice. You were fed up with people trying to fuck you one way or another. Tired of the greed and the manipulation.

You caught Ada looking at you. She appeared moved. Or maybe she just pitied you. Ed looked distressed and confused. You couldn't blame the old bugger. He never could have imagined, *not in a zillion years*, as he would put it, that he would witness an A-grade royal meltdown, when he had naturally assumed the night was going to be all about him.

'Does what?' asked Rex. He shrugged, as if he didn't have a clue what you were going on about. Straightening up, he glanced at the others in a bid for their sympathy.

You paused and smiled to yourself. You knew it was pointless explaining.

'Well, then,' he said, with open arms, trying to resolve the situation.

Your rage had cooled, replaced by sober resentment. Discovering Eloise's scam had shaken you to the core. What had happened to you made you question yourself, your values, as well as the sort of people you surrounded yourself with.

Holding your finger millimetres away from his nose, you whispered plainly, 'You and I are over.'

And from the disappointment in his beady eyes, you could tell he knew you weren't just throwing words into the air.

You turned around to Ed. He looked like he would be much happier if you would all just bugger off. That way, he could have a chance to meditate before going to bed and perhaps restore his easily disrupted inner balance.

'I'm sorry, Ed, for all this nonsense, but I think it's better we call it a—'

But Rex didn't allow you to finish.

'Just give us a minute. We have to talk,' he interrupted, then clung to your arm with both hands.

Instinctively you tried to shake him off. 'What on earth are you doing, Rex?' you tiredly protested. You caught the panic in Ada's eyes as he pulled you away to a quiet corner, like some adolescent about to be punished by the headmaster.

It's all right, you mouthed to her.

You heard Ed's voice diplomatically suggesting, 'Maybe it's best we all head downstairs. My goodness! It's already quarter to ten.'

'Don't worry, we're off. All I need is a minute,' Rex reassured him, as he kept pulling you towards the entrance of the room, as far away from the other two as possible.

'What are you doing? We have nothing left to say to each other,' you hissed, though with little resistance; you didn't want the situation to develop into a full-fledged wrestling match. As soon as he let go of you, you said, 'Jesus, Rex, I meant what I said! I don't want your fucking friendship. And stop making such a scene!'

With trembling hands, he held you by the collar, and whispered, 'No, don't say that.'

'If you genuinely cared about me you wouldn't have engaged in your usual antics back there. Not with her.' You gave him one good look and then repeated it: 'I'm done with you.'

'No, no, don't say that,' he breathed, caressing your face lightly with the tips of his fingers.

Staring back, you could now see right through him: the sad, deeply insecure and angry man that he was. But you could not find it in your heart to forgive. There was no longer any place for someone like him in your life.

You pulled away and saw his desperation quickly turn to humiliation and deep sorrow.

You reached out to give him a supportive pat on the shoulder – a friendly impulse – but he pushed your hand away.

'Oh, just fuck off!' he snapped, before storming out of the room.

You looked up at the dark, cloudy sky. 'Interesting evening, don't you think?'

She smiled and gave you a look. You pulled out a cigarette and lit up, then briefly turned around to look at Ed's house. The realisation this could well be your very last visit gave you goosebumps.

'Where are we going?' she asked.

'Where do you want to go?'

'To your place. I want to see where you live.'

You walked down the street hand in hand. As you passed them, you studied the semi-detached houses on either side. Many of them had soft light seeping through their curtains. The thought of other lives existing independently of you, behind those tall exteriors, no longer made you feel desperately lonely. Not now you had Ada by your side, holding your hand. And you had more pressing things to consider: you were at a turning point in your life. As much as you dreaded the challenges that lay ahead, you also knew a change could do you some good.

ADA

I

SOMETHING ABOUT HIM IS DIFFERENT TODAY. The thought resounds through my mind again and again. Almost immediately, it begs the question: *How well do you really know this man?*

We lie on his bed fully clothed, my head resting on his chest. His stare is fixed on the dark ceiling above as he caresses my hair and occasionally kisses my forehead, as if to emphasise that – though we have hardly spoken a word to each other since we arrived at his flat ten minutes ago – we are still very much connected through touch.

I hear his muffled heartbeats, and occasional sounds running through his abdomen (finding it strange and fascinating to recognise that his body, like everybody else's, has to perform its vital yet prosaic functions). I listen to his inconsistent breathing, interrupted from time to time by a sigh, sometimes a gulp.

Still affected by the heated moments I had witnessed at Ed's studio earlier, I revive them inside my mind; they feed my assessment that he's been acting very differently today. His nonchalant attitude in the days prior had given me the impression that he wasn't someone who could lose his cool easily; I keep pondering the reasons behind the withdrawal that gradually took hold of him after we walked out of Ed's house. Was he still upset about the incident with Rex, or just drained by it?

The bold crayon scribbles on the walls of his living room also keep reappearing inside my mind as yet another pressing question about who he is. What kind of a father is he? One that leniently allows his children to draw on his walls, or the sort who cannot exercise an ounce of discipline over them?

If it had been yesterday or the day before, when he had adopted a consistently accessible front, I think I would've found the nerve to ask about the scribbles on the wall. Though it's the first time he's been this tender with me, there seems to be an invisible barrier between us that doesn't allow me to interrupt the strangely comforting silence he has initiated.

I stroke his chest a few times – his inwardness reminds me of a purring cat's unwinding yet reticent companionship – then lift my head up off his chest, pull myself up and begin to kiss his slightly parted mouth.

Running his fingers softly up and down my back, he responds with a playfully elongated 'Mmm,' as if he would be content to lie there and continue to be on the receiving end of my advances. Further encouraged by his composure – willing but unassertive, in sync with the behaviour he had eventually adopted the night before – and the liberating effect this has on me, I get on my knees and climb on top of him, feeling his reassuringly soft yet sturdy torso between my legs.

We look into each other's eyes. Light bleeds into the room through a half-open door; traces of streetlight come through

the unobstructed windows. I can barely make out his eyes –
but even so I can spot the teasing glimmer in them; this time
they're accompanied by an expression I've become accustomed
to seeing in people of my parents' generation, and which I therefore associate with a maturity only achievable by weathering,
over decades, the ups and downs of whatever life throws at you:
a tired acceptance of how things are.

As I press myself into him and begin to kiss his mouth
once again, enjoying the tang of nicotine on his breath only
because it's *his*, I think about the primal factors at play behind
my strong desire for him. I think about the wildlife documen-
taries – intrigued by the unfussy rationale behind most peculiar
animal behaviours – I have become hooked on watching in the
evenings. My attraction towards him is a much more convoluted affair. But why, ever since *the incident*, is it *he* who has
managed to get this close? Could it be down to the animalistic
pull we ignited in each other? Or his tolerance the night before,
in the face of my indecision? Or is it because he's come into
my life when – as Marlene mentioned during our most recent
session – I'm already showing signs of recovery (though I tend
to receive such statements from her as mere ploys to encourage
me, unsupported by evidence)?

In between tender kisses, he pauses. 'Will you stay the night?'

I look into his eyes and nod. He pulls me down on top of
him and whispers, 'Thank you,' before embracing me. I reciprocate. When we eventually let go of each other, we giggle as
I slip back on to the bed ungraciously, like a sack of potatoes.

I lie sideways next to him, my head resting in my palm, and
carefully observe the outline of his face – a blissful temporary
state, I already know, only possible at the very beginning of

a dalliance which bears the potential to become serious, if it doesn't unexpectedly fizzle out.

My fingers wander down the slope of his neck and over the width of his chest, as if they're following a winding stream that takes shape according to the topography of its terrain. I begin to unbutton his shirt, my pace quickening as I move to the next button, then the one after that. Just as I'm determinedly unbuckling his belt, he holds my hand and says, 'Wait.'

He lifts his upper body, adjusts the two pillows behind him, and rests his back against them; I also adopt a seated position on the bed, leaning on my arm and tucking my legs beneath my thighs.

'I need to tell you something,' he says all of a sudden, in a particularly gravelly voice, before momentarily looking away, as if he's struggling to find the right words to explain what's going on inside him. The prospect of what he's about to reveal instantly ignites panic in me; my mind touches upon one dramatically bleak hypothesis, then another, until – by now assuming *we* are about to come to an end – I picture myself rushing out through the front door of his flat, never to set foot in it again.

This too will pass, I whisper internally, a simple consolation I tend to use whenever faced with disillusionment or trouble, as I had also done on the night of my shattering ordeal back in Turkey. This passing observation prompts me to compare the futility of my current situation to the imminent threat I had been up against that night – and to my state of mind when I had been let down by other potential love interests. I realise, regardless of what blow I might receive from Lucian, its effects on my mood will be transient, unlikely to last longer than a few days. I wait more calmly.

Looking tired and stressed, he rubs his forehead.

'I met my new accountant this afternoon. Apparently, I've been fucked left, right and centre.'

I immediately ridicule myself for being so preoccupied with thinking everything had to be about me.

He leans forward, caresses the hand resting limply on my lap and stares at our overlapping hands.

Without looking up, he reveals, 'I've been dying to tell you about this the entire night. But now that I'm about to, I'm worried it might push you away from me.'

I observe him worriedly.

'Come closer,' he whispers, sounding forlorn and desperate for my proximity. He pulls me by the hand and our bodies slide back onto the bed. With a heavy-hearted sigh, he mutters, 'I guess it's only a matter of time before you learn what a fucking loser I am.' Still tightly holding my hand, he turns his back, and I cradle him.

'Don't say that,' I mutter into his ear. I don't know him well enough to say more.

'There's a chance I'm on the brink of losing the gallery.'

Astonished by his revelation, I respond, 'I'm so sorry!' What a catastrophic let-down this must be for him; the humiliation and the self-doubt it must cause. I think about the strangeness of being so emotionally invested in his life when I've known him for barely three days. 'But why?' I ask cautiously.

I sense his stomach momentarily expand as he reflects on the question.

'I tend to trust others too much. I'm drawn to highly manipulative, charismatic types like Rex.'

He lets out a faint chuckle.

'Within weeks of hiring her, I gave Eloise the keys to the gallery. I gave her the password to my business bank account, and the authority to do whatever she wanted with it, as if I didn't really care if she went ahead and destroyed what I'd painstakingly built over the last six years.'

Feeling his agony and fury, I mumble, 'Everyone can make mistakes of judgement.'

I lift myself off him as he shifts and lies on his back.

'I quickly recognised her penchant for sucking up to rich clients, and her remarkable flair for talking people into buying just about anything. Selling has never been my strongest point, and I was keen to capitalise on her capability, of course – yet I did this without considering how far her potential to deceive could take her. I preferred to look away, as it were.'

Able to imagine what Marlene's most rational response to Lucian might be, I channel her calm and self-possessed demeanour: 'Maybe it's easy for you to make these assessments now – but when you're going through whatever you're going through, it's not always that easy to see things for what they are.'

'But that's just a lame excuse, don't you think?' he responds, lethargically, scratching the top of his head.

Provoked, I involuntarily tense. 'Every person has the potential to be talked into things they think they will *never do*, or be tricked in such a way that they remain oblivious to the scam happening right before their eyes.'

I can't help but blame myself, still, for my crumbling composure on the night of my interrogation. Towards the morning, I had broken down and surrendered, agreeing to sign several documents confessing to offences I had never committed. At the time, I had been too distraught to read them. I continue to blame myself, too, for having succumbed so easily to a suicidal frame of mind upon my release – unable to sleep or eat, I sat in the corner of my room, trembling with fear, crying deliriously and repeating to my parents (who tried to comfort me as much as they could) that I had no will to carry on, that, dead certain I would be locked up for good, I would rather face death than have to turn up at my trial. I wish I had possessed the fortitude at the time to set my all-absorbing fears aside and see things for what they were; that instead of absconding like an outlaw I had embraced the role of the wrongly accused martyr, and had demonstrated endurance others could take strength from. I would be in a much better place, and things would probably have resolved themselves by now.

Too distracted to sense my growing tetchiness, he responds, 'Listen, I'm all up for playing the victim and blaming everything on that traitorous bitch – but let's not forget, there's also what's known as free will.'

My limbs seem clumsily foreign to me as I sit up, pointlessly trying to suppress the despair that has overcome me. I've become accustomed to how it progresses. Once I'm abducted by this overwhelming emotion – as if it were a poltergeist possessing me whenever I'm at my weakest – I inevitably have to submit to it before I can move on.

I reply, in a muted voice, 'Sometimes they can even take away one's free will.'

As tears emerge from my eyes, I turn away and start to weep uncontrollably. My body keeps clenching itself, as if it were a large muscle going into painful spasms.

I sense his hand on my shoulder, his fingers softly digging into my flesh in an effort to console me – how easily we have switched roles. I decide to open up about my past, particularly when the past keeps infiltrating the present whenever our intimacy gains momentum.

'I was arrested the last time I was in Istanbul. It was during the Gezi Park protests in June 2013. I was one of the protestors who peacefully lobbied against its demolition. I haven't been able to go back to Istanbul since.'

After wiping off the dampness under my eyes and on my cheeks, I turn towards him.

'Why did you get arrested?' he asks calmly.

'You could say I was in the wrong place at the wrong time. I was on a narrow side street just off İstiklal, a major pedestrian high street in Istanbul, on my way to a supermarket where they were donating bin bags and other supplies. Suddenly, a police van came charging through, turning on its loud sirens at the very last minute. They arrested anyone they could get their hands on. I was handcuffed and kept with the other detainees, some who had been severely wounded by resisting, inside a sweltering police van for over two hours.'

Like livestock, we were jammed in the back of a truck, waiting to be driven off to the slaughterhouse. I was sweating, trying to breathe in humid air that stank of sweat, breath and blood. My hands were handcuffed behind me, and the terror of what could be in store for me, for us, kept pacing in my mind – as if it were a wild animal gone delirious inside a tiny cage. Initially, time passed torturously slowly – but by the time one of the men warned, 'They're coming!' it seemed hours had simply *evaporated* in a handful of minutes. Then that crushing fear returned in full force. Sinking down in my seat, looking downwards, I had shut my eyes and wished to disappear. After a few seconds, opening my eyes to face the inescapable reality at hand, I saw a quickly expanding patch of moist darkness on the crotch of the trousers of the young man beside me.

After some deliberation, Lucian said gravely, 'That doesn't sound fun.'

'No, it wasn't.' I shake my head, feelings compassion towards that past self – something Marlene points out I should grant myself more often than I do.

'What happened after?'

I turn away towards the window, and find myself observing the purple sky outside. The clouds resemble light smudges of oily pastel, impressionist gestures on a depthless monochrome plane.

'Ada, you don't have to tell me anything if you don't feel like it,' he adds, affectionately rubbing my shoulder.

'I know.'

As we smile softly at each other, I tear up once more; the growing bond between us makes me think about how, like tragedy, serendipity can strike at any time, when one least expects it. Having assumed my work with Quinn would have no life-altering effects of any kind, I never had imagined I would meet someone – let alone be willing to open up to him on our second date. Yet getting to know Lucian has made me appreciate that there is life beyond what happened to me.

'After I arrived at the police station, I was strip searched.'

The nauseating shame and paralysing horror of that night returns. How I nearly tripped when I'd tried to balance on one foot, then the other, as I discarded my stained trousers, followed by my disfigured T-shirt, in front of two uniformed strangers – two women – who chatted about their daily activities as if I wasn't in the room.

'They asked me to remove everything I had on, including my underwear.'

'God!' He rests his forehead against his index finger and thumb and remains in that position, as if he needs time to take it all in. When he looks up, I see disillusionment in his tired eyes.

'It's okay,' I say, to give the impression I've gotten over it by now.

Made to bare every inch of my body in a brightly lit room, I had at first pointlessly tried to cover up. When one of the guards knelt before me, my immediate response had been to try to match her action to some official, routine procedure, though really I already knew it was not. I froze on the spot and sobbed in silence while she took her time to observe the area between my legs, as a mere taster of the human rights violations they were capable of committing behind impenetrable walls and locked doors.

'Bastards!' he angrily hisses as a sports car whizzes maniacally down the street below. Precisely whom he has just scolded is unclear.

'After putting my clothes back on, I was interrogated by two male officers, then released by sunrise,' I explain. I follow the car's roaring, spitting engine until it fades into the indistinguishable murmurs the city generates nightly.

'It must've been *terrifying.*'

I draw my legs closer to my body, squeezing them tightly with both arms, and then look up at the large photograph hanging on the opposite wall. I can just about make out the intricately over-lapping bodies of naked women. The objectification of women's flesh confronts me wherever I go; in its least malevolent state, it advocates obsessive adoration and lust. At its worst, women's bodies become an easy target for frustrated male inadequacy, brought on by the pressure to exhibit macho tendencies not all men naturally possess. And a vehicle for patriarchal control they're frequently unable to exert to the desired level.

'My only tool for survival at the time was *hope*, but I gave up on it quite rapidly,' I say, again, feeling a churning sensation in the depths of my stomach.

'Have you ever gone up to the mountains?' one of the two detectives had asked, in the midst of unstrapping his watch.

My heart rate immediately shot up. Squinting at him, I muttered, 'Sorry?' I thought I must've misheard his question; I couldn't possibly see what could make him imagine that someone like me – a girl born and bred in Istanbul, with no strong political aspirations until now – could join the Kurdish rebels in the Qandil mountains all the way at the other end of the country – but it also seemed unlikely that he was asking me a casual question about whether I hiked in my spare time.

Immediately regretting my response, I said, 'Of course not!' torn between my determination to prove my innocence and my cowardly desperation to set myself apart from an organisation, as if it were a deadly plague that could be passed on to anyone just by false implication. Why had he taken off his watch? He now placed it lengthwise on the table in front of me. Minutes prior, he had removed his jacket and hung it on the back of a chair.

'I live in London,' I had quickly, nervously pointed out. Surely once they found out what my real story was, they would acknowledge they had no reason to keep me there.

Gesturing at me with his chin, he retorted, 'You don't say!' in his loud and brassy voice – as if whatever came out of my mouth could only be some implausible cover-up.

'What do you do there?' the other detective – standing at a distance behind me and also dressed in civilian clothes – asked neutrally, as if I were someone he had happened to meet socially. Slouching on the low stool I had been made to sit on, I briefly turned in his direction but was too timid to look him in the eyes.

'I'm a student at university. I'm studying—'

'After all, the organisation is very established in London,' the one beside me interrupted.

'London is one of their main breeding grounds. But of course, these fucking whores all claim to be students.'

He rested his fist beside me, his knuckles on the table, the gun he carried on his belt millimetres away from my face.

'What were you doing in the back streets of Beyoğlu, defying the Turkish police like that, ha?' he demanded, shaking his head, as if scorning an underage shoplifter he had just caught red-handed. Spite oozed from his every word.

'But I wasn't defying anyone.'

The truth had no leverage at this point; any kind of denial was deemed another act of defiance.

'Why do I even bother?' he yelled furiously, lifting his hand in the air.

When he leaned on me, the leather case of his gun now pressing against my cheek, I had tilted away – and he, in return, had leaned further in. His growing erection pressed against me through his trousers. Paralysed, trembling and breathing audibly, I had directed my glance in the opposite direction – as far as my vision would allow me – to a random point on the skirting board. All the while, I was overwhelmingly preoccupied with the knowledge that, if what I was being threatened with were to actually happen, something in me would be left permanently damaged. This preoccupation had been set in motion by the increasing verbal and physical abuse I had withstood during the long hours of my captivity. I was periodically taken back to the cell, then brought to the interrogation room again, stuck in a vicious loop of psychological torture I was convinced would never end.

Lucian cups my face in his hands.

'Listen to me. You are exceptionally brave and strong for having gone through something like that and coming out the other side.'

Embarrassed, I roll my eyes at him defensively – but eventually nod back. As his words sink in, I sense my face contort into a tearful smile until, unable to hold back, I'm flooded by tears once more. Lucian wraps his arms around me and keeps whispering 'Shh' in my ear, caressing my hair, and soon my sobbing is reduced to deep breaths and occasional sniffles. Exhausted but comforted, I stay in the moment – as my motionless limbs begin to lose sensation, his body begins to feel like an extension of mine, and for a dreamlike moment we're floating inside the dark stillness of the room.

'You know, you should paint again.' Loosening his grip, he adds, 'As clichéd as it may sound, making art can be very therapeutic.'

'So should you.'

Able to find a bit of humour in our dire straits, we smile at each other.

'Actually, I did a still-life painting last night when I got home,' I reveal, a ripple of new excitement passing through me.

'Really?'

'It turned out to be much more promising than all the other attempts I've made since moving to London.'

'Why do you think that is?'

'For the first time, I felt I was moving forward.'

11

Gently roused by the distant sounds of cupboards being opened and shut, and the appetising whiff of freshly toasted bread and filtered coffee, I take my time to stretch my limbs. As my bare legs lightly brush against each other, I think about how, through the night, we had kept waking each other with unexpected shifts and shuffles, the different snuggled-up positions we quickly adopted setting off bizarre narratives in my dreams that felt remarkably real, as if they were continuations of reality in a parallel dimension. My eyes still shut, I search for him under the duvet (as I do, it secretes hints of his smell), my hands extending all the way to his side of the bed, where the mattress has become cold. I return to my end, where it's still delightfully warm.

Daylight has transformed his bedroom, leaving no corner hidden. I emerge from his cupboard-like en suite, tiptoe bare-foot out of his room, and poke my still-drowsy head into his living room – where the scribbles on the walls now appear less prominent. I make my way to his kitchen, from which the sounds of human habitation emanate.

I appear before him, standing on one foot while balancing the other foot on top. Suddenly conscious of exposing my bare legs in broad daylight, I pull down on the sides of the extra-large T-shirt he had handed me (along with a plastic-sealed, folded toothbrush that came with its own mini toothpaste) when, around one in the morning, I had proposed we go to sleep. After exhausting the topic of my pending trial – due to take place in four weeks – we had resumed talking about what Eloise had been up to. He had immediately been swamped in self-blame and resentment – demonstrating an incapacity to show himself the compassion he easily could spare for me.

Yet he greets me in a surprisingly chirpy mood, as if a night's sleep has cast a whole new perspective on things. 'Morning, sweetheart.'

I sleepily smile and nod back, studying the effort he has put into making himself presentable. In a sombre tie and blazer jacket, he looks boyish, his days-old stubble shaven and his hair combed backwards. I recall how he mentioned the appointment he had with a solicitor this morning – peevishly, his temper showing itself, as if it was a complete waste of time.

Fretting – had I become a hindrance to his plans? – I say, 'You should have woken me up. Are you late for your appointment?'

He opens his arms expectantly, putting down the mug of black coffee in his hand. Reassured, I revel in his warm embrace and his freshly applied cologne. He plants a kiss onto my temple. I close my eyes and reciprocate his gesture by softly tilting my head against his lips.

'I need to make an exit in twenty minutes – but you, my dear, *you* can stay and relax for as long as you wish to.'

I shrug, debating whether I should. Even though the distance from his flat to the Fair – due to open its doors to the public at noon – is a much shorter ride on the Tube than from mine, and therefore I could lounge about here all morning, I am unable to set aside the aimlessness and voyeuristic awkwardness I'm likely to experience, being inside his personal space in his absence – albeit his flat resembles a temporary arrangement rather than someone's home.

'You can read the morning papers in bed,' he proposes, lifting his eyebrows – as if to imply the leisurely pastime can easily lend itself to other self-pleasuring activities – directing my attention to the unread pile resting on the kitchen counter as he gets up to fetch a mug from one of the cupboards above the sink.

'You've been out.'

'I had no choice. This kitchen is usually as bare as the Sahara.'

I observe the countertops, which lack the usual bits and bobs that accumulate over time.

'Milk?' he asks, casting a glance at me while pouring the cafetière. I shake my head, then place myself onto the stool next to his. He hands me my mug of coffee, then says with regret, 'I was only able to make it as far as the shitty off-licence down the road, so I'm afraid the breakfast menu is somewhat limited.'

I nod appreciatively, examining the newly bought pint of milk, box of cereal, jar of jam and loaf of sliced brown bread deposited on the island.

'But even so,' he says, bringing his hands together, 'what can I get you?'

'Maybe some cereal.'

Watching him tip a lavish amount of cereal into a bowl and pour milk over it – on both occasions I have to abruptly caution him to stop – I reflect on the blissful ordinariness of the moment. An exchange with Marlene early in our relationship comes to mind, an encouraging reminder of the progress I have made, and where I could be one day, perhaps in the not-so-distant future.

Her hands resting on her lap, delicate fingers loosely intertwined, Marlene explained, 'With time, you will see. Things won't feel so painfully raw. The incidents will stop popping up in your mind as often as they do. You will start associating things less with what happened to you.'

I could understand her argument from a logical point of view, but I was unable to relate to any of it.

'From where I stand, it's very hard to imagine that will ever be the case,' I eventually managed to respond in a low, quivering voice.

Her eyes projected warmth and sympathy as she smiled confidently at me, as if to imply that it was normal at this stage for me to be incapable of acknowledging what was plainly visible to her. 'Trust me. Us humans, we have a great capacity for healing. Think of all those people who have gone through much worse than you. Who have lost their loved ones. It's terribly difficult, and seems impossible at first, but eventually most are able to move on.'

◆

My eardrums fill with the rhythm of cereal being crushed between my molars. Lucian sits back onto his stool – and, after taking a quick bite of toast, he turns his body towards me.

'When I woke up, I watched you as you were sleeping. Your eyelids were moving a little, and at one point you had a smile on your lips. I wished I were inside that mind of yours, to see what was going on in there.'

I smile demurely, my gaze momentarily escaping his – it's odd that he's behaving as if his troubles are no longer distressing him. 'Has there been a new development?' I ask.

He lets out a bitter chuckle. 'Not to my knowledge. I'm still just as fucked as before.'

I nod, trying not to let my disappointment show. I take another spoonful of cereal, this time imagining the loud crunching as footsteps on thick, icy snow. As I do, my spirits are instantly lifted by how the unlikeliest of things resemble each other – which lures me back into the understanding I now and again entertain about the mystical order of things. That all existing things, however distant or seemingly unrelated, are connected by an invisible web. A cigarette butt discarded on the kerb of a bustling street, trodden on for days on end by countless individuals, is eventually picked up by a diligent street sweeper or a nestmaking sparrow. Now its journey takes a significantly different turn. From its making to consumption, it can be linked to so many other living and non-living things – not to mention many human beings. And, in this way, it not only connects lives separated by continents but also shared histories, in the process of its manufacture – and the exploitation of people and natural resources it nevertheless always entails.

Suddenly, Lucian gets off his stool, as if he's been beckoned by a time-sensitive task. He begins to pace alongside the island, his head dropped pensively and his hands resting resolutely at either side of his hips. After a few seconds, he finally stops and speaks; as he does his eyes project a mad kind of exuberance.

'I've been up since seven just thinking about things.'

'About what?' I ask, concerned, cautioning myself not to get ahead of myself with baseless suspicions again.

'Where I wish to go from here, from this charade I've been a part of for so long,' he says feverishly, walking up to me in his squeaky-clean black loafers. I've not completely got used to his altered appearance. Upon reaching me, he rotates the seat of my stool, turning me towards him.

Unable to wait any longer, I ask, 'Well, so where do you wish to go?'

I'm more amused than surprised when he backs away from me and giggles. I've got used to his ways by now; how many situations carry the potential to evoke a rush of laughter in him.

Taking a moment of pause and rubbing his moistened eyes with a hand, he comes up to me. His fingers seize mine.

'I was thinking of Istanbul.'

The mere mention of *Istanbul* engulfs me – an accumulation of impressions: street vendors wandering on foot along congested highways, disabled beggars on dusty pavements, Turkish flags hanging off balconies, electronic beats fused with Arabesk, flashy, recklessly driven cars, roving yellow taxis badgering pedestrians with their horns, long queues in front of metrobus stops, packed public transport reeking of sweat, taverns and restaurants pouring out on to the pavements, newly built, soulless shopping malls in every neighbourhood, propaganda posters of moustached heads, backgammon in men's coffee houses, rowdy football hooligans blocking traffic in front of football stadiums, young glue-sniffers with lost expressions, waste-pickers dragging large carts across the city, skinny stray dogs wandering in packs after midnight, police barricades, well-fed stray cats lurking next to fishmongers, soot-covered buildings, school playgrounds with a bust of Atatürk, blue seas, blue skies, suspension bridges, yelping seagulls, secluded waterfront villas, old, grand apartments in striking Art Nouveau, Neoclassical buildings, tattered fishing boats, ostentatious yachts, token barriers for ferryboats, imposing palaces, magnificent mosques, calls to prayer, misty silhouettes of minarets and overbuilt concrete spread across seven hills.

'Istanbul?'

Lucian shrugs his shoulders plainly, as if to say, *Why not?*

He crouches in front of me. Our very first encounter springs to mind like a funny anecdote – how I had given him advice on the best times to travel to Istanbul. In the span of four days, we have travelled full circle and returned to where we started.

He moves closer still. Staring intently into my eyes, he says, 'I want to go there with *you*,' his fingers tightening their grip encouragingly.

I stare back into his eyes, waiting for further elucidation, before I nervously blurt, 'For a holiday?'

'If that's what you want to call it,' he replies.

'But you know I can't go back.'

'Didn't you tell me last night that there's a good chance they're going to let you off?'

I sigh. 'I was merely reiterating the opinion of others, but nobody really knows what decision they will come to.'

He runs his hands down my bare thighs and lightly presses them against my kneecaps to lift himself back to an upright position. When he holds my chin up, I expect him to console me with a tender kiss, but instead he observes me with kind eyes before uttering, 'I have a very strong hunch that in a few weeks you will again be a free citizen of this world.'

I nod back, with the frail kind of hope I continue to cling to.

He releases my chin. 'Your face lights up each time you speak of Istanbul. Once the coast is clear, you and I both know you'll be on the next plane there. I want to be on that plane with you.'

I'm impressed that he's able to read me so well, deeply touched he cares enough to want to share that moment with me – if it ever happens.

'I want to see Istanbul through your eyes. I want you to walk me through the streets you grew up in, the places you love the most.'

Before he reaches the end of his sentence, I'm already imagining us strolling hand in hand through neat rows of sprouting vegetation in a secluded orchard planted by local residents. It resembles an oasis, tucked away behind slender, colourfully painted wooden houses in the coastal, bijou district of Kuzguncuk. Elif and I had only visited twice; so mesmer-ised had we been by its tranquillity and character that we had dubbed the place our own.

'I would love to do that,' I admit, for once not doubting this would be achievable – or, for that matter, whether either of us would want it as much in a month's time.

I part my legs as he brings himself forward. Our lips finally touch, and I'm again given the taste of his warm breath – which as usual carries a whiff of nicotine; the day's first cigarette has already been had – and the playful stroking of his tongue. In a matter of seconds he interrupts our moment to convey an idea that's too thrilling, it seems, to hold back any longer.

'Who knows? I might like it so much out there that I might just want to stay.'

Several questions rush through my mind, none of which I can bring myself to put forward. Eventually he breaks the growing silence between us by repeating himself, as if for him all answers lie in that pivotal moment.

'I've been up since seven just thinking about things – about important stuff. Like what I plan to do with the rest of my life since I've *completely* hit rock bottom – at the exceptionally tender age of forty-three, might I add, my dear,' he adds, having easily slipped into his usual entertaining persona, before he regains his sober front and continues.

'When I opened my eyes, it felt like just any other morning at first – but then the reality of what I found out yesterday hit me. I quickly rose above it, as a plane does when it takes off, shuddering and shaking as it ascends through the clouds. And then soon you're thirty-five thousand feet off the ground, gliding at a tremendous speed towards God knows where, and the sky appears spotlessly blue along the stratosphere. The sun is shining brighter than ever, and all you can see below you is the buoyant layer of heavenly white clouds stretching to eternity – or so it seems. Looking at it always gives you a different perspective. If what's out there is *real*, then pretty much anything on a personal scale is achievable. For the first time, I was able to register what's happened to me as a wake-up call – a blessing in disguise, if you will. How many people end up being enslaved to a set-up that, had they been proposed it when they were younger and full of high ideals, they would've spurned? But life can gradually draw you, like an invisible tide, to places you never imagined you would go. It's hard to say what I would've accomplished, if anything, had I continued to pursue the career of an artist. One thing is for sure, though – I would've been in a more honest place than *this*.'

He exhales a deep sigh of relief, happy to have come to such a conclusion.

As soon as the thought crystallises in my mind, the words roll out of my mouth. 'You want to paint again.'

He pauses. 'You know as well as I do that it's never as straightforward as that.'

Casting my eyes downwards, I nod.

'Having said that, this morning I had what can best be described as *a vision*.'

I look up curiously.

'When I saw you lying right beside me, fast asleep, your curls scattered across the pillow like some sultry siren who had mysteriously slipped into my bed in the middle of the night, I did think to myself, *It's not really as bad as it seems*,' he mutters softly, his hands loosely around my waist. 'I just watched you for a while, and your eyelids began to move. When you smiled at something – I wish I knew what it was – I suddenly had it. The vision, I mean. We were in Istanbul, inside a large studio that we shared, *painting*.'

I too entertain a snapshot in my mind: the interiors of a penthouse studio inside one of the old apartments in Beyoğlu, laid throughout with gracefully aged parquet floors, its large windows overlooking other charming, old apartments – some decrepit, some displaying colourfully subversive graffiti – every one of them an artefact of the many different cultural transformations the city has seen in recent centuries. Below the windows, and further down the narrow roads tourists (trying their best not to get run over by motorbikes appearing out of nowhere) roam around in wonder, among locals who carry on with their routines. Sooner or later they track down historic churches and synagogues, ancient ruins and enchanting antique shops discreetly tucked away. At night, popular gay bars and taverns set the tone. Exclusive art gallery openings have people spilling out onto the pavements with a wine or beer in hand, while fast food and takeaway joints remain open till the wee hours of the morning. Just some of the usual perks of Beyoğlu's round-the-clock street life – which during Gezi Park had been ignited, right down to its dead-end streets and obscure alleyways, by an unprecedented festive spirit. People of all ages and backgrounds flocked in, day and night, chanting in unison, happily coexisting, demonstrating, if only for a limited time, how mutual tolerance could easily be attained once no offence was taken by how others chose to live.

'But Lucian, we barely know each other,' I can't help but say, having finally realised his travel plans for Istanbul are of a long-term nature.

As he tilts his head closer to me, a dreamy look surfaces in his eyes.

'You just know when something is *meant to be*. Something just clicks – and all of a sudden, it paves a way to a future you didn't know could exist a week ago.'

Overjoyed, and instantly seduced by his conviction, a smile hovers over my face – but seconds later I find myself disorientated as I question my own sanity – and his sanity, of course. Even if what he's proposing feels strangely *right*, what we have is so new and so very unpredictable – as is what awaits me back home, which lies solely in the hands of officials who could easily give me a prison sentence for a list of crimes they know I have not committed. Liberals have become just another unwanted minority in a system where minorities – at the instance they dare challenge authority, even if by only seeking their fundamental rights – are demonised and imprisoned. Sudden backpedalling on liberally inclined policies, sidestepping legal procedures, or passing new laws overnight are par for the course for the ruling elite to serve this very purpose, and to continue to expand their power and immunity by enforcing a culture of fear and intimidation.

'How can you think of moving to a country you've never stepped foot in?' I say, trying to talk some sense into him. My own words only manage to amplify the dread that it might well be *me* who never again sets foot there.

He cups my face with his hands and looks straight into my eyes, as if he's trying to reach deeper, to a place where I'm still receptive to the connection we have.

'Cause I'll be going there with you.'

And, however briefly, he *is* able to woo me with his spirited earnestness, and with the daringly romantic notion of us eloping to Istanbul together, where we would inspire each other to pick up painting again, plunging headlong into a relationship. The enchantment of this moment is quickly disrupted. Unlike him, I'm unable to relish such free-flowing fantasies when what the future might bring has such an unyielding hold on me. Despite this, I entertain a vision of my own: we're seated on the crowded top deck, overlooking the beauty of the sinuous shoreline as it unfolds before our very eyes. I imagine the heaving concentration of buildings, the noisy traffic we have just left behind. Sensing the wind against my skin, blowing through my hair, I picture the rusty surfaces of the vessel, hung with bright orange lifebuoys. I inhale the iodine, the occasional hints of petrol I imagine the wind carries from the engine, and hear the yapping of rowdy seagulls fed by small pieces of *simit* thrown overboard. It seems only yesterday that I last boarded a ferryboat.

'Tell me what's on your mind.'

'I think a part of me has never really left,' I quietly respond, then drift into thought again.

One by one, with compassion, I imagine the faces of my parents, then of Elif and Tijen. I consider the support I've received from other family members and friends, from numerous acquaintances as well as complete strangers – lawyers, journalists, human-rights activists, and others who were just ordinary citizens with a strong sense of justice. Of which, I have discovered, there are plenty, having stood shoulder to shoulder with an ever-multiplying throng of them in the summer of 2013. And as I acknowledge the millions and millions of likeminded others I know are out there, I'm suddenly filled with hope – not just for the verdict of my trial, but for the future ahead. Though I know this buoyant outlook is not meant to last – it never does – I remind myself of Marlene's advice – that it's within my capacity to reverse the heaviness of despair, by reflecting on how it *feels* to be in a calm and content place, and adopting this state of mind. *Like flipping a light switch inside one's awareness.*

QUINN

QUINN'S IN A MUCH chirpier mood than usual, having finally closed the deal on a multi-million-dollar sale after weeks of manoeuvring slippery negotiations with tight-lipped discretion.

He stretches his legs and rests his feet on his desk, careful not to shift the piles of folders on it: one with sale proposals, one with itemised gallery bills, and another with a large stack of invites to private art functions he has no desire to attend, having concluded from a quick browse that none of them are worth his time.

His new PA knocks, then pokes her head through the door with a file in her hand.

'Hi,' he says. 'I need to get on to something – but do you mind bringing in another espresso?'

She's beginning to understand how difficult he can be to pin down – even on a quiet morning like this. Trying not to lose her cool, she nods back, then closes the door behind her.

Quinn interlocks his fingers over the back of his head and stretches his torso as far as he can in his chair. Holding the pose for a few seconds, he glances over to the only artwork currently hanging in his office. A Devora Miller *Line* painting. Equally set horizontal lines in soft pastel hues on canvas – simple yet effective. He has the work on loan from a client in a financial rut and in need of some quick capital. The painting will hang without a price tag on his office wall until it's snatched up by another client. Quinn is visited daily by other dealers, art advisors and collectors who come to pick his brain about what to buy or to sell or trade-in next. Of course, with Quinn, no advice is given out of goodwill. If it's another dealer or an art advisor, he will seek out various secondary market deals they can do together; that's where he earns the real dosh. The exhibitions are just window dressing.

Leaning forward, he dials a number on the gallery's landline, then leans back in his chair. When she eventually picks up, he casually says, 'Hi, it's Quinn. How're you doing?'

It takes her a few seconds to answer. 'Fine, thank you.' She sounds gobsmacked. 'How are you? I hope things are okay at the gallery,' she adds anxiously.

'Everything is just hunky-dory,' Quinn replies, tapping his fingers on his desk. It's one of those rare days he's not feeling as if he's on a knife's edge.

One of the windows of his office has been left ajar, and street noise is seeping in. It doesn't hurt that it's an unexpectedly pleasant winter's day outside. The air is crisp and there isn't a single cloud in the sky.

'Listen, I've been meaning to call you.' He removes his legs from the table and sits up straight.

When rival galleries opened up outposts in Hong Kong and started hiring Mandarin, Urdu or Russian speakers, he'd had no aspiration to follow suit at first. Yet Quinn has come to understand that if he wishes to continue running a successful business, he has to broaden his reach, to acquire new, rich clients from emerging markets. Recently, he signed up a locally renowned Chinese artist, and hired a young Russian socialite – someone not his first choice for the position of a PA.

Turkey is another country that's been on his radar.

'I'd like to offer you a job.'

She gasps. 'I don't know what to say, Quinn.'

'I had a chat with an immigration lawyer. Apparently, it's not that simple for me to apply for a work permit on your behalf. I need to prove why I can't hire someone British, or someone with an EU passport, in your place.'

'Oh.'

'But the immigration lawyer said that you, as a Turkish national, can apply for a self-employment visa – in this case as an art consultant, or an art advisor, or whatever you want to call it. He says it's a pretty straightforward procedure. It's some visa arrangement all EU countries have with Turkey. I can help you with your application. I can provide a letter of recommendation and whatever else they're after. Once you receive your permit you can come and work for me. I'm happy to hire you two days a week to begin with.'

During the Fair, Quinn had been highly impressed by Ada's discipline – and by the number of Turkish collectors who had turned up at the booth to cosy up to her. He had kept giving her new assignments every day to challenge her – and to get his money's worth, of course. He had her send out offers to clients. This involved emailing a client a professionally photographed, high-resolution image of the artwork, information about its medium, dimensions and price, along with press clippings and an impressive biography of the artist. She had tracked down a sought-after, out-of-print artist's catalogue raisonné and arranged the delivery of an artwork to a private collector's home for viewing.

On the very last day, she had spent the whole afternoon next to two technicians dismantling artworks from the display, before wrapping them in bubble wrap, placing some works into card boxes and others into large crates. When she had completed this huge task – when it was nearly time for her to leave – he had asked her if she could send out a few more offers. She had compliantly stayed longer to complete this final task.

'It's a no-strings-attached proposition,' he tells her. 'Once you get your visa, we can try it out for a month and see how we feel. Whatever happens, you'll have a work visa to fall back on. A work permit for the UK is as good as gold. It's a win-win situation for you.'

The day after the Fair ended, he typed her name into Google. He practically fell out of his chair, coming across endless news articles about her – all in Turkish, of course. He got a rough idea of what was being said thanks to Google Translate. Then, a week ago, he happened to sit next to a Turkish investment banker at a charity dinner for Cancer Research. The woman forthcomingly gave him the full story, right down to the decision the court had very recently come to at its final hearing.

'If they hadn't given such a verdict, half the country would now be on their feet!' the investment banker told him.

With her notoriety and fame – and being the daughter of a painter whom the investment banker had dubbed 'a living legend' – she seemed the perfect candidate to attract rich Turkish collectors to Quinn's Mayfair gallery.

Ada sighs deeply down the phone, as if this is all a bit over-whelming. 'I don't know what to say,' she repeats.

'You don't have to decide right away. Why don't you sleep on it?'

'It's hard for me to make a decision about anything. I'm in a bit of a limbo right now.'

'Limbo? What do you mean?'

There's a pause. He thinks he hears some rustling in the background, then it stops.

'I'm actually flying to Istanbul tomorrow.'

Quinn picks up on her apprehension. He's not surprised. *She must be barking mad to be returning.*

'Good for you!' he says. 'Are you going to hang out with your folks?'

'Yes!'

'You must *really* be looking forward to that.' His conviction makes it obvious he knows about her situation.

She tearfully admits, 'I might actually kiss the pavement when I arrive.'

He briefly struggles with the schmaltz of the moment, then finally blurts out, 'I'm really happy for you. Well, have a good one then.'

He hears some more rustling on her end followed by a man's whispers: *We are flying to Istanbul.* She shushes him.

Quinn's PA knocks again and enters. He vacantly watches her place the cup of espresso before him and leave. While this is happening, he hears some faint giggles followed by more whispers on the other end of the line. He cannot make out what's being said. She must be covering the phone's microphone with her hand.

He doesn't know what to make of it, but he's starting to lose his patience. 'Is this a good time for you? I can call back if you're busy.'

'I'm so sorry! No, no. It's a perfectly good time,' she responds, abashed.

Quinn hears the man once more. This time, his voice is coming from further away, but it sounds louder and clearer: *Tell him we'll send him a postcard.*

He *knows* that voice. *It's Lucian's – goddamnit! But how can this be?* His mind travels back to the Fair. *That shameless seducer – I bet he never listened. I bet he went straight behind my back. He obviously couldn't waste a minute to get into her pants.*

Quinn briefly closes his eyes. He lifts his glasses and presses his thumb and index finger against the bridge of his nose.

Everyone's heard that Lucian's gallery has gone under. Rumours have been circulating: a fraudulent employee forging invoices and sucking the gallery's account dry. It's Quinn's biggest nightmare realised. He had wanted to hear it straight from the horse's mouth, but it's been impossible to get hold of him. He had naturally assumed Lucian was stuck in a drug den somewhere, on a binge.

Quinn clears his throat. Pretending he hasn't heard more

than he's supposed to, he asks, 'So, how long are you planning to be out there?'

'That's the thing – I don't know yet. It might only be a few weeks, or it might be longer than that.'

'So you wanna have a proper break, huh? Can't blame you.' He takes a sip from his espresso. 'And I don't see why you shouldn't be able to apply for your work visa while you're out there.'

'I suppose it's doable,' she answers hesitantly.

'I can wait for a month or two – but don't expect me to wait any longer than that. You should see the *enormous* pile of CVs we receive weekly. Let me tell you – those graduates would give an arm and a leg to be in your place.'

She sighs tensely. 'I am so flattered. I really am. But, well, you see, I used to paint. And—'

'Like father like daughter, hey?'

'I guess.'

'Nice to take up a relaxing vocation on a long break – will help take your mind off things and give your days a bit of structure.'

'Well, you see,' she nervously begins. 'It's becoming a bit more serious than that. That's why I'm planning on renting a place out there. A studio, I mean. With a friend. If we do, we might stay longer.'

Quinn pauses. 'A friend?'

She hesitates. 'Actually, it's a boyfriend.'

Quinn gulps down what's left of the coffee. *What is she going on about? Is she seriously turning down the offer of a lifetime? So she can paint pretty pictures and hang out with some middle-aged washout? Provided she doesn't get rearrested while*

293

she's out there. Is she high on drugs or something? And what about him? Leaving the carnage behind, just like that, and going on a freaking sabbatical? What the hell does he plan to do for the rest of his life – paint?

He puts the coffee down. 'But you are planning to come back, aren't you?'

ACKNOWLEDGEMENTS

I am grateful to my husband James and my son Henry for their patience and continuous support throughout the many years I have locked myself in my room to write this novel – and our cat Louis for his comforting presence while I did.

I wish to thank Christina Nebel for her guidance and inspiration over the years.

I am indebted to everyone who read this book at its various stages of conception and completion including Simon Petherick, Hanif Kureishi, Jacob Smullyan and Didem Karasulu. A special thank you to Aydın Mehmet Ali for her translation of Küçük İskender's quote. And of course, I wish to express my gratitude to my publisher, Henry Rowley for his thoughtfulness and dedication in every step towards its publication.

Lastly, I wish to thank everyone who generously shared their experiences of the protests with me and helped me recreate their milieu and explore their psychological impact.

MUSIC THAT
INSPIRED THE BOOK

Birsen Tezer, 'İstanbul', from the album *Cihan* (2009)

Dilek Türkan, 'Hazin Teraneler', from the album *Aşk Mevsimi* (2011)

Henryk Górecki, *Symphony No. 3, Op. 36* (1976)

Charles Mingus, *Charles Mingus Quintet & Max Roach* (1964)

Fazıl Say, 'Gezi Park Sonata, Op. 52' from the album *Say Plays Say 3* (2021)

Gaye Su Akyol, 'Uzat Saçını İstanbul' from the album *Hologram İmparatorluğu* (2016)

Gwilym Simcock, *Good Days at Schloss Elmau* (2011)

Beynelmilel Notalar feat. Merve Göktemiz, 'Çav Bella' (2022)

Erik Satie, 'Gnossienne No. 1' (circa 1890)

Pamela, 'İstanbul' from the album *Şehir Rehberi* (2004)